TOMORROW'S WRATH

J.M. CLARK

Tomorrow's Wrath
by J.M. Clark

Copyright © 2018 J.M. Clark
All Rights Reserved

Cover art by Panagiotis Lampridis
Edited by https://espressoeditor.com/
Formatted by FastFormatting@gmail.com

Fraternity Rose Publishing

FRATERNITY ROSE
PUBLISHING

ISBN: 9781980948292

Join the mailing list and receive free giveaways and exclusive content:

Website: http://www.writtenbyjmclark.com
Email: writtenbyjmclark@gmail.com

CHAPTER ONE
Prelude

THERE WERE NO KIDS IN THE neighborhood anymore. Only him. His mother and father said that when they were kids themselves, tons of children filled the streets. He walked alone. They rode bikes together, played jump rope and a game called tag in groups. He wanted very much to be a part of all those activities. Someone his age to talk to would be nice; it all sounded like so much fun.

Branden could not even fathom the idea of other children. At thirteen years old, the only people he'd ever seen in his life were his parents. That was it—no other human beings. They moved around the neighborhood from home to home, ducking the big white vans whenever they drove into the subdivision he and his family lived in. Alone.

Sometimes he wondered if his parents were being truthful about the people in the vans. Were they really so bad? Would it really be so bad if they knew his family was there? Maybe they wanted to help?

Every few months the vans would come to do something called a sweep. Branden's father, Morris, said a sweep was when they drove the streets of the neighborhood checking to make sure no one was around. To make sure everyone was still...dead. The van quietly moved up and down the roads, the big tires flattening the grass growing through the cracks in the gravel.

1

In some spots it was hard to tell where the curb and grass began because of all the overgrowth. His parents told him that at one time—before the sickness, people would cut the grass, clip the bushes, make things look really nice. To Branden it looked fine enough, but he had nothing to compare it to, other than pictures. Pictures did nature no favors though.

When the sweeps happened, he and his family would go into the attic of whichever house they were staying in that month and peer out the windows, making sure the van, or sometimes vans, were long gone before coming back out. In his entire life, Branden had never seen the drivers stop the vehicles and get out. They just drove through. Nothing to worry about, his father always said.

"They have a route to take once a month, and this neighborhood is just one part of the route. They wouldn't waste their time getting out of the vans." He was right, they never did. So over time they lost their boogeyman effect on Branden. They became a monthly inconvenience, nothing more.

Branden was playing in the backyard of a house around the corner from the house his family was staying in that month. When he had left earlier in the day, his mother, Karry, was getting lunch together, and his father was in the study of the house, sharpening knives and making traps. They caught their food that way. His father was really good with a bow, but his mother was better.

Dad never wanted to admit it, but they all knew that when food got low and all the chips were down, Mom would be the one bringing home the bacon, so to speak. His father always brought up the "bringing home the bacon" joke. Branden never quite understood it, but his parents laughed so hard whenever it came up.

He'd been shooting jump shots at the basketball hoop for an hour. The sun was high in the sky and sweat was pouring down his head, but he liked it. It meant he was working hard. His father always said, "If you aren't sweating, you aren't working hard."

He didn't mind being alone or doing things alone, because it was all he knew. Most of the time, playing was a solo act. Sometimes his parents would join him, but for the most part he was left to it. Independence was the way of the new world, and it was best to become accustomed to the current reality he found himself living in.

His father had a small brown recorder for when the vans came. He would blow on the musical instrument, and the sound served as a signal to come running home and hide in the designated spot of the house. For the most part, Branden happened to be with his parents when the van came. But for the few times he was on his own when a sweep took place, the plan had worked out just fine.

Nothing to worry about. Come home, hide, be quiet, and when the van was done with its business, he could go back to whatever he was doing. The sound of the recorder was easy to hear even if he was a few houses away; there were no other sounds in the world, minus birds and small animals, so the high-pitched warning could be heard quite loudly.

Branden stood at the free-throw line in the backyard of a home that no longer had a family. The previous residents no longer had any use for the makeshift court, or the home for that matter. Their bodies had been found in the house and placed in the cellar of another home.

All the bodies that had been left behind were in that cellar. His mother saw to the burial of any children from every house they'd lived in. She was great like that. Branden hadn't seen many bodies, burials, or cellar visits, as they'd been in the same area for so long, but he could remember a time or two.

He remembered.

Bend your knees, flick your wrist for rotation, and hold your hand in the air for the follow-through. His father had played varsity basketball in school, and he taught Branden everything he knew of the game. None of the lights in the houses worked any longer because electricity was cut everywhere, so they used candles to light the homes at night, and they talked a lot about the past. There wasn't much else to do besides reading (and they all read a lot), so Branden knew all there was to know about the world before everything changed—the way things were in his parents' youth.

Hearing the stories made him happy he didn't have to live through it; you can't miss what you never had. Friends that never were, vacations only existing in a child's imagination, could not be truly missed, for they were never experienced. They would remain future possibili-

3

ties if things were to ever get back to where they once were. Nothing in his short life made him think this would ever be the case though.

Swish. The shot went through the net, silky smooth. That was forty-one shots in a row he'd made from the free-throw line. His best was eighty-seven. Most days he would come back here and shoot a bunch. It helped pass the time. If he couldn't be found shooting at the rim, he would play in the creek not far from the backyard of the house and try to catch frogs, crawdads, and other small animals they could eat. Doing his part.

As he strolled over to retrieve the ball, Branden remembered his mother had told him to come home after a while to eat lunch. He liked to stop on a winning streak so that when he came back, he would already be in the positive. Wiping sweat from his brow and sweeping the dark brown locks of hair from his eyes, the young man turned to leave. He opened the metal gate and closed it behind himself, abandoning the basketball sitting still on the concrete beneath the rim.

He came running from the side of the neighbor's yard and jumped over the curb, cutting through the yard and high-stepping over the grass and weeds now occupying what was once the best-looking lawn on the street so many years ago. Branden burst into the door of his home, meeting the smell of some kind of meat. The scent invaded his nose the moment he walked in the door. When they were able to have meat with dinner, that was a good supper.

"Mother, I'm home," he yelled as he kicked off his gym shoes and went into the bathroom near the front door to wash his hands. He already knew his father would make sure he did just that the moment he saw him, so he planned to earn some responsibility points by anticipating the request.

The handwashing was always a half-assed job anyway. There was food begging to be eaten, and he wanted to get back out to the ball court to try beating his record. He finished quickly washing up in the bin of water they collected from the creek daily for just that purpose, then wiped them dry on a towel. With that out of the way, he rushed from the bathroom and headed to the kitchen. They would soon be eating together at the table and talking about different things; sometimes his mother would give an impromptu math or science lesson. She

4

was a teacher before it all happened, so she was happy doing just that still to this day. Even if most of what she taught him was no longer useful, old habits died hard.

Branden went jogging into the kitchen, nearly sliding on the linoleum in his socks. "Let's ea—" he began to say, but stopped mid-sentence, the words climbing back into his mouth, retreating down his throat and back into the voice box from which they came. He was frozen in disbelief at what he was seeing. He bit back a scream. From inside the sound of a thousand souls cried out in the very depths of his heart—but no sound left his lips.

What he saw didn't look real to him; his brain couldn't process the image. He looked away and down to his feet, searching to give his eyes a better image to report to his brain.

The once white socks were now soaked in red...in blood. He had slid into blood. How could something so lighthearted like sliding through the kitchen in socks, filled with excitement to have supper with your family, end up morphing into something so...disturbing? Branden thought about walking back outside and coming into the house differently. What he was seeing could not be real. At the same time, it was the most realistic moment in the whole universe.

His eyes followed the blood on the ground to his mother's body. Her neck was cut open, and blood still rolled from the deep wound across her throat, creating a small red lake settling around her shoulder, which then came to be a small river that streamed past her feet. His blood ran cold at the realization of what was before him. Branden said nothing, he couldn't speak. Finally, his eyes noticed something that they hadn't picked up on with the shock of finding his mother... the way she was.

There were two men standing next to her body, staring at him. They did not make a move toward him; they just watched. They seemed almost as surprised as he was.

Branden found the courage, or maybe it was just shock and fear to call out to his other parent. Although something told him it would be for naught. "Father! Father! Where are you!" He had screamed loudly, though the scream was void of hope or feeling, never looking away from the men in black uniforms standing next to his mother's dead body. He backed up into the living room area, an involuntary reaction to the situation, Branden was not aware of his body moving at all, his legs did all the work on their own.

He felt like he was watching it all happen, perched safely on the ceiling like a fly. He saw his body backing up, and he wanted to warn himself about what was slowly walking up behind him, but he found out too late...

A hand from behind grabbed the collar of his shirt. Branden nonchalantly turned to look at the hand. Before seeing the man's face, he knew it didn't belong to his father. The voice was not familiar, and the hand on his collar had blood on it. Most likely the blood of his father...

He was the only person alive in his family? The thought would be unnerving for anyone, let alone a child.

Of the three people left in a neighborhood in Mt. Healthy, a small suburb of Cincinnati, there was now only one. "You are coming with us, son," the man holding his shirt said. "As you can see, this place is not safe for you. Everyone else here is dead."

"Bring the van around, and let's get to the Palace." The voice was calm and steady, bored even. It did not match the scene in the kitchen or the fate he knew his father had met in the study. The knives he'd been so proudly sharpening didn't help in the end, it seemed. *All the hand-to-hand combat practice was pointless in the end*, he thought, still staring at the bloody hand gripping his shirt.

Unable to speak again, Branden simply walked out of the house with them and waited on the sidewalk while someone pulled the van up. He did not weep, he did not curse the men who killed the only people he'd ever known. As the vehicle pulled up, he wondered how many shots he would have made if none of this had happened and he'd been able to go back to his make-streak after dinner.

CHAPTER TWO

Carla

S HE'D LEFT CAMP TWENTY MINUTES PRIOR, walking the same hidden path she'd been sneaking off to for the last year. Nothing sinister in mind; it was simply a place to get quiet time, to reflect on things that were important to her outside of the group. That was important. How could she be of help to the many if she didn't take the time to care for herself? She didn't tell them because she didn't want them to worry about her.

Carla made her way along the river's edge, stepping over big rocks and vaulting over fallen trees, being sure not to make too much noise. There were those in her group who watched out for...things like this. Believed defectors or even someone else from a would-be competing group. She knew where they were all stationed though, so there wasn't much worry on her part. But it was still good to keep a low profile.

After another five minutes of traversing the creek area, she made her way to a small cave located in the side of a small rock structure. She wouldn't call it a mountain because it was not quite that, but it was big enough. The entrance to the cave was covered with shrubbery and sizeable tree limbs. She didn't want small animals getting inside and walking off with the few things stored there that she held dear to her heart.

Carla slowly removed the obstructions from the entrance of her secret hideaway. The cave was dark, as was common for such places; they were not meant for humans. Caves were the homes of nocturnal animals that were gifted special optics for such a setting. She was not bestowed those same gifts, but the good lord did see fit to give her the gift of common sense. She had brought candles.

Carla struck a match from the box she stole from the common room of her group, lighting the candles and placing them in strategic spots of the dark, dank cave so that she could see all things. She wanted to make sure she was safe and that no predators had found a way inside, waiting to attack. Carla had a hunting knife and a pistol fitted with a silencer. If a shootout with a badger took place, she wanted to remain incognito of course.

All was safe and secure in the hideout, so Carla relaxed, removed her pea-green Army Reserve jacket, and laid it on the floor next to a milk crate where she usually sat. She had not been a part of the reserves before the sickness came. Carla was a Sunday school teacher at St. Andrews First Church of Louisville in Kentucky. Carla's husband, Mark, had owned a successful construction company, which left her time to do what was important to her full time. Teaching the Lord's word to kids is what she enjoyed, so, that's what she had done for years.

When the sickness came to claim the lives of everyone, she was in church with her children and about seventy-five other members. Those that were still strong enough to drive to the Lord's house the day the sickness came were lucky enough to die within those walls. She was not so lucky though.

Carla walked to the southern right corner of the cave and lifted a big stone with two hands just a few inches off the ground. She then set it just a foot away from where it was. Carla smiled. The thin brown wallet was still there; of course it was still there. Who the hell would be looking to lift a big-ass rock in a cave, in a world that had moved on long ago? It was a miracle she was still going through the motions of survival. She knew she was lucky to have found the Eagle group though. Prior to that she was trying to decide when she would slit her own throat.

Now she found herself clinging to any life she could find motivation for. Who she was today was nothing like the Sunday school teacher. The woman who read Bible stories to children, frequented Kroger grocery store, and read a book a week from the Kindle Fire that her brother had given her for Christmas. She now coordinated attacks, carried and trained with high-powered weapons, and whipped women and men alike into shape. Carla was a fearsome personality among her group.

She picked up the wallet and made her way back to the blue milk crate. She sat there and placed the wallet on her knees. Opening it always made her so emotional that she would cry uncontrollably. That was why she had to hide it so far away from the group. Even in death, there were things that you could not tear yourself away from. Death was final in some ways, and in other ways it was the beginning of a new link. A terrible, torturous, and sleepless link that left one party emotionally maimed and the other party unaware...because they were gone.

This was the link that Carla found herself involved in. Letting go was hard, impossible even, for a person like her. Why would the good Lord see fit to do this to her? She could understand why the world ended; everyone knew that was coming a hundred years before it did. The signs were there. But why was she left behind? Why couldn't those she loved most be spared? She asked herself these questions on a daily basis, a million times a day. Her eventual answer: she was being punished or tested. Her resolve was being tested. Could she endure...?

After opening the wallet, Carla closed it again quickly, looking away. She stared at a candle on the ground close to where she sat. Glaring at the flickering flame dancing in the darkness was calming for her. She wanted to be the flame. To have the power to bring the light when there was nothing but darkness before. It had been twenty years since they were taken away from her, and here she sat, still crying over them. Before she could become what she needed to be for her squad, she needed to move past this. It was so hard.

Without thinking, she opened the wallet and pulled out two pictures, throwing the wallet to the corner where the big rock sat. She took a picture into each hand and stared at them, stared at the beautiful faces. Inside, Carla could feel her rigid and strong bone structure turn into cooked noodles. She immediately fell apart once she saw their faces.

One picture was of her family. Her husband, Mark, herself, and their two children: seven-year-old Delilah and three-year-old Jolie. The picture was taken at Christmas. They'd been at Mark's family's house for Christmas dinner sitting on the couch, when his brother came over with the camera and began snapping photos. It was one of those in-motion, half-smile, half-trying-to-keep-the-kids-from-smashing-mashed-potatoes-into-the-couch pictures.

The other picture was of her and both of her daughters. It was a selfie she'd taken from her smartphone at the museum. Carla took her daughters somewhere interesting once a month when she could find the time. They'd been so happy that day. It hurt to see their faces, but she could not bring herself to get rid of the pictures.

For the last twenty years, between the running, killing, being hurt, and being chased, the only constant in her life was the brown wallet that had belonged to Mark and the pictures within. There was even a twenty-dollar bill inside. It had no value in the new version of the world she now lived in, but she kept the bill inside because Mark had put it there at some point in his life.

The idea of doing something over and over again that you knew would hurt you was insanity in itself, she knew that. It was akin to a woman taking a man back who constantly abused her—even though she knew he would hurt her, it would hurt even more to be without him. That's what the pictures were to Carla. It was a form of abuse, not physically but worse; it was emotional and mental torture.

When everyone died, it was the worst thing that could be imagined. She sat there waiting on her turn to get sick and die, but it never came. The pain and loneliness felt otherworldly, and every time she looked at the pictures of her family, it was like reliving it all over again. But she would endure, and for Carla, the pictures were a part of that struggle.

The day everyone left her alone, she was in the church with her children. Mark had been away on a job when people seemingly started dying within hours. She drove the kids to the church while calling

Mark time and time again, but she never got an answer from him. Her daughters were in the back seat, spitting up mucus and vomit the whole time. The drive was filled with tears, moans, and sounds that the human body emitted when death was near.

By the time she got to the church, there were close to seventy-five people there with the same idea that she had. Looking for Jesus to save them and their loved ones. No one stopped to think that maybe what was happening *was* the work of Jesus. Obviously, no one was spared; the divine plan that was engineered by the most high but carried out by those from elsewhere went as planned.

Carla, a woman of only twenty-six years old at the time, sat in the church pew with her dead children sprawled out over the length of the wooden bench. They lay on either side of her with their heads on her lap, Carla stroking their hair and easing them into the afterlife with her touch. At least that's what she told herself. Death was all around her within the church. All seventy-five people had died by the next morning. Only she survived the night. Mark never answered, and after a while his phone went straight to voicemail.

That morning, Carla eventually snapped out of her trance and knew that her daughters deserved a burial. She went down to the basement of the church and retrieved a shovel. She dug one big grave and gently put her children into it, crying like a mad woman as she covered the grave with dirt. Ending her own life was on the edge of her mind with a toe over the cliff that morning; it was all she could think about while burying her children.

She had the fleeting thought to bury everyone in the church, but she couldn't possibly—she hadn't slept all night, and her body would not be able to carry out such a workload. Carla said a prayer, asking Jesus to accept everyone into his kingdom. Then she kissed everyone's forehead and walked out of the church, where she sat on the steps and screamed as loud as she could. She screamed until her voice cracked and sound would no longer escape her throat.

Carla drove back to her home, hoping that her husband was there. He was all she had hope for at that point. Their home was only five minutes up the road from the church. There were no cars but her own on the road that morning; she didn't see a single soul out and about.

She did find Mark in their house, and to her astonishment, he was there in bed. Somehow he had made it back from work and must have been so exhausted that he'd crashed before he could charge his phone and call her. Just as her hopes were heightened at the idea of not being totally alone in a dead world, it was destroyed by the realization that he had moved on with everyone else. His skin was cold and felt like rubber when she went to touch his arm, which was the only thing sticking out from under the covers.

Carla did not cry, could not cry. She had reached her daily maximum of tears. Her voice box refused to evoke more screams. She could not carry his body to bury it, she was tired, and the only thing she wanted to do was die. Carla never liked being left behind; even as a kid she loathed the feeling of being left out.

Sitting there on the blue milk crate these twenty years later, nothing had changed for her. Sure, she was now part of a group that had managed to survive and had even accomplished some incredible things as far as colonizers go. But when she looked at the pictures of the remnants of her old life, she was transformed into the Sunday school teacher who had been left alone on the steps of her church.

She cried until she could not cry any longer, then she walked back over to the wallet and slid the pictures inside before dropping the big stone over it once more. The pictures needed to stay safe. She feared that if she could no longer gaze upon her children and Mark, she would fully lose herself. Those faces kept her linked to the past. Her devotion was based upon those memories of who she was, who they were.

A big brown paddle was propped against the cave wall on the opposite side of where the stone-covered wallet rested. Carla removed her green tee shirt. She wore no bra; most women didn't bother with them in the time they were living in. The coldness of the cave hardened her nipples upon exposing her chest to the elements.

Before getting the paddle and beginning her normal routine of atonement, she put her back against the cave wall, feeling the jagged rocks and pebbles pressing into her skin. She'd performed this act too many times to count, and it barely hurt anymore. The skin on her back had been so damaged, she thought the pain sensors on that part of her body were nearly non-existent.

Carla squatted down with her back pressed firmly against the cave wall. She wiped tears from her eyes and hardened her face as her full lips curved into a slight smile. The time of crying and feeling sorry for herself had ended; it was time to atone. To show the good Lord that she was willing to punish herself time and time again until He saw fit to call her home.

Carla rose from the squatted position, scraping and pushing her back against the wall. The jagged rocks ripped into her already scarred skin as she heard and felt rocks falling from the wall. Slowly she rose, making sure the pain was real enough to feel every bit of it. Her facial expression did not change. She deserved it, she knew that. There was a reason He left her in this world, and it was not to cheat her way out of it with suicide. Her purpose was to atone for the sins of man.

She was the chosen one. Children were the most important thing in a woman's life, and hers would not die in vain. Carla believed she was charged with bringing in a new era and, with the discipline from her group, she would remove the threat to the planet.

Once risen to her full height on her tiptoes, Carla repeated the same action but in reverse, crouching down while scraping her back again. For the next five minutes, she repeated this routine until her legs became weak. She could feel warm blood dripping down her back, and the wall had become slippery as she moved up and down against it.

Carla put her shirt back on and removed her boots first, then her pants. She wore black panties, nothing pretty or sexy. They were period panties as her good friend Ashley always called them when they were in high school, passing tampons back and forth in class. She walked over and grabbed the heavy paddle, smacking it against her hand violently while making her way back to the milk crate. She sat down with her knees together.

Carla raised the paddle as high in the air as her arms would allow. Then she slammed it down across her thighs. She repeated this same brutal action over and over until her thighs were swollen and blood could be seen beneath the skin. This punishment hurt worse than what she did to her back because she needed her legs to walk and train with the squad. Paddling her legs always left her with a limp for a day or two afterwards.

The sound of wood beating against flesh could be heard throughout the cave and went on until her arm could no longer rise with the paddle in hand. The pain was miniscule in comparison to the sacrifice she was making to God.

When finished, Carla set the instrument of atonement back against the cave wall and put her boots and fatigue pants on. Walking out of the cave and covering the entrance with the tree limbs and other shrubbery, she thought to herself that her physical atonement was for the best, and it would benefit all someday. Jesus went through it, and mankind still found a way to fuck things up. She would make sure that the sacrifice of her family was for a reason. Carla made her way back through the wooded area and back to her team, limp and all. There were a chosen few among the group who were ready to move against any and all at a moment's notice. Even treachery and loyalty could go hand in hand for a righteous reason.

She would tell them she sprained her ankle but would not allow a medic to check her body. The green jacket would cover the bloody carnage that was her back. She'd gotten adept at bandaging her back after a nice cold shower. Another day of paying for the sins of all, and another day of no one in her unit finding out about her own personal mission.

CHAPTER THREE

Phase 2 - Mary

S HE HAD LEARNED NOTHING IN THE last nineteen years while inside the Palace facility that would have prepared her for living out in the world. The fear, the anxiety, the feeling of being lost, and even more than that—the beauty of it all. The colors and smells alone left Mary encapsulated in a state of wonder. If only he was here with her to enjoy it all, to protect her and just touch her... A touch from him would be everything to her. But that would never happen again.

It was the fourth day since she had escaped, or, more accurately, been permitted to leave the Palace. And still she wandered the forest, looking for an exit of some sort. Mary's body had begun to fail her. Hungry and distraught from seeing the life sapped from her love, Jacob, the emotions that she'd dealt with over the last four days had become a wildly boiling cauldron of feelings. The very bones in her body ached for him, and the feeling was unlike anything she'd ever encountered.

Her days were filled with fascination of the forest, seeing all of Mother Earth's beautiful creations. There were so many things she had never seen before, had never even learned about in Old World sessions. She found herself enjoying every timid footstep over the grass, every afternoon spent near a meadow, or simply watching a stream carry leaves and small minnows off to wherever they belonged.

The nights though, those were different. The darkness brought a blitz of misery, flashbacks, and confusion. She felt hunger pangs so severe they threatened to make her delirious as her body consumed itself from the inside out. The visions were another factor. No matter where she looked, everything became a vision of Jacob's body lying on the ground with a hole in his chest the size of cereal bowl, blood and gore falling from the wound and his life fading into nothingness. Their lives fading. Faded.

Most nights she chased sleep in an endless maze of zigzags and obstacles, sometimes not finding rest until nearly morning just as the sun came peeking out of the clouds. The darkness scared her. Being alone scared her, and she was alone now...truly alone.

Where there had once been another person in every direction she looked, now there was no one. She was overcome with grief, as thick a feeling as one could experience. Where there had once been a schedule full of sessions, classes, activities, and social events, now there was nothing to do but frantically search for an exit to the labyrinth of trees and shrubbery she found before her.

When she felt her self-pity becoming primary over the anger she had for the Order, she mustered the strength to keep going. Thinking of what had been taken from her made her tremble with fury. The sacrifice Jacob made for her would not be in vain; she would make it out of the forest and she would find help. First, she needed to find food, but help was coming in at a very close second in the hierarchy of needs. The only problem was that she felt like death, and moving around was difficult to say the least.

Mary found several types of berries—some she recognized, some she didn't. She ate them all, even tried eating leaves and other foliage from the ground, which tasted terrible. But you'd be surprised what you would put in your mouth and attempt to keep down when you hadn't eaten anything for a full day. She'd gorged herself on the unknown berries, knowing that it could mean her life if they were poisonous. They were not particularly good, but she forced down the sick feeling while eating them.

That afternoon she felt sick. Not the nausea from being pregnant, but something different. The morning had been filled with vomiting and fits of diarrhea, which she knew was making her dehydrated. That was very dangerous for the baby growing inside of her, and she had not found a stream to drink from since waking up that morning. A layer of dried, cracking skin replaced the soft skin on her lips.

Mary stumbled through the forest until she found an opening in sight—but she felt she might not make it there. She could barely make out a small trail leading outside of the last few massive oak trees to her right. Sweat poured down her forehead into her eyes, burning them, making it hard to see straight. She walked hunched over, clutching her stomach the whole way.

Her pants were filthy, saturated in mud. The tee shirt she wore when she and Jacob had made a run for it was now tied and knotted at her side. The standard white shoes for Palace members were now brown and damaged from dragging them beneath her as she lurched through the woods. Her once flowing jet-black hair now lay over her shoulder in a tangled, kinky remnant of a proper ponytail.

Her balance faltering, she made it to the clearing of the forest and tumbled past the last tree, which made up the blanket of trees that had shielded her over the last four days. The forest had both protected her from any who were pursing and imprisoned her into a gauntlet that nearly took her life. She was still unsure if she was out of the woods as far as being sick.

Mary lay there in the grass, struggling to get to her knees, digging her nails into the dirt, trying to power though the pain in her stomach and weakness in her legs. Calling upon the inner strength that Jacob taught her to have, she made it to her knees with the forest behind her, looking up into the sky. Squinting and blocking the sun with her dirty palm, she realized this was the first time the sun looked upon her face without hiding behind the cover of the tree tops.

The day was beautiful, the sky the most breathtaking color of blue she'd ever seen. The clouds danced with each other, and all she could hear were the insects, birds, and small animals in the woodland setting at her back. *What a crime it has been for the Palace-born to never have seen this in so many years.*

Using her inside wrist, Mary wiped sweat from her eyes and forehead just as she leveled her gaze to what was directly in front of her. She blinked a few times, making sure she was seeing it correctly. She stood up and took five wobbly steps toward the thing that had caught her attention. Falling to her knees just before reaching it, she crawled.

Reaching out, Mary was able to grab it. Her hand gripped the stick and pulled it from the ground. Anger and sadness filled every fiber of her body. Sorrow began at her feet and rose to the crown of her head. She wanted to snap the object in her hand but lacked the strength. *Was it all for nothing?*

In her hand she held a stick with a small red flag on the top—the same type of red flag that circled the Palace in a hundred-yard radius. The same hundred-yard radius that symbolized the quarantine area of a Palace facility. She knew it was no more than a guise put in place to keep the Palace members afraid to leave, and the thought still angered her.

Mary looked up and past the other red flags littering the well-kept grass field she lay upon, and there it was in all its strong, powerful, and unrelenting stubbornness. She gawked upon the Palace, but not her Palace, not her home, the only one she had ever known. Not the same place she had run away from hand in hand with her love, who'd died on a field much like this one. This was different. It was smaller, but there was no mistake being made here. It was another Palace.

She could feel her body begin to get hot as hatred filled her thoughts. If she could blow the place up with her eyesight, it would be a mushroom of smoldering brick and glass. She could not though, and she needed help. Mary was with child and needed to eat. She needed medical help, not to mention a mental evaluation. But she would lie there on the grass and die before she wobbled up to those massive glass doors and asked for help.

If she could only move around the hundred-yard radius of this Palace, maybe she could find safety elsewhere. Mary attempted to stand up once more to drag herself around the perimeter of the structure, hoping she wouldn't be seen by anyone inside. For all she knew, they would be as likely to gun her down like they did...*Jacob*...than to come out and help her.

After trying to make it to her feet, she could feel the bones inside of her weary body scream *NO MORE!!!* She collapsed to her side, head lying in the grass, facing the Palace. She could barely make out men in black security uniforms running toward her with guns in hand. They were screaming something at her, but she was too weak to care, too sick to bother scurrying back into the wooded area only a few feet behind her. Maybe this could be the end. Maybe she would meet up with him in another life.

CHAPTER FOUR

Lonnie

IT MADE THE FOURTH DAY IN a row. In the beginning, it was hard for him to deal with. No, maybe that was the wrong word. It was sad for him; he felt empathy for them. From what Lonnie could see, it was hard for all of them. They had never seen anything like that. Not even close. Rules were rules though, and the fate of the very planet hung in the balance. Sirus said so.

It all happened so fast. One day, everything was business as usual. Same old Palace schedules that had long become repetitious to everyone there. Then it all changed with a boom and a body lying motionless in the field.

The last of the Palace-born individuals were trickling into the auditorium and taking their seats. Everyone was dressed in white uniforms, which they had been given a few days ago. All of the women had their hair pulled into tight ponytails, and the men were sporting short buzz cuts. Lonnie didn't understand why the change in hair and clothing, but he was sure the Order had their reasons.

He sat there daydreaming about the events that transpired directly after they'd all watched that old guy, Jacob, get shot down outside the Palace. Everyone was made to come to the central plaza and watch through the glass as Jacob and one of the Palace-born women made a run for the forest. She made it, but he didn't. *Her name was Mary. She is probably dead by now...or taken and being enslaved by the others out there.*

Lonnie still remembered the screams of everyone in that moment. In unison, there were rounds of panicked gasps, hands covering mouths and eyes, and outright blood-curdling screams. He noticed that the teachers and security didn't budge; they didn't seem to be surprised at all. Like they expected it...he supposed they did. Especially considering what happened next.

He sat there in his seat and stared up at the stage, watching the Old World individuals on their knees, hands tied behind their backs with white blindfolds over their faces. The sight made him feel...indifferent at that point. On the first day he was empathetic, but now he felt as though it was simply another session. A lesson to be learned about how things worked. Sirus and the Order were calling this the beginning steps of Phase 2.

Lonnie looked away from the stage and noticed the person to his right. It was Melinda. She was a few years younger than him, maybe fifteen years old. She looked visibly unsettled, her hands gripping her knees tightly. He saw she was trembling in fear of what was to come. Her right hand shot up to her face to wipe away a tear, then back down to her right knee. He leaned in close to her so he could whisper.

"You have to relax. They won't like to see you crying. Calm down."

Melinda straightened up in her seat, sniffled, and looked straight ahead to see more Old World members lined up in rows on their knees. There were three rows of them at this point, and more were being brought in from behind a theater curtain on the stage area—all of them blindfolded. There was no sound but that of their cries, mumbling pleas for mercy, and negotiations to be banished from the Palace. They were speaking to no one, because no one was listening. They were the enemy.

"You've seen the videos playing on the pod televisions. They are not good people and must be eliminated if we are to go back into the world and start anew. Those recordings do not lie, you must accept the reality that is," Lonnie said, whispering quietly enough so that no one noticed.

"I know...I know. It's just so bad. I know those people up there."

Melinda held her eyes open as wide as possible to keep the tears from dropping. He knew that if she only blinked, the tears would come streaming down once more. Maybe someone would notice and believe she felt bad for the criminals up there...then maybe she'd end up on the stage next?

"You saw how they were all trying to corrupt us," he said. "They showed us on the television. You even saw that guy Jacob confuse the Palace-born woman and convince her to leave the only home she'd ever known. We watched it. Those people up on that stage are not the people you thought they were." Lonnie moved away from her sharply, returning to a straight position. The last of the Palace members were in their seats, and the Old World members were in four rows on the stage now. It was time for another cleansing.

"I know," was the last thing he heard from Melinda before the lights in the auditorium went dark.

Security came through the back exit in a single file line. They walked up to the first row of seated Palace-born members in their white uniforms. They hadn't had a chance to cleanse a group yet. Lonnie did though, on day two. The security team placed a gun into each of their hands. Same as yesterday, and the day before that.

The security team split into two groups and made their way to opposite sides of the auditorium. They placed their hands behind their backs and stood up straight, staring at the stage of crying, blindfolded Old World members.

Just then, Lonnie felt Melinda's hand graze his. She seemed to be trying to hold on to him to brace for what was to come. Even though he felt annoyed with her and the crying, he allowed this kindness and took her hand.

The first row of Palace-born members got up from their seats, guns in hand, and walked up to the stage, also in a single file line. They made a circle around their blindfolded friends of the past. Those who were once seen as loved ones and comrades were now targets to be shot down.

Lonnie could hear the guns being cocked back, a bullet moving into the chamber ready to be disengaged. Melinda's small hand squeezed, and he felt his own hand apply a firm grip in return.

He and hundreds of others sat in their seats, eyes fixed upon the dark stage as if they were attending a Broadway musical from the Old World. They watched in half amusement, half eagerness to see problems from the past extinguished. Some faces were smiling, and some looked distraught, much like Melinda next to him. He felt nothing, and that bothered him. He wanted to feel something.

It didn't matter either way. He and Melinda held hands tightly as the stage lit up with gunfire. A strobe light show of sparks, smoke, blood, and smiles from the shooters. *They are smiling...*

And still, he watched...and felt nothing.

CHAPTER FIVE

Mary

MARY COULD FEEL HERSELF BEING LIFTED to her feet. Her legs now nothing more than dangling limbs of weary muscle and bone, she couldn't stand straight if she wanted to. And she did want to. The security guards in all black each had one of her arms over their shoulders as they helped/dragged her toward the Palace.

She wanted to scream at them to stop, to drop her where they stood. Jacob had not died for her to just end up right back in one of those facilities. Unable to scream, she couldn't even formulate a decent mumble no matter how much she tried to conjure the strength. Her throat felt nearly closed, and her dried lips were cracked and bleeding. Any energy remaining in her body was being used to keep her alive.

Other than the two security officers carrying her toward the Palace, six others surrounded them as they walked. All were armed with automatic rifles. *Why do they have such weapons?* The guard in front of the security rescue team urgently barked at someone on a small black device. Something about "target acquired." Then she heard only static. Drifting in and out of consciousness, she couldn't bring herself to care what they said.

The seed of fear that her child was dying inside of her had begun to sprout flowers after day one of being in the forest alone and hungry.

Those flowers were fully bloomed at the moment. She wished Jacob had known he would be a father in the coming months. A real father. Things would have been different, she thought. Mary had planned to tell him when they were safely away from the Palace. But it was too late. He died, and maybe the baby was dead as well. She felt like she deserved to die right there on the quarantine field, as he did.

Sirus would come to this Palace and take her back. She knew he would. If that happened, she would kill herself in her pod. A knife would be ordered with dinner, and she would open her throat with it. *How disappointing this has turned out to be,* she thought as her body was hauled through the field, her feet dangling, the toes of her shoes dragging on the ground. Birds flew overhead, searching for food or resting in their homes, unaware her life would be coming to an end the second she got the first chance.

Mary labored to look up at the sky once more, sweat dripping down her forehead and into her eyes. She wanted to view the open sky before being taken into the Palace. One more time at the very least. She'd paid the cost for this brief gift of freedom. Then she lowered her gaze and saw they were but a mere twenty yards away from the doors, where other security officers waited, their cold faces chiseled like stone into a never-changing mask of indifference.

Then it happened. A loud boom, much like the sound accompanying the bullet that stole her love away, sounded off. The guard holding her right arm over his shoulder crumpled to the ground, his legs collapsing beneath him like a folding table. Mary was so delirious at this point that she didn't notice the spray of warm blood wash over the right side of her face and shirt. She was already looking down at the ground, so she witnessed the pieces of his head chip off and go flying all over the grass like so many rocks. Gray brain matter fell from what remained of his skull.

Before she knew it, she was on the grass field next to him. The guard on her left had let her arm go, and she could not keep herself up. Mary lay next to the boy; she knew it was not a man grown by the look in his dead eyes: fear.

The other guards were frantically turning in circles like chickens with their heads cut off, looking for where the gunshot came from.

Panicking and screaming orders to each other, they swung their guns this way and that, but there were no targets to shoot. At least none that she could see from her limited view on the ground. She was far too spent to roll over or even turn her head in the opposite direction.

In short order, she watched three of the security guards get mowed down by more gunfire. It all seemed to happen in slow-motion, flying metal ripping through the air and puncturing flesh. Creating small holes upon entry and even roomier holes when the shells exited the corpse. They were corpses before they hit the ground, even she could see that. It all reminded her of a video she saw in a morning enrichment class.

Thinking back as she lay there watching the human bodies drop, she decided it looked like ballet, but at a much slower pace. The men were more like bags of blood than actual bodies with muscle and bone. So much blood. When she broke it all down, she realized they were just that—bags of meat and blood. The bullets cut through the men like they were cotton candy tearing apart. It was effortless. The body armor they wore was about as effective as a tee shirt the way the shots pierced and exploded on impact.

As the shots rang out seemingly from every direction, the guards were forced to perform pirouettes. Spins and turns were on display as their bodies served as homes for the bullets from whoever was shooting. She'd never seen anything like it in her life. It was more amusing and interesting than it was scary. After losing Jacob, Mary didn't think fear lived inside of her heart anymore. The only thing she ever really wanted was taken away. Death would be a gift to her.

The gunfire stopped. Two of the guards managed to make it back to the Palace doors. They both ran inside without looking back, leaving the others as food for the earth. They were but crimson stains on the grass. A mess of all the things that keep the human body functional. Mary lay there, staring at the things that had been men just seconds ago. How fleeting life could be.

One man lay a few feet from her, his arm now in two pieces, blown off at the elbow. His eyes bulged from his skull as he went into shock. The man's chest pumped up and down faster than a chest should be able to move, and then just like that, he was gone. His body relaxed, and the frayed nub finally rested on the left side of his body. Mary closed her eyes and waited for her bullet. The security guards had been chased off or shot down, and now it was her turn. So, she waited. She hoped.

The sound of footsteps could be heard running up behind her. *More than one.* She couldn't turn around on her back to look, nor did she care to. Maybe the person or persons would end her without a word and then run back into the forest on either side of the Palace. *Why would they come this close if that was the intent?* She didn't bother to open her eyes. She would let them do what they came to do.

Mary felt a hand slide beneath her stomach. Then she was being flung into the air like a rag doll and over the shoulder of a man.

The stranger whirled her around so fast that the others accompanying him were a giant blur, but she guessed there were about ten other people.

"The cavalry has arrived, ma'am!" the big man carrying her bellowed in a booming voice as he galloped off into the nearby wooded area. *The cavalry?* Mary closed her eyes again and nodded off into darkness. The sounds of gunshots and return fire faded out, right along with her consciousness.

CHAPTER SIX

Kate

MAYBE IT WAS BECAUSE SHE WAS the last one left in the room, or maybe it was simply because it didn't matter anymore. They spoke freely, knowing she could hear them, but not caring. Almost as if she weren't even there.

The ropes gnawed away at her skin. Her wrists had been rubbed raw days ago, and now they were bleeding and swelling. They had even begun to give off a rancid smell. Kate had stopped caring about the pain the day before. There were much more pressing matters to worry about.

Yesterday she still thought there was hope. She was always optimistic like that. When the world itself began to fight off and eliminate most of the population in the form of the sickness, she still thought there was a chance. And there was. Now she wondered if she'd been stupid to believe that things really hadn't ended twenty years ago.

The Old World members were brought to the gym the day Jacob and the Palace-born woman went running toward the forest. For the last five days, they'd been taken out every six to twelve hours for what the guards had been calling a "cleansing."

Whole groups at a time, but not her. She didn't feel lucky for that though. She heard the ringing of gunshots, screams, and sometimes even applause. There was no mistaking what was going on out there.

"I'll be happy when we're done with this part of the plan. It's kind of dragging on, ya know?" Kate heard one of the faceless men say. From what she understood, they were charged with guarding everyone occupying the gym. She only heard two of them.

"What's to come won't be any easier for you than this. You sure you cut out for this, Danny?"

"Of course I am. What kind of question is that? I gave the pledge, didn't I? Don't come at me like that, Nathan." She heard the man named Danny clear his throat after speaking. He sounded like he wanted to cry, and she wondered if Nathan was right, if Danny was indeed not cut out for the job. Not that he was doing anything more than guarding a bound woman of forty-eight years in an empty gym.

"Yeah, I hear ya. But anyway, did you get the correspondence today about those"—Nathan paused—"Others? They attacked a nearby Palace, and good lives were lost. Damn good lives were squandered away for nothing. Just walked up to the front entrance and shot at everyone they could before hurrying off like the rats that they are. I don't feel bad because we are getting rid of the leftover rodents still living among us. It's either destroy them or allow them to finish destroying the planet." Kate heard the man spit.

"I know that," Danny said. "You don't have to explain it to me. It's in their nature to be that way. Sirus said so." She heard Danny's voice fade with his words as his footsteps carried him across the room. It sounded like he was wearing heavy boots.

"They are just now clearing out the bodies from the last cleansing," Danny said. Kate's heart nearly stopped beating. She felt she had never been the sharpest tool in the shed, either out in the real world prior to the sickness, or inside the Palace. But she was smart enough to know that they were being killed in that other room, and her number was fixing to be called next. Or *fixin'*, as her Grandmother would say when she was a child.

Grandma had been lucky she died long before the sickness. What a gift that she never witnessed any of this going down the way it has. *All things come to an end*, Kate had been telling herself over and over for the past few days as she listened to her friends being chopped down through the walls of the gym. She thought that if she could just accept the fate that awaited her—awaited everyone—then when her number was called, she could be fearless and take her death with pride.

"Tomorrow we start Phase 2 of the new teachings. Teacher Paul gave a short lecture on it today. I believe your floor goes tomorrow. Something about learning their ways to better get rid of them. He says the time we have spent around the Old World people will serve us when it's time to go out and deal with them." She could hear Nathan moving toward her.

Kate sat there on her bottom with both hands tied behind her and a white kerchief over her eyes. The steps continued to come closer until she could feel him in front of her. She could feel his energy, and it felt wrong. It felt hateful.

Suddenly a strong hand grabbed on to her red hair. Kate squealed in pain as she felt him wrapping her hair around his fist like a boxer bandaging his hand before the gloves were slipped on. He dragged her a bit, laughing as he did so. She felt embarrassed, and even that emotion at this moment and time seemed out of place. *I'm on the docket to die and can still manage to feel embarrassed because I'm being manhandled.*

"Hey man, stop doing that!" Danny screamed at him from near the door. The hand continued to yank on her hair. She thought it was being pulled from her skull. Nathan's hand freed itself from her tangled hair, allowing her body to fall to the ground. Kate cried beneath the cloth over her eyes.

"Relax, relax. She isn't much to scream about! You and I both know what's about to happen to her anyway. Hell, she knows as well. I'm just having a little fun," he said in a playful tone.

"I don't care, man. That's not our job. Let the ones in the auditorium handle that kind of stuff. We were told to guard the room and make sure no one tried to run. That's it. I'm not getting in trouble because you want to play around." Kate could hear from the direction of their voices that they were close to each other. *He got in his face?*

"Don't get all angry with me for playing with the little rat—"

BOOM! BOOM! BOOM! A loud knocking came from the door. Both men stopped arguing immediately and ran toward the sound of the banging. The door opened, and Kate only heard whispering. Then the door closed. The hushed voices got louder, and she heard Nathan say, "You do it...I'm going to my post. I mean, since you seem to care so much. I doubt you can even go through with it. Freaking rat lover." With that, the door opened and shut once more.

For a few moments the room was quiet. She wasn't sure if both men had left the room. Her body began to power down from all the adrenaline that had just poured into her nervous system. Those final words made her believe she was about to be killed right then. No auditorium group execution, but a cold, lonely death not even deserving of an audience. Odd she felt offended by that.

Kate felt calm for a split second as she lay there on her stomach, head aching from the hair pulling. She thought her skull might be bleeding a bit. She didn't move, remaining frozen in the same position the young soldier had left her in after abusing her like a seventh-grade bully.

Then the boots slowly began clicking against the floor, coming toward her. Slowly at first, hesitant even, and then they quickened. Kate panicked and began to beg.

"Listen, you don't have to do this. I'm sorry! Whatever I did, I'm sorry. Please just let me go, and you will never see me again! You can let me out the back door. No one will know..."

She didn't think she would beg to live in the end. It was past time to leave this plane of existence. In fact, it was about twenty years delayed. She felt that the people from the Old World were living on borrowed time since the sickness had spread. They were the ones not special enough to be taken, the lost tribe of the human race. Somewhere deep inside their minds, they had all been waiting to join their families in whatever came after this.

In that moment though, she did not want to die. Not in an empty gym, not alone, not without anyone to ever remember her—because all those people were dead as well. What happened to the memory of YOU when there was no one to remember any of the pieces that encompassed your entire being?

She thought about all these things in great detail. It may have only taken about three seconds of reflection, but it felt like a lifetime. Was there going to be anything else after this? She'd always thought so; many people did. But was it true?

The man named Danny put cold steel on the back of her head, pulled the trigger, and stopped all of her thoughts in an instant.

DANNY ENDED the woman's shameful existence, her life blown away in a terrible cloud of red and pink mist floating about the room. No fanfare or even a soul to watch her body take its final breath.

He walked over to a table, set the gun down, and exited the gym. He headed back to his pod, where he would eat the roast and mashed potatoes he'd ordered on the nutrition dispensary earlier that day. He didn't think about the woman, or any of the other Old World Palace members from the past. Nathan was right. They were but disgusting trivial things eating away at the planet, spreading plague time and time again, same as rats. Man had never cared about the fate of a rat, and he would not be the first.

CHAPTER SEVEN

Sirus

To: NCP GROUP [Palace Division]
Server: Unknown OC

From: O'Sullivan, Sirus
Date: May 19, 2040 16:24:36 EST

Subject: I loathe terrible news

I'VE BEEN MADE AWARE THAT PALACE 114 has lost the target. Please help me understand how this has happened? I provided direct coordinates to where she would be coming out of the forest. Mary is a very small woman with no combat training of any kind. She has no idea about the outside world other than what she learned inside the Palace —which are VERY basic survival skills. So, help me understand how a young, confused woman was able to get away from armed SECURITY!

I don't care about the meddlesome rebels and their pea-shooters; they should not have been powerful enough to take out so many security guards and make off with the target. I'm expecting a full breakdown of the situation by tomorrow. If I do not get it, I'll have my men chopper me to the 114 Palace, and I'll just start killing people until I get the answers I want. Death has always been a motivational tool for your kind.

She was permitted leave because I didn't want her to see Phase 2 in its entirety. NOT BECAUSE I WANT HER DEAD OR IN THE HANDS OF THOSE DAMN REBELS! Mary is very important to the plans the Order has in store for this world. It is of the utmost importance that I have her back here with me. There are lots of things I can be loose with; retrieving her ALIVE is not one of those things. I look forward to your response.

Thank you,
O'Sullivan, Sirus

CHAPTER EIGHT

Mary

MARY HAD TROUBLE OPENING HER EYES. She struggled to lift her hand and wipe the sleep from her eye lashes. They felt glued together. All she could see was a bright shining light above her head, nothing else. *What happened? Am I dead? What's going on?* She'd tried to say it out loud, but it was in her mind, echoing inside of her.

Managing to get her arm to move, Mary touched her cheek, then began to wipe her right eye to better see the room she was in.

"Whoa there, little Palace girl. Not so hasty!" The soft but strong voice scared Mary so badly she thought she would jump out of her skin. Her body lifted off the table she was lying on. A small scream escaped her lips just as a hand grabbed her arm.

"Relax, we are not here to hurt you. We have been doing all that we can in order to keep you alive. It's cost us a lot of our meds and a bed, neither of which we have enough to spare." The voice was that of a woman. Mary's vision was still too hazy to see clearly. She felt as though she had been sleeping for weeks.

In a panic, Mary yanked her arm from the woman's grasp and began wiping her eyes vigorously, clearing the cobwebs. *Why can't I see clearly?*

"Who are you!" Mary screamed. "Let me go. I don't want to be here. Just leave me alone, please!" she pleaded as she jumped up from the bed, backing up against a nearby wall, still not able to see exactly who was in the room with her. Her hands shot out in multiple directions, trying to fend off whoever was coming for her. She could just make out the forms of multiple people gawking at her.

She'd never been made to feel like an animal inside the Palace, but now she felt exactly that way. Cornered, afraid—desperate. She could see enough to tell that the people in the room were not dressed like teachers or workers in the infirmary. Where was she?

"Listen chick, you need to calm your ass down," came another voice. She recognized it as the same booming voice of the man who'd carried her away from the quarantine field. "If we meant to kill you, then we would have done so outside! Sit back down—"

"No, Derek, don't. Stand down soldier. I'm giving the orders here. Don't forget your place." The strange woman's tone suddenly became cold, and an awkward silence fell over the room.

She moved closer to Mary, taking small steps toward her. Mary's vision finally cleared a bit, at least enough so that she saw the woman holding one hand out, squatting low as she took steps in Mary's direction like she was cornering a wild animal. The strange woman's posture was appropriate for how Mary felt.

"Listen to me, young lady. We don't know who you are, and now you're beginning to scare us. That's not what you want to do here; we saved you from the colonizers, and those of our kind that work with them." She moved close enough to glide her fingers softly over Mary's forearm, which she had lifted to shield her chest and face. A defensive position that, to her surprise, came naturally.

"I'm confused," Mary said softly. She wasn't sure if they could hear her.

"I know you are. Just sit back down and let me explain a few things to you. You are indeed safe here with us. We brought you here to help you, remember that."

In that moment she thought about the baby growing in her womb and wondered if they found out while she was asleep. Had they run any tests on her? She wasn't far enough along to feel the baby moving around, but she wanted to feel something. To be assured that the baby was still alive. If they, whoever they were, had somehow found out, she was sure it would be brought up at some point.

Putting the thought out of her mind, Mary moved her hands back down to her side slowly and walked over to the bed, feeling defeated in a way. There was a lot going on inside of her body. Anxiety and fear ran rampant in her mind as well. But she needed to remain calm and not be shaken.

There were approximately twelve people in the room. Upon another look around, she noticed they were in an infirmary. It looked exactly like the infirmary in the Palace—her Palace. Only it was more rundown than the infirmary she knew. But why were these people inside of a Palace? *Where are the teachers and security?* she thought, trying to get her bearings to deal with the issue at hand.

There were five men and seven women, not including her. They wore clothing and gear like she'd seen in Old World clips from wars. Wars of the past where men would kill each other by the thousands, millions even. These wars took place for little to no reason, mostly based on the greed of the few.

The strangers wore vests that looked like they could stop bullets from penetrating their skin and black-and-green-colored clothing that seemed to be created to blend into the forest. Mary could not get the word off the tip of her tongue and out of her mouth. Army fa... fa...something.

Even in the midst of a dire situation, it bothered her that she couldn't think of the name of their style of clothing. If she forgot something at the Palace, they would have added it to her file, making it harder for her to get into the Greater Understanding Program. Which really didn't exist anyway, she remembered. It was all a ploy created by the Order and Sirus to give Old World members something to reach for. A cruel lie that ended up being no more than death in the end.

"Can I have a little bit of alone time with our newest find?" the woman said loudly, her voice echoing throughout the room. There was a sense of authority in her words, and everyone made their way to the exit without a word. When they were all out, one of the men carefully closed the door behind him. The woman sat next to Mary and tilted her head down, looking up at her the way a mother would when trying to speak to a scared child. Mary stared at the dirty shoes on her feet, swinging them back and forth as she sat on the gurney. She was afraid to meet the woman's stare.

"What is your name, young lady? I'm Carla," the strange woman said.

"My name is Mary...Are you and your friends going to hurt me?"

"Of course not, Mary. That's a lovely name, by the way." Carla slowly grabbed both of Mary's hands and rested them on her knees. "Look at me. You have nothing to be afraid of—you are safe here." Mary lifted her head, finally looking at Carla and finding a smile on the woman's face. A warm smile that told her things would be okay, but there was an intensity hidden in her eyes. Mary could see that as well.

She hadn't felt safe since before she and Jacob ran away from the Palace only days ago. Felt like years to her...every minute felt like a day without him. She would need to learn how to deal with that fact since she would be living through the day. The suicide she planned would be put on hold for the time being. These strangers were definitely not with the Order.

Mary tried a smile. She felt like it came off as more of a grimace than anything else. "Where are we?" she said in a whisper to Carla.

"Where do you think we are? Something tells me that you may already know the answer to that question." Carla pointed down at Mary's shoes. "Those are pretty standard issue sneakers for individuals who have been living among the colonizers."

"Colonizers?" Mary spoke slowly, articulating every syllable.

"Okay, I see that you're still out of it, which does not come as a surprise. When we found, or rather saved your life from the facility guards, you were already out of it and near death. Dehydrated and sick, and you likely are still sick as we speak, but you are doing much better than you were yesterday afternoon when we got to you. The medic here says you ingested something bad for you. While it wasn't deadly, it did make you very sick, and it's the reason you had issues seeing. Your vision will be back to normal in a day or so. Nothing to worry about now, it's an effect of that particular plant. But Derek thought you were a goner for sure."

Carla got up from the gurney and walked over to the service desk area of the infirmary. Mary noted a slight limp when the woman walked away. Carla leaned over the desk and pulled out one of the drawers from the other side, grabbing a file. She sat on the edge of the desk facing Mary and began to read the paperwork inside.

Mary cracked her knuckles, watching the woman licking her thumb as she went through the pages. Every joint in her body felt stiff.

Carla seemed strange to Mary, but in all the right ways. She'd never seen a woman command such authority in her voice. Studying Carla, she noticed that her long arms were thick and muscular. Her hair was tied in a tight ponytail that pulled her eyebrows up into her forehead in a way that looked almost painful. She was beautiful, and it was hard for Mary to stop scanning her. She looked to be about five ten, one hundred and forty pounds. Mary had no clue why those particular numbers came to her; they just did. She was sure they were accurate.

"This is what you would call a Palace, as I'm sure you're already aware. We call them facilities. So, if you hear that word, just understand we are talking about the same things." Carla set the file to the left of her, grabbed a cup on her right, and took a big gulp of what Mary thought was coffee or tea judging by the steam whirling around the lip.

"And you don't work with the Order in some capacity? Or is this something different?" Mary asked with a confused face. "I know that not all Palaces work the exact same way... Are you going to send me back to the Palace that I came from?"

Her voice cracked when she spoke those last few words. The fear of coming face to face with the evil that was Sirus came back to her mind. She would die before she did that. Of course, it didn't fit that Carla's people had shot down security agents at the Palace near the forest, but maybe there was in-fighting among sections of the Order? Nothing was adding up, and Mary's fear made it impossible to think clearly.

"One question at a time dear." Carla rested the weight of her body on her hands behind her as she kept her butt on the edge of the desk. It seemed as though she was trying to keep the weight off her legs. Mary wondered what happened to the woman that made her walk so gingerly.

"Were you hit in the fight when you all helped me? Did you hurt your leg saving me?" Mary expressed sincere compassion and concern in her voice.

Carla looked shocked, but quickly caught her expression then smiled and waved the statement off. "No need to worry about that. Everyone here is hurt in one way or another. Had nothing to do with you or taking out a few security guards. Don't worry your pretty little head." She smiled then went on speaking about the matter at hand.

"This is what you would call a Palace, one of four in Indiana, or Old Indiana as we now call it. My group, the Eagles, took over this Palace about a year ago. We lost many lives, but in the end, it was worth it. There are now over two hundred soldiers here, and we're fully equipped with Old World weaponry. Some of those same weapons and soldiers tore those guards to pieces to liberate you from the clutches of those from elsewhere."

Carla stared deeply at Mary, and her gaze became cold and unfeeling. "I would like to know why your facility allowed you to leave. I've never seen that happen before."

"You all killed everyone here? The teachers? Security? Everyone?" Mary thought she would be sick, even sicker than she already felt, at the thought of so many lives lost. She knew that the Order were not good people, but so much death made her feel terrible.

"Of course." Laughter came bursting out of Carla's mouth. "We killed everyone that they themselves didn't kill first. Not sure if you noticed while creeping through the forest like a magic fairy, but you probably did not run into any other people along the way, correct? The good Lord has not seen fit to make them invincible. They are gone, child."

Mary shook her head. *What does she mean by everyone they didn't kill first?*

"Listen, I want to be honest with you about who we are and what we do. After I tell you things you need to know, I'll have a question for you. Depending on how you answer that question, you may get a chance to see another day."

CHAPTER NINE
Melinda

ER KNEES BELLOWED IN PAIN, HER knuckles white from holding on to the sides of the toilet bowl in the bathroom of her pod. She'd be in this position for over an hour. It was pointless to get up and try taking a shower before bed. The images would come back to her, and so would breakfast, lunch—and dinner from that day. She couldn't believe she'd eaten that much food, but apparently, she had. The toilet and the constant flushing would serve as proof of this.

When she'd looked in the mirror before the most recent round of vomiting, Melinda's face had been the pale color of sickness, every ounce of color driven away from her cheeks. Vomiting would do that to you, and vomiting on and off for an hour would do worse. Tears streamed down her face, drying on her cheeks after a while, only to be replaced by new streams when the time came to heave up more of the Cobb salad from earlier.

She'd always hated being sick for this very reason. The vomiting was so painful on the stomach and carried a bit of shame with it. In this case, she worried that the shame of the day would keep her up for many nights to come.

A feeling came to her that others from the cleansing were doing the same thing at that very moment. While some of the Palace-born had watched in delight at what was happening on the stage, the majority either looked disgusted and sick or altogether distant. She'd been wondering since returning to her pod why this was the case. Why were people who had lived through the same experiences having such different reactions to the traumatic events that had taken place in the auditorium over the last five days?

Melinda's back hunched upward as she retched into the toilet bowl once more. At that point she was violently expelling no more than water and what looked like bile from her belly. The sight and smell of it made her want to vomit even more. Her stomach felt wound up and irritated. She wanted nothing more than for it all to stop. Sleep would be a welcome visitor; she didn't want to think about anything anymore. She wasn't sure if she wanted to live anymore; the cleansings were that terrible.

After another five minutes of resting her head on the toilet seat, she thought it safe enough to get up and begin to clean the floor of the bathroom without having to vomit again. That was the hope. Unfortunately, she hadn't quite made it to the toilet upon coming into her pod from the cleansing session. There was much to clean up before getting into the shower.

Melinda got to her feet, relieving her poor knees from the hard linoleum she'd been digging them into for the last hour. Her young fifteen-year-old knees popped as she moved. Age meant nothing to her, or to anyone in the Palace after the age of ten, which served as the age of adulthood. She felt like a woman grown, and even more so after witnessing the deaths of so many that she'd come to know and care for.

That day she went through a change that she'd never be able to reverse. Those images would haunt her, even when she closed her eyes...the sounds were as graphic as the visual.

Irony came to mind as she grabbed two towels and a washcloth from beneath the sink. The Palace-born had been made to endure the same things that the Old World members first experienced upon coming to the Palace. To watch as people they knew and "loved" were exterminated like animals. On a much smaller level of course, but to her and the other Palace-born, this was "the world," and it all seemed to end for her during the cleansing. What was there to do now? She felt lost.

Melinda had of course watched the video clips that played on an endless loop on every television in each pod and in the central plaza. She'd read the literature provided on each floor from the Order about what the remaining Old World members were doing on the outside. It didn't matter though, right was right, and wrong was still wrong. She couldn't see things any other way. They were being forced to believe that the Old World members were no longer human or deserving of love and empathy. Just like that, they didn't matter.

She'd spent her life learning not to hurt people, not to wish ill will on any living creature born of Mother Earth's bosom. Now all of that was being turned on its head because these people were out there suffering from mental illness and confusion? None of it made sense to her, and she hoped that a better explanation would come down the pipeline later. There had to be more to the story than what she'd learned at this point.

So much needed answering before she could fully get on board with something that seemed so wrong to her. How were people still alive out there? Why were survivors of the sickness trying to kill good people of the Palaces? Why had she and others from the Palace been made to believe that they couldn't go outside the hundred-yard radius or else they'd suffer the same sickness that killed so many over twenty years ago? *Were they trying to protect us from the bad survivors out there the entire time?*

She knew that they were supposed to just listen and believe whatever the teachers said, but it needed to make sense to her. She would not simply gloss over all the contradictions and begin to foster hate for people on the outside she didn't even know. From this situation, she had learned that things clearly were not what she once thought they were. Doubt invaded her thoughts, and doubt was a sickness of the brain in the Palace.

After cleaning the bathroom and returning the floor to the pristine white that everyone had come to expect in the facility, she tossed the vomit-soaked towels near her pod door. The cleaning crew would come to get those tomorrow while she was away at a session. *If we are still doing sessions.*

She hoped that the cleaning crew would not make a big deal of the vomit all over the towels. She desperately hoped they would not tell a teacher. If they thought she was too weak to fall in line, there was no telling what would happen to her. The violence of those in charge and the security group had been on display for days. She now knew what they were capable of. The nightly ritual had changed, and she had no reason to believe that the day activities would remain the same. Phase 2 of the Palace was leading them down a harsher path.

The clothes she wore from the day sat in a pile next to the stand-up shower in her bathroom as she stepped inside and turned on the water. This would be the hottest shower she'd ever had; it was necessary. Melinda would scrub at her skin with a white wash cloth, trying desperately to wipe away how dirty she'd become. How they'd ever come to be what they were that day was beyond her, and it had been challenging to even look in the mirror while she'd brushed her teeth and tongue for ten minutes straight before the shower.

She hadn't pulled any triggers that day, but she also hadn't stopped any from being pulled, and she would have to live with that. For better or worse, she'd allowed something wrong to happen because she did not want to end up on that stage.

Even though the guy next to her had taken her hand and said they deserved it, she could feel his pain as well when the guns began firing. *The strength in his grasp was all fear*, she thought as she let the water rain down on her face. Maybe she should try to find him and pick his brain on what exactly was going on. She was pretty sure his name was *Lonnie*; she often saw *him running* in the gym.

Melinda's mind went right back to the event in the auditorium. She was seemingly unable to think about anything else longer than a few seconds before going back to the cleansing. Maybe the thing that haunted her the most was the fact that she felt like a coward. The same cowardice that allowed the Old World people to let atrocities happen before the sickness came to claim most of their lives.

Before the sickness, people had remained idle while the powers of their world destroyed the ozone layer, the oceans, wildlife—all while constantly waging war on each other. They thought they had no power to stop what was, and maybe they were right. She had no idea, but she felt like someone should have tried. Now she felt no better than any of them, because when the time of truth had come for her, she hadn't answered the bell.

If Mother Earth released a pandemic into the atmosphere to kill off those who were not just, did not care for each other, and were destructive to their own detriment, how would She view what they'd done all week? The thought made her dry heave right there in the shower. Nothing came up though; she was empty.

The steaming water from the shower fogged up the glass. It made her feel protected, hidden even. Tonight she needed that because she was feeling small and weak. The water washed away the filth of the day. She had a feeling that showers would have a whole new meaning if she was to witness or take part in such things.

Melinda washed her body and got out of the shower, dressed, and hesitantly headed down to a newly opened room on the sixth floor. A shooting range. It was part of the nightly schedule now. She had to go if she didn't want to be singled out as being against the mission. The video clips playing throughout the Palace all said as much, and on the bottom right of each screen were the words: "Complete the Mission."

Instead of nightly dinners saying Mother's prayer with Sirus through the television and eating together, they would now eat alone while watching videos of unfathomable violence on the televisions. After dinner it was time to change clothes into something more fitting for blowing fake targets to bits, then head down for killing practice. Teacher Paul said they would be using the skill a lot in the days to come. That worried her.

On the elevator with other Palace-born members heading to the sixth floor, Melinda remembered something Sirus said in a letter drafted for each person in the Palace. They were to be soldiers in a "holy war to end all holy wars." This was meant both figuratively and literally.

CHAPTER TEN

Lonnie

"HAVE A SEAT RIGHT THERE, YOUNG MAN," Teacher Luke said to Lonnie, sitting back in his own seat on the opposite side of the table. The teacher had a welcoming smile on his face as he nodded in the direction of the chair. He placed both his palms flat on the table, a manila folder laying face-down in the middle. The youngest of all the teachers in the Palace had a knack for grossing out anyone who had ever spent more than a few minutes with him. He'd been called eccentric by others around the Palace, among other things.

Lonnie didn't feel that way about him though. He thought the man an oddball, but he didn't get the creeps from him. "Hello, Teacher Luke, how are you doing today?" Lonnie pulled out his metal chair at the white table and sat with his hands on both knees. "May the Mother's blessings rain down upon you and me alike."

The teacher waved his hand dismissively at Lonnie's words about Mother's blessings and tossed his wild black hair away from his brow. "No need for that song and dance. We know that you are committed to our mission and getting back out into the world." He reached across the desk to shake Lonnie's hand. "I'm...hmmm, how can I say this? I'm excited to meet with you today, Lonnie."

After a firm handshake, the teacher looked at Lonnie, and the smile disappeared all of a sudden. "I just wonder if you are ready," he said, regarding the young man with a troubled look. The teacher tapped his finger on the desk, as if he were trying to figure something out by simply staring at him. His eyes were abnormally big and brown, even more so when he was staring at Lonnie the way he was just then. "With such sensitive information and choices, one must be most careful as to who can be trusted. You understand?"

"Am I ready for what, Teacher Luke?" Lonnie began to feel uneasy. He'd been doing everything in his power to prove he was ready for the Greater Understanding Program (which no longer seemed to exist) since he came into the adult pods at the age of ten. He'd even stomached the cleansing without losing his shit all over the girl next to him.

"Well...it's what I called you down here for. The Order, myself, and Sirus have need of a young man like yourself for what's to come, but..." He paused, removed his hands from the desk, and placed them in his lap while continuing to stare at Lonnie. "There are things that have come to our attention with you. Things that could take you out of contention for such a role."

A swarm of emotions flew around in Lonnie's mind at the sound of those words. *My god, what have I done? Is it about the cleansing? Did they see me holding that girl's hand? Maybe they saw me close my eyes for the last half of the...slaughter.*

He adjusted his sitting position, moving his fingers around the small pricklies that replaced the tight small curls on his head. He was still getting accustomed to the buzz cut. The grooming folks at the Palace were not as good at cutting the hair of those of African descent. They did manage to not cut his skin during the shave, unlike some of his friends—so, that was something. Lonnie snapped out of the brief distraction to find Teacher Luke getting up from his seat.

Lonnie decided he would come right out and ask. "I'm sorry, but I don't know what you mean by that, sir. Could you be more forthcoming with any concerns? I'll do all I can to make sure everyone involved knows that I'm not a problem and will not become a problem." Lonnie didn't want to end up on the stage. But they wouldn't do that to the Palace-born, would they? He was pretty sure that treatment was reserved for the Old World rats. *Right?* He became warm all of a sudden and felt his body starting to perspire. He was sweating like a pig, hoping the teacher wouldn't notice. Sweat meant nervous, nervous meant lying or hiding something.

Teacher Luke sat on the edge of the white table in the small room, which housed nothing but the table and the chair. Long bright lights lined the ceiling, and there were no windows. Lonnie had never been in a room like this in the Palace. He wondered what the function of such a room could possibly be, other than a talk like this.

"We know things, Lonnie. We see things, and more importantly, people talk," Teacher Luke said, rubbing his freshly shaven chin and looking down at the young man. "You see, we have stumbled upon something about you and your stomach, or lack thereof, in regard to... How should I say? Messy situations, some would call it."

Lonnie felt his throat tighten at hearing the words.

"Now, I only say this because it's very important to the Order that we promote members who are ready for any situation. Things in the near future could become grim, hard to deal with—tough decisions may need to be made." The man stared into Lonnie's eyes as he spoke. It made Lonnie feel as though the teacher were peering into his soul for fear or weakness. Searching his soul for what he needed to find. After all this time, Lonnie was finally becoming creeped out by the teacher.

The weakness was in there, but Lonnie would not allow it to show. He was scared; letting down the Order was the worst thing anyone in the Palace could ever do. The thought of not being helpful to the cause, or worse, getting in the way of what needed to be done, hurt his heart.

Luckily the Palace-born were all too familiar with masking their true emotions. It would not be a problem for Lonnie to convince Teacher Luke that there was nothing fragile hiding in the confines of his psyche.

"What's been found out, sir? I'll do anything to right any wrongs I may have inadvertently been involved in or committed myself. Please tell me so that I can beg for forgiveness." Lonnie sat straight up in his seat like a soldier at attention. He stared straight ahead at the wall, never looking directly at Teacher Luke. He'd seen the security squad do that when talking to the guys in yellow coats. He wasn't quite sure, but he had the feeling it was a sign of respect.

"I like that. I do like how eager you are to please. That actually excites me even more than I thought it would." Teacher Luke bit his lip as his eyes lit up with intrigue and excitement.

"Someone said you couldn't keep your food down the day you found the dead child in the pod. Is this true, Lonnie? Was it all too much for your tender heart to bear?" He pulled the chair from under the desk and put one foot on the seat. He leaned on his knee with his arm, cutting his eye at Lonnie. "Now, I don't believe that, but that's the word from some who were on the scene. Tell me that's not true. If you honestly can, that is. Lies are not allowed, as you know."

Feeling both embarrassed and relieved at the same time, Lonnie found it hard to find a reply. He didn't want to lie, and he also didn't want Teacher Luke to think him a coward. "I, uhh...I did become sick, but it was not for the reason you think. I mean, if that is what you think.

"I became ill because I knew that someone was dead in the Palace. I knew one of those rats did what they do best, and I arrived too late to stop him. I was only able to alert everyone to the death of Michelle. Honestly, I still become filled with rage when I think about it." Lonnie slowly turned his head to look directly at the teacher. "They fuck everything up."

"You're right, that's exactly what they're doing. Same types of things that led us all to where we are today. Those from the Old World are not capable of being happy. No matter what you give them or do for them, it could never be enough. We gave them a safe place to live, we saved them all, and look at what we got in return. Housed and fed them for years, and in the end, they have no problem smiling in your face before shoving a dagger in your back just as soon as they get the chance.

"I want to tell you a few things about them, who they are, what they are. I don't want you to have any reservations about doing what must be done if the Earth is to continue to give life, if we are to continue to exist as a people and species." Teacher Luke's voice was building up anger with every word. Lonnie could see he had no love for those from the Old World. Even though he himself, the other teachers, and every member of the Order, were also from the Old World.

"Why are they that way though?" Lonnie asked. "Is there anything that can be done other than killing them all? I ask not because I'm opposed to doing what needs to be done, but because I'd like to understand the psychology of their mental sickness that causes them to be this way." He looked up at Teacher Luke questioningly.

"Unfortunately, no, there is no other way to handle them," he said, holding Lonnie in a cold stare. "We have been trying to show them the error of their ways for the last twenty years. People like us, I mean the teachers, the Order's workers and staff, we have learned from the ways of the past. We had lots of information on ourselves and the old civilization as a whole. We had the ability to learn, but they simply do not. They must be put down so that we can get back to the mission. And that mission is to give the Earth children who love and appreciate the gifts she brings us with every rising and setting of the sun."

A memory came to Lonnie just then of a time in the courtyard. He was walking the trail with others from his age group, and they'd passed a few people from the Old World sitting on a stone bench. As he and his group walked by, he heard one of the women whisper, "Fucking nigger," under her breath. Until this week, during a session about racial topics from the Old World, Lonnie hadn't understood the implications of the insult. But at the time, by the way it was said and the snide look on the woman's face, it just felt wrong.

SHE'D KNOWN that he and the other Palace-born wouldn't understand what the word meant. That was likely why she'd said it, so in that way it was a double offense. It was bad enough that she called him that, and she did it knowing he was too ignorant to even understand she was offending him.

HE HAD DONE nothing to upset that woman, and she'd been in the Palace learning about the correct way to do things for fifteen years at that point, and still...the hate came seeping out. She could not help herself, and the others on the bench had smiled right along with her. They were all hateful, the whole lot of them.

He thought of the man getting Mary to run away with him. The rat named Dwight killing Michelle in her pod, forcing Lonnie to have to see it, smell it, experience such a thing. He tied that together with the group of people known as Caucasians in the Old World sitting in the courtyard, looking down at him, one having the nerve to call him that dirty word. Teacher Luke was right, he could truly see that now.

After a few moments of tense silence, the teacher walked over to his side of the desk. "This brings me to what I needed to discuss with you today, sir. You are a young...and a strong man." He put a hand on Lonnie's shoulder, giving it a hard squeeze.

"We need people like you. Strong, intelligent, and logical. Logic is an underrated strength. In lots of cases, the lack of logic can allow the heart to tell you lies, lies that your brain can come to empathize with." He removed the hand from Lonnie's shoulder and got down on one knee next to his chair. Lonnie kept his gaze looking straight ahead at the wall, taking in everything that was being said to him.

"I'll be frank with you because I trust you, I believe you, and I think you are strong enough for the job. Some among the Order have questions about that, but I'm not among the ones hesitant to this promotion..." Teacher Luke tapped Lonnie on the knee, getting him to break his stare and beckoning him to make eye contact.

"All you must do is tell me what I'm needed for and I'll take care of it," Lonnie said. "No questions asked. I have heard you today, and I know the things you say to be true. The one question I had, you answered when you didn't have to, and I appreciate that. I agree with you, and you have my word and service from here on in. I'm a tool for the Order on behalf of Mother Earth." Lonnie nodded in assurance at Teacher Luke, who was still on one knee, smiling at that point. A devilish smile. "Use me in any way you see fit," Lonnie said, repeating the sentiment once again.

"I was hoping you would say that. We are looking for special individuals to help lead those who remain in the Palace. To teach them, to be an example. Not that we the teachers, the watchers, and the security team aren't doing a great job, or that your kind—I mean those who have only lived in the Palace—would not follow our lead, they will. But the transition would be much smoother if it came from someone like you. One of their own."

Teacher Luke leaned in close as he continued. "The time spent among the Old World members for the last twenty years has created an atmosphere in which they were and still are being seen as brothers and sisters. And they were, don't get me wrong, they were. But it's vital that we stamp out a small candle flame before it's tipped over and creates a wild forest fire. We need men like you to help blow out that small flame. Can you do that?" Teacher Luke rose to his feet and walked back over to his side of the desk, sitting down in the chair. "You can be that for us, correct?"

"I can, and I will. I feel as though I was created for this moment, and I'll never give you or anyone else in the Order reason to doubt my resolve or my stomach for the harsh stuff ever again." Lonnie spoke with tears in his eyes. He felt strong now, he felt driven...valued even. He'd never felt valued before. It was a good feeling.

Teacher Luke extended a hand across the desk, smiling and nodding his head in agreement. "I'm gonna vouch for you. Don't let me down."

Lonnie proudly shook his hand.

CHAPTER ELEVEN

Andrew

STEPPING INTO THE ELEVATOR WITH HIS small gym bag, Andrew was more afraid than he'd ever been in his life. At only sixteen years old, things had been easy for him...up until last week. He grew up in the child center with over seventy children around the same age, and that life was fine...it was normal, it was all he'd known. It was as normal as could be, growing up around other children, no parents, and only the occasional adult to make sure nothing terrible happened to anyone.

But things were terrible now. The Palace had become a place of anxiety, fear, and murder. No one could convince him that what he'd witnessed was not murder. Andrew spent the last two nights crying to himself beneath the covers in his room. How did things become so bad so fast? One week he was laughing in morning enrichment classes with friends, and the next they were all in the auditorium watching Old World members being filled with holes on stage. And they were the gallery...he was made to watch, was supposed to feel nothing.

But he did feel, and he knew that others did as well. Fear was a strange thing though, it would allow you to hide your true nature and go along with the crowd. Andrew did not want to be a part of that crowd.

He hoped that no one would stop the elevator on the way down. His plan was to get to the eastern courtyard and make a run for it, the same way that Mary and Jacob did. Andrew couldn't forget the gruesome image of the Old World man being shot down, but Mary had made it. And maybe Andrew would too. He was willing to risk death getting out of there—the situation had come to that. And if he could avoid all human contact from there to the courtyard, maybe he had a chance.

He hit the button for the first floor and felt the elevator come to life beneath his feet. Moving down, he became more and more nervous as the numbers lit up: seven, six, five, four...Then the elevator's movement paused. It came to a stop. Andrew thought he would be sick right then.

Please let this be anyone but a teacher or security officer. Anyone at all. The elevator door slowly opened. Andrew looked down at his shoes, not wanting to face who may have stopped the elevator. His heart had fallen into his legs at that point, banging off his knee and coming to rest somewhere near his calf muscle. If it was a teacher, he would scream for help. It wouldn't do anything for him, but he would not be able to stop himself from doing it regardless.

"Hello, how are you?" a strong male voice greeted him as the owner of said voice stepped into the elevator. Andrew still did not have the courage to look up at the man, and he kept his eyes on his white sneakers. Then he noticed that the man wore the same shoes. Relief filled his mind like sun through open blinds on a beautiful Saturday morning. Andrew allowed himself to calm down.

"I'm doing fine, and how are you?" Without allowing the man to answer, Andrew decided to double down on the pleasantries, not wanting to raise any suspicion. "May Mother bless us all in the days to come."

"She will, my friend. I believe that she will do just that."

Andrew reluctantly lifted his head, finally looking over at the man now that he was sure it was not security or a teacher. The other Palace member was not much older than Andrew, but he was a great deal bigger. He had round brown eyes and short brown hair. The face was familiar to Andrew from his time in the child center so long ago. It seemed to be a past life now, even though it was only six years ago when he ascended into adult pod living.

The other man smiled at Andrew and pushed the button on the elevator to close the doors. Returning the smile, Andrew hugged the bag beneath his left arm tighter and looked forward.

Again, the elevator came to life. Three, two, one...

The doors opened, and both men walked out. They walked in the same direction, heading toward the eastern courtyard. Andrew tried walking ahead; he loathed awkward conversation and was not in the mental state to fake a talk with someone while planning a breakout from the only home he'd ever known. He might accidentally confess his plan to whomever he spoke to if he began running his mouth.

"Heading out?" the man asked, keeping pace with Andrew. "I'm Milton, by the way. I've seen you around. Maybe in the gym, but I think your age group was a year or so behind my own."

"Yeah, gonna get some fresh air before this afternoon's activity class," Andrew said in a low voice, averting his eyes back to the ground as he walked. He felt Milton looking at him.

"Same here. I need the air. Things have been really weird here, if you know what I mean," Milton whispered to him, leaning his own head closer to Andrew's as they made their way down the corridor.

"Tell me about it, man. Those who offend against mankind and the planet as a whole must be extinguished though." Andrew repeated the words he'd heard Sirus say in one of the video clips now showing repeatedly on the televisions. The same televisions that for the last twenty years hadn't displayed much more than "Please Wait" until the runaway incident. Then the week of cleansing followed thereafter.

"Mother's grace upon those that offend, you said it, man." Milton laid his left hand on Andrew's shoulder and opened the glass door leading out to the courtyard with his right. Andrew didn't like being touched, especially by someone he didn't know well. He shrugged the hand off his shoulder with a smile while walking through the doors.

Both young men walked out into the hot humid day. It was warm, but the sun wasn't bright in the sky. Rain was coming; black clouds could be seen off in the distance. Andrew noticed a security agent to the right of the door. There was just the one, and he was not near the area that Andrew planned to escape from, so that was a plus.

There were others out in the courtyard. Some were walking, and there was a group of people near the big Planet Earth statue, talking about something that looked important based on their faces. He thought they would be talking about killing more Old World members; that's all anyone seemed to talk about lately. He needed to free himself from what his home had become.

"Alright man, it was great talking to you. Maybe I'll see you tonight at the range if that's on your schedule?" Andrew said, walking away from Milton and waving at the same time.

"I'll be seeing you. Have a great walk, Andrew." Milton returned the wave as he made his way to a group of women walking on a trail that, which fortunately, led in the opposite direction.

There was fear within his mind for what could happen after he went past the red flags in the ground. He knew they signaled the end of the quarantine area around the Palace. The thought of falling to his knees, vomiting up his guts, and stroking out was a real threat. It's what they had all been told, and that's how the deaths looked on the TV. The Order wanted them to see footage of how most the population had died; maybe they thought it would be a deterrent for anyone tempted to run away. He wondered how they got such footage but did not ask. He didn't want to think about it.

Even with the thoughts of dying a gruesome and painful death by sudden sickness stuck to the top of his brain, he was still going to leave. He had to leave. Andrew could not play a part in the deaths of others, no matter what the Order said these people did. He was not an executioner and would not play any role in the extinguishing of other human beings.

Andrew walked along the trail by himself, trying his hardest to build the nerve to take off and run. He'd walked around the area at least six times, getting the lay of the land as far as security, if there was any (there wasn't), and checking for any nosy Palace members who could see and alert security.

No one was paying attention to him or even cared about what he was doing. He still got the feeling he was being watched though.

Whenever he thought about running off into the woods from the eastern trail of the courtyard, he would hear something, or someone would come out of the Palace, talking loudly and drawing attention.

The bag under his arm had his breakfast from that morning inside, along with a few washcloths and deodorant. He didn't know what he should bring with him when he escaped, so he added the most practical things he could think of. What did one bring along when running away from home? Things small enough to fit into a small bag, he supposed. He would prefer a gun over a croissant roll, but he had to take what he could get.

If what they'd learned over the years was true, or even partially true, the world outside of this quarantined oasis of sorts was a mess. There was no telling what he would run into making his way through the nearby forest. Not only that, but there was always the possibility that he wouldn't make it to the forest. *What if they shoot me down? Like Jacob?*

If that was the case, then he would just have to take that chance. His plan was fragile and would surely fall apart, he knew that. He also knew that he could adapt and find a way. He had no one in particular he was going to find, not even a location in mind. All of that was up in the air, and in a way that was exciting.

Andrew was one of the more promising Palace-born of his age group, some thought the top of the group. He had no delusions of grandeur about what he planned to do and the chances of failure involved, but it was worth a shot for him. He could not remain in the Palace another day, and if it ended in his death, then so be it. There were things worse than death, he truly believed that.

Andrew stopped on the trail, looking behind him to make sure no one would see him run off into the wooded area near the trail, where he would make a mad dash into the forest outside of the quarantined area. He touched his chest; his heart was pounding so hard and loud he thought the people in the courtyard might hear it. Stress was building, and he knew if he didn't pull the trigger on this whole thing, it would just get worse the longer he took.

Looking into the sky, seeing the dark clouds were closer now than they were when he walked outside, he swallowed hard and then took a deep breath. Swinging the bag over his shoulder, Andrew took off in a full sprint, off of the trail and away from the Palace.

While doubt and horror accompanied his every thought, there were threads of liberation and freedom floating around in there as well. He jumped over a big log about one-hundred yards into the wooded area. Running so hard and fast he tripped on a stone jutting from the ground, but Andrew did not fall. He gained his balance, continuing to sprint through the wooded area. He could already see the field with the red flags ahead. The side of his lip began to turn up in a smile at the thought of being away from what the Palace had become. Then something jerked him to a sudden, violent stop. He felt whiplash in his neck and back as he whirled around, thinking he would see a tree or something his bag had snagged on.

There was no tree, there was only Milton, his strong hand gripping Andrew's writst. Andrew pulled his other arm back, ready to swing his bag at the young man he'd just been sharing pleasantries with minutes ago.

"Let me go, man, let go of me!" Andrew said quietly in a pleading tone.

That's when he noticed that the bag was no longer in his hand, and it was a labor to even lift his arm. Milton let Andrew's arm go and stepped back, staring at him like something he didn't quite understand, cocking his head to the left a bit. Andrew tried to shout at the young man to go back to the courtyard and to not say anything to the security agent about seeing him make a run for it. No words came out of his mouth that time; nothing came out but what felt like a pint of blood.

The thick red substance came bubbling over his lips, pouring down his gray sweatshirt and turning it a rusty shade of brown. He reached out with the one arm that would move and took two steps toward the man in front of him. Milton, still staring awkwardly at him, stepped back, snapping twigs and rustling leaves while shuffling backwards. He almost looked afraid of Andrew. Still he said nothing; he just watched, studied.

Andrew felt a warm liquid running down his back and down his leg. There was a stiffness coming from his back. He reached around to touch it, and that's when he felt the handle. *A knife? Is there a knife in my back?* Andrew's eyes widened as even more panic flooded his brain. He tried to pull the handle—the knife—from his back. He spun around in circles, spitting up blood, trying to pull the knife from his body. Milton gazed at him wth inquisitive amusement.

After what felt like an eternity but was likely a few seconds, Andrew grew tired, and lost balance, he slammed his right shoulder into a nearby tree. He slid down to the ground with his back against the tree—feeling it move the knife around in his back as he tried to catch his breath, but it was escaping him. He thought if he just calmed down, he would be okay. Milton would take him back inside the Palace, and he would be fixed up in the infirmary. There would be a punishment of course, but maybe it wouldn't all be over for him. Suddenly he didn't want to die anymore; it did matter now. *In the face of death, you do care.* That was clear to him at that moment.

Milton then did something so weird and out of place, Andrew stared at him with the same quizzical look that he was being watched with. Milton sat down with his legs crossed under him a good five feet away, right there in the dirt. Watching him...watching him die.

Andrew spit a huge clot of blood out close to Milton, now aware of the fact that he would not be taken back to the Palace, it was clear that the weirdo planned to sit there and watch him pass away. He eventually brought his arm back to the front of his body and allowed the knife to stay in its new home. He couldn't remove it no matter how hard he tried...even if he could, it would not change what was happening. He'd die this way.

Andrew's head fell to the side, too heavy to hold up. He had no idea he was being watched by another Palace-born the whole time. So, things had progressed that far already? The last thought in his mind before falling into a forever sleep: *They have begun using us to watch and hunt down our own. That's smart. Sitting in a small pool of blood there against a massive oak tree, dying. He had to admit... That was smart.*

CHAPTER TWELVE
Mary

"WHEN IT ALL HAPPENED ROUGHLY TWENTY years ago, it was the worst imaginable thing that could have occurred. A pandemic," Carla went on, "and one with amazing range. I mean, it wiped out nearly the entire planet in a matter of three days. Those who had a reaction to the sickness could not be saved, and the amount was close to ninety percent. I'm aware that you have been told ninety-five percent.

"You are not the first Palace-born person we have come across over the years. The first alive and well Palace-born, but not the first." Mary's eyes widened at the words. Carla waved off the look on her face. The gesture said, *Don't worry, we'll get to that part.*

"You see, as you were growing up in their human factory, we have been out here fighting against those you call the Order." Carla spoke with no tone of disgust or anger; to Mary it sounded more like proto-col. *How many times has she had a talk similar to this one?*

As Carla went on speaking, Mary got up from the gurney and limped over to a window in the infirmary. She peered outside, thinking she would see the finely cut grass of the fresh green field that surrounded the Palace she grew up in. That was not the case, of course. The grass was overgrown, there were no red flags, and there were lots of people dressed like Carla and the others who had saved her (or perhaps taken her?) from the security guards at the other Palace.

"There are three Palaces in this area?" Mary asked.

"There are four. The one you came from, which serves as the main Palace, seems to have the most security. We are left to believe that's because there are higher-ups there. There is the facility where we found you, which as you could see had...not so good security." Carla winked at her.

"And then there is this one, which we are in control of now, and there is another. All of them are hidden in forest areas. That's the crazy thing about all of this—it was executed under our noses the whole time. Who knows how long it took them to build all of those Palaces. We never even saw them being built, or heard of such things. They were put in place by a conglomerate we know of as the NCP Group. That name is the only information we've found on them."

"I see..." Mary said, her words trailing off for a moment. "So ask me." She turned away from the window to look Carla in the eyes. "Ask me now. I'd rather answer and be killed if that's my fate than to listen to a full lecture and meet the same ending." Of course, she was bluffing the woman. Mary was not so indifferent about dying. If not for her child, she would in fact be okay with moving on. But now that she'd been given a second chance at life, she wanted to live. No, she wanted the child to live. That was more accurate.

"First of all, facility brat, you don't make the rules here. As I said before, I'll tell you some things that you will need to know before you can properly decide. So, sit your ass back down before you fall over. You aren't even close to being healthy enough to be moving around independently." Carla got up from the edge of the desk and walked over to Mary, grabbing her arm once again and leading her back to the gurney. Mary thought that Carla could use a little help as well with that terrible limp, but she accepted the woman's assistance. The look on Carla's face was that of an adult teaching a stupid child not to stick metal into an outlet and shock themselves to death.

There was a mini fridge near the desk. Carla limped over, bent down, and grabbed a bottle of water. She twisted the top off and handed it to Mary. "Drink this, shut up, and listen." The strong older woman made her way back to the edge of the desk, where she clearly preferred to sit rather than the chair.

Mary drank the water like she'd never had anything to drink in her life. She poured the water down her throat, consuming the liquid faster than her stomach could take it all down. She coughed some up, and it spilled from her dry lips and down to her neck. While drinking like a mad woman, it occurred to her that Carla was staring. Mary then realized how ridiculous she must have looked at that moment. She lowered the bottle of water and took a few small sips before sitting it next to her and wiping her mouth with the outside of her hand. "I'm sorry. I was quite thirsty. Go on please."

"Yeah, I see that. No reason to drink so fast, we have plenty of food and water. Not enough to waste, but more than enough so that you don't need to drink like it's the last bottle in the city," Carla said, smiling at her.

"Anyways, I was saying... It may come as a shock to you to find out that those who paraded around as your teachers, your guidance counselors and such, are not from this planet." Carla paused, watching Mary with fascination in her eyes. The woman seemed to be waiting for a reaction at that bit of news. If not words of disbelief, at least a look of confusion and fear from Mary.

Carla would not be rewarded with such a reaction. That big bombshell was only a sparse firecracker to her at that point. Mary simply blinked and nodded for her to continue.

Carla cocked her head to the side, moving her thin bottom lip over her top lip while raising both eyebrows. "Those that go by the name NCP or the Order are here to destroy any human life that will not bend to their will. We do not know what they want, other than all of us dead if we don't do as we're told, so we must fight back, which is what we've been doing. We are not the weak and helpless creatures they believe us to be.

"Our Lord and savior Jesus Christ saw fit to give his life for our sins. We will not allow that sacrifice to be in vain."

Carla mumbled something and stared off into nothingness, looking right through Mary. Something about her family members, but Mary couldn't quite make out the exact words. As fast as Carla had zoned out, she popped back into the present as if nothing had happened at all.

"We must stop them from stealing human lives and stuffing them into these facilities, which are, from what we have been able to gather, located in every state. Maybe in every country, we have no idea. Taking over this Palace was not the treasure trove of knowledge we thought it would be. We believe that most information was burned before we were able to take over. It's clear that this was all planned very carefully by our enemies, and the sickness was the first step to their plan."

Mary raised her hand as if she were in class. Carla stopped talking. "Can we skip all the parts of your story that have to do with who the Order is and what they have planned?" She then grabbed the bottled water and took another huge gulp, finishing it off. She twisted the cap back on and placed it at her side.

"I'm sorry, is that something you don't want to hear about? Is it too troubling and scary for your weak Palace-born mind to deal with? Or maybe it's not interesting enough for you?" Carla began to raise her voice, her cheeks filling with the color red. Every feature on her face got tighter all at once.

"No, it's not that at all. I'm interested to hear anything you have to say, just so long as it's not something I'm already aware of. Things I may even be more in the know about than yourself. I've heard as much from the program director, Sirus," Mary said matter-of-factly, a touch of arrogance in her voice. She didn't know why, but she wanted Carla to respect her, to know that she wasn't just some kid from the Palace. To know that she'd experienced trauma in this life as well... that she did know things. Carla's eyes lit up when she heard the name.

"I heard about their plans from his very own mouth before he allowed me and Jac—" Mary stopped talking and looked away, breaking eye contact with Carla. "Allowed someone like you, a man from the Old World, and myself to leave. He told us who they were and what their plans were, then he let us leave, just like that. At least that's what he wanted us to think." Mary could feel the burning anger rising from her belly to her chest.

"They ordered someone to shoot... my friend (He was much more than that) down just before we made it into the surrounding forest. The same forest that I basically crawled out of before your people found me." She took a breath and allowed herself to calm down. Even though she was full of disgust for Sirus, she would not allow herself to be seen behaving unlike a woman grown. Not by this particular woman who already saw herself as superior in many ways. Something in the tone of her voice and the look in her eyes said as much.

"Could you repeat that name once more for me? I want to make sure we are on the same page here." Carla's face grew graver than it looked normally. Mary had just met the woman that day but already could see that her default expression was brooding.

Mary did not want to start talking about Jacob, but if she must then she would. He meant a lot to her, and she thought it was important that this woman knew what brought her out of her home.

"I was going to say Jacob, but, well it—"

"No, for Jesus' sake I don't care about who that is. You said a different name, it began with an S." Carla walked toward Mary, who lowered her gaze to the floor. The mention of Jacob's name hurt too much to even utter, and there was a stinging pain in her chest at the way Carla had spoken of him. So easily dismissing him. Beneath the pain she could feel anger boiling in her stomach again. She grabbed the empty plastic bottle at her side and squeezed it, hard. She felt every muscle in her body become rigid. Since leaving the Palace, her anger had been off the charts. She felt furious all the time, easily aggravated.

Even while wandering in the forest, she'd felt angry every minute of the day. Surrounded by beauty but still too angry to truly enjoy any of it. Her love had been killed right in front of her, and that was obviously part of it. But there was more to her rage than that.

"Sirus," Mary said through gritted teeth. "What about him? He is in fact the director of the Palace program. I've sat here listening to you toot your own horn about what you've accomplished; how much could you possibly know about what's really going on if you don't even know who's running the operation you're trying to take down?" Mary's voice was getting louder, her face heating up as she spoke and began to rise from the gurney.

"And stop bringing up your nonsensical religious figures to me. This is a real-life conversation about real things and real people that actually exist. I don't want to hear about Jesu—"

Before Mary could finish her sentence, Carla's limp vanished as she covered the distance between them in what felt like a second. In a quick whirl of her right hand, Carla pulled the blade on her belt loose, spinning it in a circle with her fingers. Mary could see the reflection of light bouncing off the shiny metal as it whizzed by her face, cutting through the air near her ear and finding a home on the skin of her throat. Carla was so close, Mary could feel the peach fuzz from the woman's face lightly brush against her own cheek. She spoke in a whisper, pushing the blade against Mary's throat and forcing her to sit back down on the gurney.

"Listen to me, you blaspheming little cunt. I'd love to get the intel you have on this Sirus character, but let's get something straight first. If you ever fix your ignorant mouth to speak against the only true savior or put down the efforts of great men and women who have given their lives to win back this dead planet from those that created...you, I will open your throat where you sit, stand, or sleep." She spoke with a snarl in her voice. Mary thought she sounded like evil incarnate. She'd never been around anything so...rabid.

"Never mistake me or any one of my team members for those you are accustomed to," she went on. "We deal in death, a life lost is a life lost. Where you were raised makes no difference to me. The price of life is now cheaper than it's ever been in the real world, and let me tell you, money no longer exists. So, opening you up so that we can take a look at what those bastards created could even be seen as...an experiment of sorts."

Mary slowly turned her head to look at Carla. The teeth of the blade nipped the skin on her throat as she turned her head, and she felt the small droplets of blood blooming. She suddenly felt calm, in control of the situation. The fear was there for sure, but there was something else...something that made her feel as though nothing could hurt her.

Mary spoke to the older woman in a whisper. "And Carla, you should never mistake me for someone who values living at this point. I do not care to have this conversation with you or to help you with anything. I never asked for your help to begin with. So, if you think providing help would award you information from a lost Palace-born, well, you are sorely mistaken." While responding to the woman, Mary moved her right hand to her midsection, hoping to shield the child in her belly from harm if things were to escalate further.

"I would have been fine with dying, Carla. So, if you believe that threatening me with what I desire is going to be a scare tactic, again—you are wrong," Mary seethed. "Also, never speak like that about Jacob for as long as your miserable life continues."

She couldn't believe the words that were coming out of her mouth. She'd never spoken like that to anyone. A part of her was afraid of being hurt while she carried Jacob's child. The other part wanted things to go further. She wanted to end Carla, needed to erase her from the face of the Earth, in fact. Her own mouth transformed into a sinister smile, and she quickly kissed Carla, right on the lips.

Mary felt outside of her own body. She wasn't sure why she'd done that. She was just so angry. It felt like Carla would take offense to it, and that's exactly what Mary wanted to do. Offend the older woman. Hurt her in any way she could.

Carla jumped back just a little, enough for Mary to know that what she'd done had caught her off guard. The older woman recovered quickly though, returning a smile and becoming visibly excited. "Have it your way, bitch!" Carla pulled the knife away from Mary's neck, flipped it in her hand, and pulled her arm back, aiming the blade directly at Mary's stomach. Mary stood up quickly and sidestepped to Carla's left, hoping to parry the blade once it came in for the stab.

Just as Carla was about to strike, someone burst through the infirmary door. "What are you doing, Carla?!" The knife dance that Carla began stopped right then and there, her swift movements coming to a screeching halt.

Mary looked over to her right and saw a man taking big fast steps toward her and the woman intending to murder her. When she glanced back at Carla, the woman was standing up straight, blade already back in its sheath on her belt clip. Carla then brought her right hand up to her forehead. Mary had seen the salute before, soldiers from the Old World did it to show respect. *Is she not the leader here?*

The man blew past her like the wind and got in Carla's face. It all happened so fast she didn't know if she should get out of there or sit back down and watch it play out. That whole time, she'd thought Carla was running the show.

His hair was long and the most beautiful shade of blond Mary had ever seen. His eyes were wide and intense as he'd passed by her, but she could see that they were green. He was a big man, bigger than most of the men she'd ever seen in her life. He wore the same type of army clothes, but he had a red stripe down the left side of his jacket. She thought maybe it symbolized his importance. He was an impressive man to look at.

"What do you think you are doing, soldier? This is not what we do here. We do not threaten, we do not inject fear into those who need our help." The mysterious man barked the words at Carla, getting as close to her face as she'd been to Mary's. "Explain yourself!" he yelled, only an inch from her face. Carla did not blink. But she did look down to the floor, submitting to him.

The woman's face seemed to flash from a savage look of bloodlust to shame, and a hint of embarrassment. To be reprimanded in front of the Palace brat mortified the woman. Mary could see that, and it made her feel good inside.

"My apologies, sir," Carla said to the floor. "I lost my head. It won't happen again, Commander Logan."

CHAPTER THIRTEEN

Sirus

To: NCP GROUP [Official]
Server: Unknown OC

From: O'Sullivan, Sirus
Date: May 21, 2040 16:24:36 EST

Subject: Unforeseeable circumstances

I CONTACT YOU WITH MY SINCEREST regrets. Before I explain what has transpired here, I'd like to let you know how it happened and what my plans were. I take my position very seriously, as you know. Always have, and I'd never do anything that would result in my removal from this experiment.

The staff here at the central Palace of this region of the globe were gearing up for Phase 2. We ran into what I would call small difficulties with a few of the members. Some Old World, and some Palace-born. It was Mary.

As you know, we allow certain events to play out for experimental purposes. This was allowed when an Old World member was permitted the freedom to rape and release a Palace-born young woman. This event was OK'd by me for the sake of ushering in Phase 2. I planned to use a heightened anxiety event to trigger this new phase, and I thought it would be the best way to change up ideologies with the Palace-born. It has certainly done so, and Phase 2 is coming together perfectly but for this one issue.

The man Mary ran away with was killed by a security sniper before getting very far. His name was Jacob. He was going to be a problem going forward anyway, and his relationship with Mary was one of the reasons we began to expedite Phase 2. Mary was permitted to run off into a nearby forest, under the guise of an escape. The forest was free of all predatory animals. I know how important she is to the end game, which is why I'm contacting you now.

I want to assure the federation that there was no real danger to Mary in the forest. I knew she would find her way out the other side, where she would run into the neighboring Palace. Security was put on standby to retrieve her, and I was to pick her up and bring her back. I also had micro surveillance drones monitoring her health.

My team thought it preferable that Mary was not in the Palace for the implementation of Phase 2. It's a harsh thing to deal with for someone of her...still dormant skillset. It was safer for her to be away for that portion of the transition. After all the Old World members were executed and removed from the grounds, Mary, the High Valued Target, was to be brought back in and counseled as to what had transpired. The death of the man she thought she was in love with would be spun into a lie of deception, causing her to look down upon the Old World members.

Things did not quite work out that way. When she came out of the forest, there were security guards in place to drag her into the Palace and wait for my arrival. They were killed by rebels in the area, and she was hauled off with said rebels before elite security could be dispatched. I did not think it was necessary to send elite guards from the beginning—that was an oversight on my end.

Those responsible for this happening at Palace 114 were publicly decapitated, including the head of the security team (who fled back into the Palace under gunfire), and a Palace-born member who objected. As you know, that specific Palace is also in Phase 2. The gruesome images were not out of the ordinary for the Palace-born there, so the objection was taken as disobedience.

We do know where the target is being kept. We believe she may be inside Palace 48, which was taken by rebels a year ago. They'd been quiet for some time, but are now more actively moving around the area. We have someone within the group who may be able to let me know if my assumption is correct. I'm waiting to hear from them while units search the surrounding areas for Mary and the rebels who took her.

If I do not hear anything soon, I'll be sending a team over to annihilate every living entity there, except Mary. If there are any questions or concerns, please contact me. Again, I do apologize, and I'm driven to making this right.

Thank you,
O'Sullivan, Sirus

CHAPTER FOURTEEN

Proving Grounds - Melinda

She'd been going back and forth to the shooting range for the last couple days, hoping to run into Lonnie. While never quite sure if that was his name, she was just as sure that it was. Either way, Melinda knew she would recognize his face when she saw him. He was an attractive tall man, older than her, but not by much.

The Palace members were going through a small culture shock. Living their lives with Old World members one day, and then seeing them disposed of the next. Melinda thought it was similar to what it would feel like if everyone of adult age in the Old World were to disappear in the blink of an eye. What would those children have done? She thought about that circumstance a bit longer, realizing that was similar to what actually did happen. They had listened to the Order and moved into the Palaces, walking away from their past lives. She had her answer.

While she and Lonnie never had relations exercises with each other, she wouldn't mind being with him in bed. It was just something that had never happened. She assumed the options for relations were based on logistics and scheduling, nothing more.

Melinda mostly had her relations exercises with a man named Gilbert. He was in his early forties, and she'd been with him sexually since the age of thirteen. That was the age the infirmary said she would be ready to have children safely. Gilbert was a shy and careful man, always asking if he was hurting her or if she wanted to just talk during their exercise time. He was always kind to her, but they were there for a purpose. That purpose was a lot for him to handle, and for that reason, he was her least favorite of all the men she had taken to bed.

Most of the men she bedded were much older than herself. There was only one Palace-born man, and he was her age. Needless to say, there was no satisfaction involved. The younger men had no idea what they were doing sexually. All the women would speak in private about who was decent at pleasing them while trying to conceive a child.

They knew it was looked down upon, but girls would talk. That's what an Old World woman by the name of Nancy would say. Melinda remembered Nancy had taken multiple bullets to the chest the day of the cleansing. The rifle bullets had hit her so hard that they drove her to the floor, killing her right then and there. She did not twitch, move, or scream. The lights went out, and that was that.

Melinda snapped out of the brief flashback. She'd nearly bumped into someone walking in the opposite direction. She did find herself getting bored with the men who were scheduled to be with her. It could have been their age, or simply the dead look in their eyes while doing the deed, but it served as one of her least favorite activities in the Palace. She wondered if it would be any different with Lonnie.

Melinda was hopeful he would be at the shooting range that afternoon. She couldn't find him anywhere around the Palace, and she knew everyone had to come here at some point; it was a daily requirement.

She stepped into the insanely loud and massive room, nodding to the security guard at the door as she stepped through the metal detector. Melinda often wondered why they thought it was necessary. Who would try to sneak a weapon out? Perhaps it had been built with the Old World members in mind, a precaution against their previous bad habits. She supposed the Order just wanted to make sure everyone stayed as safe as possible, so they kept the metal detector, even after the...cleansing.

There were twenty indoor handgun lanes and fifteen rifle lanes.

Each lane was twenty-five yards in length. They kept an around-the-clock schedule at the range, with Palace members occupying the place at all times. No matter what time she went, it was full of people. Shooting and reloading, always shooting and reloading. It never stopped.

"Checking in?" the surly desk attendant asked. He was practically yelling at her. Part of that was due to the noise, she knew. But a lot of it had to do with his grumpy attitude. The man had salt-and-pepper hair and a constant scowl. There were a few attendants on rotation, and she knew they had a lot to keep track of. This was more than a desk clerk. This was a security guard who had to check weapons in and out to each Palace member while at the same time making sure everyone in the range followed the safety protocol at all times.

Melinda approached the desk and checked out a handgun and safety accessories. The clerk retrieved the weapon from the huge locked case on the wall behind him while she keyed in her name and the date on the electronic pad. In less than a minute, she was making her way toward the lanes.

In a morning enrichment class the day before, Melinda could hear the gunshots going off as she tried to pay attention to what the teacher was saying. She barely believed what they were now doing—such a change in ideologies in such a brief time.

Everyone was focused on their firearms, on everything involved in this new activity that had just been introduced a week ago. Before the cleansing, no one in the Palace other than the security team possessed a firearm, and no one had ever fired one since the inception of the Palace. Now everyone occupying space in the Palace was handling them like it was a customary practice.

They all wore black, the standard safety goggles, and red head-phones to block out the sound of the loud weaponry. Each individual was focused on the target, eyes squinted before pulling the trigger—sometimes in unison. She walked up and down the aisles, making sure she hadn't missed him on her general glance of the shooting range upon entry.

No one noticed her looking around like she'd lost something important. Everyone seemed be disconnected from each other recently. Seeing but not seeing, hearing but not really hearing each other. The focus was being directed at other things.

No matter how many times she shot a gun herself, they still scared her quite a bit. Granted, Palace members had only started target practice recently, but she thought she'd done it enough that she'd be more comfortable with the loud sounds. It made her feel unsafe. It felt unnatural to her, the octave of the bullets abrasive to her ears. *How did Old World members fall in love with such tools of destruction?* Melinda knew the answer to that though. Same way her own people were now becoming enamored with them. The thought made her sad. How did no one else see history repeating itself once again? Where did the Order even get all those firearms?

BANG!

With each step she took, she jumped when a gun was discharged near her. She hated that place, but she needed to keep coming. For one, she still wanted to talk to Lonnie. She thought she could trust him, more than anyone else in the Palace. They'd shared a moment during the auditorium massacre, she knew that. And two, she had to do some shooting so the powers that be wouldn't think her behavior was suspicious.

She noticed the final lane was empty. Melinda walked up to the firing area, tightening her gloves. She grabbed the headphones from around her neck, slid them onto her ears, and just like that...all was quiet again. The sound of gunshots was gone from her own personal world, and the feeling of being alone was upon her once again. She was scheduled to shoot, so she would do just that.

The handguns were her weapon of choice; the rifles were too big, and she didn't plan on ever using one of the guns outside the range to begin with. The song and dance of shooting and sticking to the schedule was to simply buy time until she could find out what was going on. Too much was changing too fast; there had to be more to it all.

Melinda recalled the day before in morning enrichment, when a young woman had said something she shouldn't have. Trish was always saying the first thing that came to her mind, no filter whatsoever. These were not the times to have that personality type. She wasn't much older than eleven years old. Melinda hadn't seen her prior to a year or so ago, but she did enjoy the young lady's participation in class. For the most part.

Trish had asked Teacher Paul if they were allowed to leave if they wanted to. As long as it was safe outside, of course. Everyone in the class became silent, including the teacher. He stared at the young girl for a while and then went on teaching. The tension was so thick you could cut it. No one dared speak for that small amount of time where silence was better than words. He never even bothered to answer. Trish went on looking down at her book and following the lesson for the day. Even the brave lion that lived in her vocal cords knew when she'd spoken out of turn.

After thirty minutes or so, a security agent came into class and asked Trish to come into the hallway to speak to her. No one seemed to be concerned that she'd asked a question like that before being escorted out of class by security. But Melinda had been terrified. She sat there in class shaking, unable to focus on the topic of the day. It took everything inside of her not to jump out of her seat and go running out of the room. To what end, she did not know, but she felt someone should be doing something.

To Melinda's surprise, the young girl did come back to class. Again, no one seemed to notice. She wondered if they all were really just that dense about what occurred, or if they were putting on an act to avoid the same kind of trouble. The latter was her guess, but still, it felt wrong not to show any concern.

Standing there in the last aisle of the shooting range, Melinda's anger boiled as she slid the magazine into the gun. She felt so angry about it all, and frustrated with herself for not saying anything to Trish. Why hadn't she asked the girl about what happened in the hall? What was she so afraid of?

Melinda put her safety glasses on and could feel her hands shaking; that always happened when it was time to shoot. Closing her eyes, she attempted to calm her nerves and relax. After a few seconds of meditation, she took a deep breath and opened her eyes again, noticing her hands were now still. Using her thumb, she clicked the safety off the firearm and allowed her fingers to do what came surprisingly naturally.

Bang. Bang. Bang. She shot the gun three times, her hands never wavering or moving out of place. All three shots found a home in the head of the paper target twenty-five yards away. The top of the head was nearly blown off as scraps of paper went flying. Squinting, Melinda lowered her gun a little over a foot. *Bang. Bang. Bang.* She lifted the gun again and let off the last round. *Bang.*

Melinda exhaled. It was done. She set the gun down on the wooden slate in front of her, pushed the button to her right, and waited for the target to make its way to her as she removed the headphones, placing them back on her neck.

She removed the gloves and put them into her back pocket, letting the fingers hang out. She would only shoot once today, same as every day since it became a part of her daily routine. She got nothing from riddling the paper targets with deadly ammunition, but Teacher Andrew would come by her pod to retrieve today's target, so she needed to have it on hand when he did.

ONCE THE TARGET was close enough to grab, Melinda unhooked the big piece of paper from its hinges. Three forehead shots, three chest/sternum shots, and the last round landed in the neck region. Same as yesterday. And the day before. Hitting the target in the desired areas was no challenge for her, it was all about focusing and doing. All of her friends shot as well as she did, some even better.

Melinda rolled the target up, placed the handgun on her hip, and made her way back to the exit. Again, she twitched at the loud firing of the rifles the whole way. She planned to go to the running portion of the gym to see if Lonnie was there. There were only so many places he could be. The Palace was spacious, but it shouldn't be this hard to find one person. Especially since the mass exodus. It was all she could think about.

An unwanted thought occurred to her then: *if* she couldn't *find him,* was *it possible that someone ha*d *hurt him*? Why hadn't she thought about that before? He could be dead. After all, that wasn't a strange thing in the Palace as of late. Lonnie was clearly upset by what happened during the cleansing. He may have voiced his displeasure with one of the teachers or security guards, like Trish did in class...and maybe they killed him for it. Maybe they'd shot him like they did the Old World members. She'd seen them do it before; it wasn't out of the question at all.

The thought alone made her want to cry, but she would not, could not. Instead, she kept her eyes forward, making her way down the aisle and rounding the corner to the service desk. She knew things were bad here, but were they truly that bad? Were they killing off Palace-born members for not agreeing with everything? The thought crossed her mind often, but the reality of it being true was a totally different thing. How far were those in charge willing to go? Sadly, she couldn't come up with an answer for that.

She'd been going along with this new shooting range stuff for what they said was training on the defensive side of things. Just in case survivors from the Old World found their way to the Palace and wanted to hurt them. There was video footage of just that—people from the Old World invading a different Palace and killing. She was able to ignore the constant violent videos being shown on all the televisions, but if they were going to start hurting people simply for becoming upset or disagreeing, she didn't know what she would do. But she couldn't stay.

Hoping she didn't look visibly shaken, Melinda smiled and handed the red headphones, safety glasses, and gun to the security agent at the desk before signing out. She wanted to run full speed out of the shooting range and to the gym, and as she began to speed-walk toward the exit...there he was.

Lonnie was walking through the door with a few other people that looked to be his age. He was in the front, and everyone seemed to be clinging to his words and laughing at whatever he was saying.

Shocked, Melinda walked over as fast as she could. She was half excited to see him, half upset with herself for jumping to conclusions. With the rolled-up paper target in her left hand, she walked through the group of people and grabbed his arm with her free hand, halting all laughter and horseplay in the group. They stared at her and each other with confused looks on their faces.

She noticed how strong his bicep was when she tried getting her hand around it, which she couldn't do. Instead she switched targets and tugged on the side of his red tee shirt, pulling him away from the crowd. "What are you doing?" he said, still laughing.

"Come here, I need to talk to you." Lonnie's face changed from a big smile to a confused frown, almost as if he didn't recognize who she was or why she would want to talk to him about anything. That stung her a little when she identified the look on his face. *He doesn't even remember me.* Melinda felt dumb for coming over and grabbing him as if they knew each other. It was stupid to assume he would remember her simply because he was all she'd been thinking about for days.

Then his eyes brightened with a look of familiarity, and the smile came creeping back onto his lips. And just like that, she felt better. *He does remember me after all.*

Lonnie looked back over his shoulder, speaking loudly to his entourage. "I'll catch up with you guys. Same lanes as yesterday, if they are available," he said as Melinda pulled him further into the corner, away from the security desk and the door.

"Where the hell have you been? I've been looking all over for you...I thought they did something to hurt you." Melinda brought her face closer to Lonnie's ear so she could speak as quietly as possible. She didn't want people to know she'd been looking for him.

"Whoa, whoa...relax...ummm, what's your name again?" Lonnie shook loose from her grasp and put a hand up, signaling for her to calm down.

"I'm Melinda. You remember me from...you know. And you're Lonnie, right?" She looked around to make sure no one was watching or listening in.

"Yes, my name is Lonnie, and I most definitely do remember you from...the thing the other day." Lonnie offered his hand to shake and Melinda smacked it away. He was trying to come off as smooth or play-ful, and based on the nature of why she wanted to talk to him, she wasn't in the mood. He had no way of knowing what she wanted to talk about, but she felt like somewhere inside, he did.

"Answer my question," she said, annoyed. Lonnie laughed.

"I've been around. Working out, taking classes and such. You know how schedules can get busy around here, especially now. What's the problem though? Is everything okay? You looked pretty bothered when you came bursting through the group." Lonnie leaned down, bending over her as he spoke, clearly mocking her small size.

"You don't have to bend down so far. I'm not that small and you aren't that big. Stop it." She laughed despite her annoyance and punched his arm. "You can't be more than a couple years older than me." She blushed and punched his arm one more time. He scrunched his nose and pretended to be in pain. His awkward jokes were inappropriate, but he was cute, and she couldn't help but to laugh.

"But seriously, I need to talk to you about something. Something important. About the day of the cleansing." Melinda's face was no longer pleasant, and she was not smiling. The sound of those words erased the grin from Lonnie's face as well. He needed to understand that this was not a casual encounter. They'd shared the same experience during a tough time, an unthinkable time in their lives together.

He took a small step back from Melinda and looked around. She thought he looked afraid.

"Okay...yeah, we can talk, but not now. I have shooting, and then I have some other things to do with Teacher Luke. What floor is your pod on? Maybe I can come by and we can talk."

Melinda took a step closer and lowered her voice. "You sure? We can just go to the central plaza, get something to eat and ta—"

"I said later..." Lonnie's face became stern, his lips tightening and his brow becoming more prominent. "I can't talk right now. I just said that. I'll just come to your pod."

"Okay, I'm sorry." She touched his arm. "I live on floor twelve, pod L-fifteen." Melinda thought they were talking quietly enough so there was there no chance of being overheard. She was confused as to why Lonnie's disposition changed so suddenly after she mentioned the cleansing. He had his reasons, she was sure. This further cemented that they needed to speak alone. "I'll be available tomorrow morning, after breakfast. You should come over."

Lonnie casually circled around her, blocking the security agent's view of her from behind the service desk. The guy wasn't paying any attention to them as he checked out rifles to the group that Lonnie had walked in with. Lonnie didn't seem to realize she noticed the maneuver he made to block her from the sight of the security agent, but she did. As if the man hadn't seen her and checked her in and out already.

"Okay, I can do that. I'll see you then. And if you could, please don't go around talking about stuff like this with just anyone," he whispered. Then he moved in quickly to give her a hug, saying loudly, "Great to see you, Melinda. May Mother bless all who are righteous and just." With his mouth close to her ear, he whispered, "People are always watching and listening. Don't be stupid."

He released the hug and pasted the big goofy smile back on. "I'll see you tomorrow," he said for all to hear, waving like a goofball to someone just a few feet away and walking toward the service desk to join his friends. *Way to be coy, Lonnie,* she thought as he did a slight gallop back to his friends.

Melinda left the range right away. On the elevator up to her floor, she thought about the encounter she had with Lonnie. It bothered her, made her even more off balance than she had been before speaking to him. *Why was he so afraid of talking about what happened?*

CHAPTER FIFTEEN

Lonnie

H E WAKED INTO MELINDA'S POD, AS nervous as he'd been while sitting with Teacher Luke that day in the small room. Lonnie wasn't sure if this was a setup, or maybe she was just that stupid to be bringing up stuff like that in public. Either way, they needed to talk to get some ground rules in place. The situation was far too serious to think that simply whispering about things would be enough to not be heard, recorded—and erased.

"Hi Lonnie. I ordered extra breakfast from the nutrition dispensary for you. I mean, if you haven't eaten yet," Melinda said carefully, closing the door behind her. She placed her back against the door and offered what looked like a hesitant smile.

"Yeah, yeah, hold on," Lonnie said, walking around her pod and looking for...He didn't know what he was looking for, but he felt anxious and couldn't begin spilling his guts before doing a once-over. Whether or not she could be trusted was still in question as far as he was concerned.

He walked over to her closet and opened it, looking through the clothes to make sure no one was hiding behind the shirts, pants, and skirts hanging up. He reached for the clothing, feeling in the pockets of the thin jackets she had hanging.

"What are you do—" Melinda started, but she was interrupted when Lonnie raised a hand with one finger up, signaling for her to wait.

"Just a minute. I'm just being careful. One of us has to care about discretion," he said in a vexed voice, never looking in her direction. Lonnie moved to the eastern part of the pod, sticking his head inside the bathroom to make sure no one was hiding in the shower, which he could easily see though the glass.

"I don't understand," Melinda said, walking in his direction. "Why are you acting so nervous? Did I say or do something wrong?"

Lonnie stood near the bathroom, still looking around. He placed a finger to his lips. "Shhhh," he said, listening intently. He heard the television playing the Old World videos at the same low volume all the TV sets played it.

Melinda stopped near the sofa in the middle of the pod, just short of her bed. "Are you serious right now?" She put a hand on one hip, looking annoyed and frustrated. Lonnie snapped out of it and began walking toward her. He wasn't pleased with the thoroughness of his investigation of the room, but he was willing to move on from it.

"Let's have a seat and talk. We need to get something straight before I hear what you have to say. Sit." He nodded in the direction of the sofa while moving around the left side and sitting down. Melinda came around the right side of the sofa and sat next to him.

"First of all, never, and I repeat, never come up to me in public like that. It draws attention, and that's the last thing you should want, considering—"

"Wait!" Melinda said, an animated look of surprise on her face. "Are you sure you want to talk about this in front of the television? You know the rumor about the teachers being able to spy on us through them." Her tone was mocking. "We can go talk in the bathroom, you know. Come on, let's take this very serious talk into the bathroom."

Lonnie put his hands up. "Don't be smart, Melinda, I'm serious. You and I both know that if the television sets were used to spy on us, that girl would not have died the way she did. Please lose the attitude and listen to me. I know you may not like my tone, but trust me when I say we need to be very careful. And not just us...everyone."

"You're the one coming to my pod and talking to me like you're one of the teachers. I only wanted to discuss something with you, and here you are, treating me like I'm the enemy." Melinda folded her arms over her chest and looked away.

"It's not about enemy or friend, its bout being careful." He put a hand on her knee, offering a small apology for causing her to become upset. "I just want everyone to be okay. We have to be careful."

"I understand," Melinda said quietly, still not looking in his direction.

"You were there sitting right next to me when it all happened. We both know what they are capable of. I don't want to get hurt, and I want you to be safe as well. That's why you can't go around drawing attention to yourself or talking about the cleansing in any way that's not agreeable." Lonnie grabbed a biscuit off the plate on the table in front of the sofa. He bit into the piece of bread, waiting on a response.

"Okay, I said I understand and it won't happen again. I was just overly excited to see you. I'd been looking for you for a few days and couldn't find you anywhere." Melinda's voice began to break. Lonnie rubbed her knee.

"Didn't know you cared so much." He smiled at her and winked. Melinda blushed and smacked his hand from her knee. "Get your hand off me."

"I'm just joking. Listen—" He paused, looking suspiciously at the door as if he'd heard someone. He got up from the sofa and started toward the door, but she grabbed his hand before he could, pulling him back down.

"Calm down," Melinda said. "It's just people on their way to morning enrichment classes. Go on."

Lonnie continued listening, eventually nodding his head in agreement. Then he fixed his attention back on her. "Listen, things are changing, as you already know. I for one don't think it's the worst thing in the world. We've seen what Old World survivors are capable of."

He pointed to the television, which showed a video of masked men in a desert-type setting, decapitating another man. Melinda's vision followed his pointed finger. She saw the image on the screen and quickly looked away, closing her eyes. "I don't necessarily believe what the Order is doing is wrong. I'm not choosing sides here, I'm just being honest. Either way, we don't want to make enemies of them."

"I know, that's kind of what I wanted to talk to you about." Melinda turned her attention back to his face. "How are there still so many survivors out in the world? It can't be both things. We've been in this Palace our entire lives because we were told that anything outside of the hundred-yard radius was contaminated and would cause death if we left without a protective suit. How can that be the case *and* there are survivors that have been around since the sickness? They've been out there all alone in a world filled with death? How can we be sure what the Order told us is true when such a huge detail turned out to be a lie?" The last sentence came out almost like a plea for help on the Old World survivors' behalf.

Lonnie thought for a few seconds. "Maybe they had protective suits? They could have gotten their hands on some when everything went down. It's possible; don't say it's not."

"But in the video of them killing Palace security, they aren't wearing suits," Melinda said sharply. "Just regular clothes like you and me. You saw them with your own eyes."

"They were also in the hundred-yard radius in that video," he said. Lonnie didn't think she would believe that excuse, but it was a legitimate answer. "We haven't seen any of the survivors outside of the hundred-yard radius without a suit on, so it's possible that they do have some, and they remove them when they get within the quarantine area."

Melinda grabbed a cup of orange juice off the table. As she took a drink, Lonnie saw the wheels turning behind her scrunched-up eyebrows while she contemplated what he'd just said. "That just sounds really far-fetched, Lonnie, I'm going to be honest with you. It's possible, but doesn't sound very plausible. If you want to explain away things, I'm sure you are intelligent enough to do so. But try to see what I'm saying."

"But why would they lie to us about something like that? We saw that Old World member run off with Mary. How do we know he didn't make her run?" He gave her a look, lifting both eyebrows and wrinkling his forehead.

"We don't," she said. "But based on how she ran back to his body and collapsed in tears, I'd say that was not the case. I'm glad you brought that up though...Why do we have security here sniping people who try to run away? Are we going to pretend that didn't happen?" She took another sip of her drink. "And before you say they are there for the evil Old World members who want to come kill us, explain why he shot a man who'd lived in this Palace for twenty years. It just doesn't make sense to me."

"Not pretending anything, I just don't think stuff is as weird as you seem to. Shooting Jacob—the man's name was Jacob, by the way—shooting him could have been because he was kidnapping her. I just told you that as a possible reason," Lonnie said. Melinda started to respond, but he spoke before she could. "I know she seemed a mess when he was shot, crying and freaking out. But that could have been any number of things. She could have panicked at seeing the violence. She could have been attached to him in some way psychologically, even though he was her captor. We've read about that in class about Old World psychology theories. He could have even manipulated her into thinking it was a good idea."

"I'm just asking questions, Lonnie. I know you felt the same way I did at the cleansing...I know it. You squeezed my hand when the shots rained down on that stage." She set her cup back down and scooted closer to Lonnie on the couch.

Lonnie felt weak. It was the same thing Teacher Luke had said, in so many words. He wondered if she thought he was afraid or that he had a weak stomach. The implications made him angry.

"I was squeezing your hand because you were squeezing mine," he said.

"Oh...I thought you were bothered by what was happening, same way as me. It was a bad thing that happened," Melinda said, backing up on the couch.

Lonnie stood up. "Well, I wasn't. I mean, I wasn't happy about it, but I understood why it was happening. Unlike you, I believe what the Order has been telling us. I saw the videos with my own eyes. I saw the two Palace members take off and run. For all we know, Mary could have ended up dropping dead after an hour in the forest from the sickness." Lonnie thought that he sounded more like he was trying to convince himself than her. She didn't need to tell him he was being weak; he knew it.

"Okay, I was mistaken then, thinking I would have a friend in you. I thought wrong about the situation, I see." Melinda looked defeated, as if the only thread of hope she had in the world had suddenly burned into nothing but a small pile of ash. Trying so hard to prove he was strong, Lonnie wound up making a young woman feel alienated and alone. He sat back down, and for a moment, neither said a word.

"You can leave. Thank you for coming." She turned to look at him. "I appreciate your words, and now I know not to come to you with my thoughts. I would hate to get you in trouble with the teachers or bother you with my crazy thoughts." Melinda rose from the sofa and made her way to the door. "I have to get to my morning enrichment, same as you."

"Don't be like that, I was just say—"

"I know what you're saying. I get it. I'm sure everything is just fine. One week we are learning to love and care for all, same teachings as always—then the next the televisions come to life, showing us every type of violence you could imagine, and we are learning to destroy targets on a nightly basis. Sounds about right." She opened the door. "Please leave. I have somewhere to be."

Lonnie felt like trash. It was not a good feeling, watching all the color drain out of someone's face because of something you said. He had no more words, at least nothing he could say that would convince her to listen to him. The door was ajar, and he didn't want to get into an argument someone could overhear.

"I'm sorry, I'll leave now. Goodbye, Melinda." He walked out the door without making eye contact. It closed behind him as soon as he cleared the doorway, nearly hitting his back. He looked around to see if anyone was in the hall. He was alone. Maybe being alone in the Palace was the best way to survive in the Palace. Lonnie got on the elevator, skipping his morning enrichment class. He had an appointment with Teacher Simon. He knew things were on the horizon that Melinda had no idea about. Maybe if she did, she would know why her questions were so dangerous.

CHAPTER SIXTEEN

Mary

SHE'D BEEN LIVING AMONG THEM FOR over a month, and it felt like longer. Time was at a crawling pace without Jacob or any of the friends she'd had since infancy. The people she lived among now were so different from the people she'd known her whole life. More importantly, they were nothing like the Order said they were.

They laughed, loved, got angry, and showed every other emotion that humanity was capable of. She was always taught that people from the Old World were murderous scoundrels who believed in nothing but themselves. While she could not speak on Old World people prior to what she'd experienced, that was not the case among the Eagles. While much rougher around the edges, she saw many redeeming qualities in the group.

Even though she was an outsider, they treated her like an equal. Fed her, nursed her body back to one hundred percent, and allowed her to live in the liberated Palace among them. She appreciated that, because they could have left her to die on that field. Even worse, they could have allowed those security agents to walk her back into a nightmare. The Palace, a labyrinth of lies and deception.

That didn't mean there weren't some who kept their distance; that was to be expected. Carla seemed to have a real hatred for her, which was confusing based on how sweet she had been the day Mary had woken up among strangers, lost and afraid. Before the knife threat.

Whenever Mary walked past Carla or came to Eagle meetings about future plans, the woman would cut her evil looks. Looks that would wilt the most beautiful of roses instantly. Carla was still holding on to the embarrassment that she'd brought on herself.

There were whispers from some that Mary had been released by her Palace to befriend and infiltrate. She understood the fear involved with allowing someone from the enemy's home into your own, but they could not have been more wrong. In fact, she'd never asked to be saved at all.

Logan had questioned her twice since she came to be in his squad's company. She answered every question that he and any of his lieutenants had, and she answered honestly. There was no reason to lie about anything, and if they wanted her gone, she was willing to be on her way. There was a big world out there that needed to be explored; she would find a home for her and the child growing inside of her regardless of what it took. The ball was in their court as far as she was concerned.

Logan seemed to be very interested in anything she had to say about Jacob. She didn't know why he had so many questions about the topic of her deceased lover, but he wanted to know everything about him and their relationship together. He even had questions about how Jacob looked—hair color, height, things like that.

She thought that maybe he wanted to see if he could trip her up in his questioning. Surprisingly, he asked very little about Sirus and the teachers. Carla seemed to be much more concerned with information on the Palace program director than Logan was. Logan had simply said, "Oh, he sounds like a charming man. I'll kill him as well," then moved on from the topic. Mary thought that perhaps Carla was in charge of identifying threats, and Logan was more of the charismatic leader type. Everyone in the Palace loved Logan; he was clearly a great leader if they had managed to take over a Palace fully equipped with security agents and god knew what else.

For the last few weeks though, there hadn't been much questioning at all. From Logan, that is. The person in charge of information records was a young man around the same age as her. His name was Dale. She'd spent much time in her new pod speaking to him. Most days they'd spend an hour going over things that went on in her Palace.

She sat in the not-so-clean pod, talking to Dale, answering more questions. It was clear that while they were being kind to her, the Eagle squad was definitely interested in keeping her around for the intel. Mary was new to being out in the world, but she was far from unintelligent. They were doing what anyone would do if they wanted to learn things about their enemy. She had no qualms with providing information seeing as they shared the same enemy.

"Okay, last week we covered a lot of the material that was taught during what you all called morning enrichment classes. This week I've been directed to get information on the child center of the Palace. We have one here, but it was burned beyond recognition by the time our men fully took the Palace, as you know." Dale sat on the other side of the small table near the sofa and television.

Mary thought about his words carefully before responding to the Eagle soldier. She thought about how it felt to see the child center of this Palace burned to a crisp. She hadn't grown up in that particular child center, but in a way, she had. In size and design, it was identical to the one she'd spent the first ten years of her life. Logan and a few of his men had walked her down to the decimated child center on her third day there. It belonged to the Eagles now. Not to her, not to the Order. They'd won it in blood and souls, and she knew she'd be smart not to forget that fact.

The child center had been utterly unrecognizable to her. The Eagle soldiers had no idea what they were looking at because they'd never seen the space any other way. The walls, the huge stickers, the colorful carpeting—all black and charred. She couldn't even walk into the huge room, it hurt so much. She saw her own childhood in the blackened crypt.

When Logan told her that the security agents and teachers had moved to the child center and killed all the children and then themselves just before the Eagles had taken the facility, she didn't believe it. She fought them tooth and nail, called them liars and accused them of being the ones who had killed the innocent children. It had all been too much to fathom at that point. She knew Sirus was not a good person, but killing kids?

A few of the soldiers who accompanied them to the child center that day had tried to calm her down. They tried to get her to see reason as she fell apart, but she would hear none of it. Mary had thrashed about, crying and pretending that they were the monsters. Logan eventually told his men to back off and allow her the time to mourn in the way she chose, and they did. The soldiers moved away and went back to the elevator with Logan. They left her there to sort out the truth of the matter.

Mary crumpled to the ground in the doorway of the child center. On her hands and knees, she had sat and cried for over an hour, cursing the planet, humanity, and everything in between. How could anyone be so hateful? she had wondered. Didn't matter if the Order did the killing or the Eagles—humanity did it. Humanity was always the culprit, and they could not be separated in her mind. She had no idea who or what Sirus was, but the atrocity that had taken place in that child center was ordered by him or someone like him.

"The child center, Mary?" Dale said in a loud voice, trying to wake her from the recent memory she'd slipped off to.

Mary snapped out of it and directed her attention back to Dale. "Forgive me, I was thinking about something." She smiled across the table and scooped two apple pieces from a bowl with the spoon in her hand.

"Why did they keep the children away from everyone else in the Palace?" he asked in an aggravated manner. She was pretty sure he'd had to ask the same question more than once.

Mary thought on the question before answering, making sure she could explain to him in a way he would understand. She knew the ways of the Palace were foreign to survivors. "The Order thinks it best if children learn to depend on themselves and not be swayed by the fears and ideologies of their parents. To be who you truly are meant to be, and nothing else." She placed the spoon on top of the chopped apple pieces in the bowl and crossed her legs while balancing herself on her stool.

"Parents by nature desire to recreate themselves and bestow

newfound knowledge and ideas. This can be realized in the form of a child, your own child. But what does this mean for the child's free will? What's to be said for their desires and sensibilities that would exist if not for you piling your own beliefs and ideas into their brain." She finished her thought and studied Dale's face, wondering what he thought of her words. He made no expression at all.

"I see," he said. "So they separated adults from children to allow the children to grow organically. Let me ask you, are there no adults in the child center? Someone has to change diapers, make bottles and things of that nature, correct? Or do older children handle that?" Dale wrote things in his notepad, looking over his glasses as he scribbled something out and underlined something else.

"Well, the children aren't entirely alone. There are those called watchers. Adult staff whose job it is to observe. Others hook babies to feeding devices and change diapers. That's the only touching they receive. The mortality rate is high in the child center.

"Some of the Old World members said that was because young life needed 'love' and the sensation of other human life. Maybe there was something to that. To completely answer your question though, watchers make sure there is food and that no one gets seriously hurt or maimed. That's the extent of their duties," Mary said, staring at Dale, checking to see if his facial expression changed while she learned of their ways. It did not, not even a twitch. He continued scribbling notes in the pad.

Dale was the head of all information for the rebel squad. She thought that maybe he'd expected to hear these things anyway. They understood the Order in ways she did not. Sometimes she found herself feeling defensive of things she heard others say about the Palaces and the people within them. Even while she hated everything about the Palaces herself, it still felt like they were talking about her... about Jacob, about all the good people she left behind when she so eagerly made a run for freedom.

"Okay, I see. I suspected as much, but I want to be diligent. Considering the children pretty much ran the show in the child center, what was the culture—" He paused to think. "I mean, what was it like there? Were the children nice to each other? Was there violence? How do you remember the child center?" Dale stared at her through his bifocals, tapping the pen on his writing pad.

Mary thought about the question. It was a hard one for her to answer. She didn't have any other experience to compare it to, so it was a challenge to describe.

"Well, it's hard to put into words. Of course, there was violence. Quite a bit of it, in fact. There was also love, cooperation, and what could only be described as a family dynamic. We cared about each other, because we were all we had." Mary spoke slowly, trying to choose her words carefully.

"Violence is a part of life. Not being in agreement is also in the same vein, which can cause violence. An even better lesson to be learned is that if you hurt someone, you should be prepared to be hurt in return. I believe this lesson is essential in learning to treat others the way you want to be treated, and from an early age. Those that lived through infancy learned. We felt alone, we found a way to survive, but most of all, we learned to support each other. Something we were told was missing in the Old World."

Dale nodded his head in agreement, still writing in is pad. "Do you think this is the truth? From what you see with the Eagles here, do you think we don't support each other?" he asked, blue eyes surveying her over the glasses that sat perched on the bridge of his long nose.

Mary's words seemed to put him on the defensive. "I believe you've all been driven together though extenuating circumstances and *must* support each other. Or in the words of Logan himself, risk certain annihilation from those you call the colonizers, or those from elsewhere," she said, going for the spoon and another scoop of apples. Dale chuckled, causing her to pause. The man hadn't so much as cracked a grin, and now he was all-out chuckling at her response.

"What do you find funny about what I said?" Mary straightened up on her stool, watching and waiting for his explanation. Now she was on the defensive.

Dale removed his glasses, laid them on the small table, and used two fingers to pinch the bridge of his nose as if he had a severe headache. "You say that you detest those who, for lack of a better term, enslaved you and thousands of others, from what we know. But you still seem to carry some of the rhetoric with you. Things you've been told about the Old World and how we were, or how we are still. Do you notice that about yourself? It's understandable, it's the only home you have ever known, and it's how you've identified yourself." Dale offered a brief but sad smile.

Mary thought to herself for a moment about his words. She knew they were right, but she began to wonder why she was still harboring some of those thoughts even though she knew those in the Order to be worse than liars.

"I see how you can think that. And even I have issues trying to reconcile what my own thoughts are based on my own experience and what is leftover judgements from the Order. I will say that I did live among Old World members for nearly half my life, and I heard as much from them as well. That mankind was not supportive of each other, everyone was out for self—trying to make money at any cost.

"I know now that the sickness did not come from the earth fighting off the disease that is mankind; I know that it was created. However, I do think that the lack of supporting one another did have something to do with why the Order, whoever they are, decided to kill off everyone but the few, if what Sirus said is to be believed. And I am inclined to trust his words regardless of how vile they were."

Satisfied with her analysis of humankind as she understood it, Mary went back to the spoon and the bowl of apples sitting in front of her on the table.

Dale once again chuckled, staring at her with real amusement. She wanted to know what was going on in his mind, what he was thinking about. Maybe he thought she was no more than a young dumb girl, engineered by the Order. She wasn't so sure this was not the case. Without him saying the words, the chuckle and the look said it for him.

"Did Sirus tell you why some humans were allowed to live? Why did most die from the sickness, and others still walk the Earth today?" Dale winked and flashed a bright smile, showing the top row of his teeth. "I'm going to challenge your thought processes now, do not take offense. It's all part of reversing the many years of indoctrination you have suffered."

"He said they wanted to keep some humans from the Old World to help teach Palace-born some of what it meant to be a human being... apart from what would be taught in the Palace. The majority of what is learned in the facility is Old World rights and wrongs, and better ways to love the Earth and all beings that reside on the planet. Without watching and learning from the Old World members, it would be very hard to understand..." Mary stopped talking and thought for a second.

"Finish what you were going to say. I think you may understand a bit better now." Still smiling, Dale circled his finger in the air, beckoning her to finish the thought before she lost it. Urging her to push the words off the tip of her tongue.

It all made sense to Mary now; she understood more about the complexities of the Order. Even when they were being honest, they were not being fully honest. Sirus said that the Old World members had become murderous over and over again throughout history, and while that may have been the truth, it had nothing to do with why they kept those from the Old World in the Palace. Mary felt like a brand-new child, finally learning something profound that the adults were bored with.

She went on speaking to Dale, finishing the sentence. "It would be very hard to understand the nature of those that came before us, the Palace-born, if we did not have them around. Only so much could be learned or understood from pictures and the few video clips we were shown over the short time period we had with them."

Part of her felt defeated for feeding the know-it-all mentality Dale had been oozing from the moment he sat with her. The other part hated the Order even more for deceiving her and all of the good people of the Palace. She didn't think they were perfect, no one was. Neither the Old World members nor the Palace-born, but that reason alone was not enough to be lied to and treated the way they were. Denied the planet, the ability to go out into the world and live among each other.

To make mistakes that could end in peril or beauty—that was what being human was about. At least, she thought it was.

Dale nodded in agreement. "I'll even do you one better. We believe some humans were left alive and brought into the Palaces in order to do what you just so eloquently explained, but also obviously for breeding purposes and an example."

Mary gave the man a confused look. "Example?"

He went back to writing in his notepad, still speaking but jotting notes down as he spoke. "Well yes, an example. To create emotional attachments and then sever them when they are at their height. To create a lasting impression. From what we have learned from your experience, if we are to believe you, you were allowed to leave the Palace with an Old World member, only to watch him get shot down like a wild animal just before attaining freedom.

"We don't believe the intent was to hurt you, but to serve as an example for everyone else still inside the Palace. Teaching them not to run, not to trust those from before, and to listen to the ruling power if they wanted to live." He circled something on the pad as he finished the last sentence.

"That wouldn't make sense though. Jacob didn't make me leave, I left because I wanted to go with him. I loved him." The volume in her voice began to rise. She could feel her anger flaring. Jacob was the kindest, most understanding and gentle person she'd ever encountered. He would never...

"Whose idea was it to run away from the Palace?" he asked plainly, not bothering to look up from his scribbling.

"Well, he brought it up, bu—"

"And is it possible that they could have overheard him saying this to you? Is it possible they could take his words and twist them to the group, making him out to be a trouble starter and you the innocent, unsuspecting Palace-born who was too young and inexperienced to understand she was being influenced the whole time?" Dale said.

"No, it wasn't like that at all," Mary explained, but she was interrupted again.

"I didn't ask you how it was, I asked if it was possible that things could be fed to the group in this way." He looked up and reached for his glasses, then began rubbing the lenses clean on the bottom of his shirt. "You have to keep in mind that most things they taught you were not true. They wouldn't begin being truthful after your departure.

"You see, it's not about what actually happened or what the intent was. What matters is how it could be twisted and served to the group as an alternative fact. You aren't there to defend the reality of what happened. So if—and this is all an *if*—if this is the angle the Order has chosen to go, which we believe is the case, those still in that Palace would only have whatever video or audio evidence and the word of the ruling power to go from. It's an old social engineering tactic from before the sickness. For you, it sounds new and diabolical, but for us? It's common procedure from before."

Dale placed his glasses back on his face. He gently flipped the top of the notepad closed and slid it into the leather bag next to his stool.

"In the days before the sickness, the governments of the world, and there were too many to count, would employ these tactics on what seemed like a monthly basis. Using video and audio files to deceive the masses into making real-world decisions based on these deceptions. Wars were created from lies, from embellishments and greed. You would have to be from our time to understand these tactics." Dale smiled. "You are among us now, and you will learn. We will make sure of that."

CHAPTER SEVENTEEN

Logan

"APPRECIATE YOU MAKING TIME IN YOUR busy schedule to speak to our new visitor. It will help immensely in the war effort," Logan said as he tinkered with a small metal weapon lying on its side on top of the workbench. His mouth slowly moved around in circles as he cracked sunflower seeds with his teeth and spit the shells on the floor to the right of the desk.

It was a habit he'd formed over the years. Helped him think clearly. It began as a thing from his days of baseball as a youth. After the world died and baseball became a thing of the past, the cracking and spitting routine served other purposes.

"Anything I can do to provide intel on those we're still struggling to understand. Having Mary here will allow us to learn things about them that would otherwise take years and more lives lost. Just when we think we have things narrowed down on their motivations, we run into another road block. Mary has provided great information about the inner workings of the Palace."

Dale sat in a metal chair next to the workbench. A bright lightbulb hung over the top of the bench, garage-style from the Old World. It looked out of place in the Palace. That was the point though. Logan had hooked the light up to the ceiling himself; it reminded him of his father's workbench. The same workbench he would watch the greatest man he'd ever known create small wonders in the garage of their old home, the home that served as his parents' burial ground. The hanging bulb gave him a feel of home, at least the feel of normalcy from before everything changed.

In a way, everyone there was looking for that, a sense of family in a world where there was none. Even something as small as a lightbulb was enough to ignite something in Logan's long-term memory, putting him at ease with what the world had come to be.

Logan kept his personal pod dark, he liked it that way. The only other light was from the bulb above his bed. Even when he wasn't working, it was that way. The curtains blocked out the sunlight from the windows, helping to encapsulate the small pod in a blanket of darkness. He had ripped the TV off the wall the first night he stayed in the pod. Even though it was not operational, it felt like it was watching him. *Better safe than sorry,* he'd told himself.

The only time he could be found in his pod was when he slept or worked on the tools that would be used in the battles to come. Logan couldn't decide if he worked on the weapons so much because he wanted to win the battles to come or if the routine of taking things apart and putting them back together kept his mind focused on something other than the obvious. Recently, Dale and others from the squad had found a case of tools or weapons that belonged to those who sought to colonize their planet.

Dale and Logan had opened the case together. What they found was possibly a game changer for their rebel squad. The Eagle captain ordered Dale to never speak to anyone about what was inside the box. If anyone happened to ask what was in the case, Logan told him to simply say there was nothing significant.

In reality though, the case contained weapons not from planet Earth. Both he and Dale could see that upon opening the lid. The metal was different. There were no bullets to be fired or magazines to be loaded. He could only hope that his group was not the only one in the world fighting. If they were, and the enemy had more firepower like what he had found—they were in for absolute annihilation.

"Good...that's good. I thought she would be a tremendous help.

Whether she wanted to be or not, it's a good thing that she cooperated. Such a beautiful young woman, isn't she?" Logan looked up from the small item he was jabbing at with his tools and smiled at the intel specialist. The smile was friendly and warm. Dale was his closest friend. The young man was wise beyond his years, and Logan could appreciate such a thing in a diminished world.

Dale's cheeks turned bright red, and he cleared his throat. Logan could see he was struggling to find the words. He laughed at Dale and went back to his tinkering. "I'm joking, soldier," he said. "She is around your age though. What are you, twenty-one, twenty-two years old?" He spit out a few cracked shells.

"Yeah, I'm twenty-one years old, sir."

"Hmm..." came Logan's only response as he went back to his work. Neither said anything for a moment.

The intel soldier broke the awkwardness he seemed to be feeling by jumping right into the meat of his briefing. "This find was one of high importance. We've never come across a Palace-born person who... was still among the living. And I would have never thought that if we did in fact find any, they would be interested in helping us. She still has some confusion going on in her head, even while seeming to hate those who brought her up." Talking about Mary and what he'd learned about her appeared to bring Dale to life. All his awkwardness subsided when he spoke of her. Logan took note of that.

"How so?" Logan said softly without looking up from his work.

"While she does in fact detest them, the indoctrination is still strong in the way she views everything. Which is to be expected. It hasn't even been two months since she left the place where mind control has been heavily implemented for the last...twenty years of her life." Dale patted the leather bag sitting on his lap. "I have a ton of notes that I think you should look at from our talk this morning. She is truly an asset to our cause."

"I don't need to see the notes," Logan said quietly.

Logan scraped his seat closer. "I'm sorry, sir, I didn't get that. Can you please repeat, sir?" Dale said.

"I don't need to see the notes," Logan said, a bit louder than before. He was generally a soft-spoken man. He liked to think of himself as a kind man—and fair. Everyone in his squad had chosen him to be the leader all those years ago in the ruins of old Northern Kentucky, in the battle for Newport Levee bridge. Many men died that day on both sides, but the survivors ended the day in control of that bridge and the surrounding area.

Their strength and resolve showed, and they managed to outsmart the colonizers. Destroying the convoy of vans and security agents looking to kill everyone living in the parking garage of the structure was a life-changer for Logan. That was the day the Eagles became a battle unit, and the day they decided to take their planet back. They had the men, they had the weapons, and that day, they found their leader. Logan didn't seem to have the same fear for the enemy that everyone else carried.

"I trust you and the work that you do, Mr. Rafferty. It's why I assigned you to the position. If you say that we have a find with Mary, then I'll take you at your word." He looked at the man seated beside him and grinned.

The truth was, he didn't care about Mary or what she had to say. She was not of the utmost importance to him. The girl was being handled by those more suited for the job. The cache of new weapons found below the burning child center was more in line with his thinking currently.

"Besides, I don't really have the time to look over the notes. We may have stumbled upon some tech that could change the tide of the war. It's a long shot, but it's definitely worth my full attention at this stage." Logan grabbed a metal ring from the workbench and screwed it onto the side of the small weapon he was working on.

"Understood, sir, but there is something she was sayi—"

"I said you can handle it," Logan said sharply without regarding Dale. A hint of anger crept into his voice, enough so that Dale sat up straight in his seat and took attention to it. "I appoint men to particular jobs for a reason, and it's not to look over your shoulders and make sure you are doing it correctly. If there is something of high importance, then you can let me know now. If not...handle it."

"Yes, sir!" Dale said.

Logan set the small weapon down on the workbench and turned

his wide, muscular frame toward the intel specialist. He knew he had an intimidating presence with his hulking neck and shoulders. Even the most murderous and cunning of the Old World rebels and those within his company would not dare to cross him. Not without the desire for a hell of a fight only one of them would walk away from.

While striving to be a noble and charismatic captain, he was known for his iron-fist way of leadership when needed. Most would fall in line with no need for strife; those that chose to go against the grain or tried to sway the leadership baton from him would be made an example of. In the most pivotal of times, order needed to exist in some way, shape, or form.

Looking at Dale with a curious and concerned face, Logan asked, "Did Mary say anything else about the man she escaped the Palace with?"

Dale opened his bag and retrieved his notepad. He began flipping through the pages quickly. He then stopped on a page and scanned it with a finger. "The man she escaped with, or, should I say, tried to escape with, was named Jacob. She fell in love with him, and he persuaded her to leave the Palace with him. Jacob was shot down before escaping into the forest area in which she took her leave from the facility. It's something that drives her; it's the root of her revenge narrative."

"I've gathered that much from her just from casual banter. I was wondering if she said any more about him beyond that."

Dale thought for a few seconds. "It's clear she loved the man, and that she saw him as a savior-like figure in her life. Someone who opened her eyes to the wrong going on in the Palace. Nothing in particular about him though. I can ask next time I speak to her."

"One more thing. Did she by chance say his age? When I asked, she played dumb with me." Logan peered down at the man sitting beside him.

"No, she did not. We know he wasn't Palace-born. His exact age though, I have no idea. It's very possible that she doesn't know his exact age. From what I gather, the Palace-born individuals are more in tune with each other than the survivors they live among. They are considered adults by age ten." Dale shoved the pad back into his bag.

"I'll speak to her sometime this week about it," Logan said as he turned back to the workbench. *Could it really be Jacob? No, it couldn't be... He died long ago.*

Dale spoke up, excited to suddenly remember something. "But we did speak a lot about Sirus. She has a lot to say about him and the talk she and Jacob had with him before they were released into the world. She says he's the director of the Palace program. A man of high importance and—"

"I don't care. I don't want to talk about him."

Dale looked around in confusion. "But you said to—"

Logan pounded the workbench with his massive fist so hard that all the tools and weapons littered about the surface jumped at least a foot in the air before raining back down with loud clunking sounds. In a low, even voice, he said, "You've made two mistakes by questioning me today. Please don't make a third. If I speak, I have reasons for my words. So, when I tell you that I wish not to speak on certain matters, let it go. I don't care to talk about this program director. I have interest in the man Jacob. I will get to this Sirus when I deem it worth talking about. Sirus is too far from our reach, and there are leagues of issues we must overcome before putting targets on him, whatever he may be. Please don't waste my time speaking about shit that makes no difference in the immediate future."

Dale closed his mouth, which had been slightly open in surprise as Logan admonished him.

"Your job," Logan continued, "is to accumulate information for when I want to speak about it. Do not bring up this Sirus character to me again until I ask you about him. I'm aware of who he is. I was told as much by Mary. Never forget who you are and where you fit into this military company. And most of all, never forget who I am."

Logan delivered the reprimand with the calmness of someone talking about flowers and the weather. He mentioned what could be interpreted as a threat on a man's life like it was no big deal at all. Logan knew that his methodical way of speaking and making decisions was why he was feared. He was a man who was hard to read.

"Excuse my words. I understand, sir. Is there anything else I can help with, sir?" the visibly shaken man said.

"No," Logan said, going back to his work. "You can go back to your normal duties. Thank you, soldier." Dale left the pod in a hurry, softly closing the door behind him.

Logan thought about the mysterious Jacob for the rest of that night, wondering, hoping. It could have been his childhood friend. The man sounded like the Jacob he knew, in appearance and range of age, but he couldn't be sure. In the end, it really didn't matter. The man was dead now. It would only serve as a reason to want to destroy the colonizers even more, but that was okay. In war, there was never enough motivation. Logan clicked the last piece of the colonizer's weapon back into place. He'd taken it apart, studied the parts of the strange source of energy that powered it, then put it back together.

When Sirus sent facility-created humans to their Palace to retrieve Mary, they'd be ready. He was betting on it.

CHAPTER EIGHTEEN

Lonnie

LONNIE FOUND HIMSELF SITTING IN A small white room, much like the room where he met with Teacher Luke, except this room was on the ground floor and there was a window. The other room had no windows, and it made him feel claustrophobic. Lonnie and Teacher Simon had been meeting up for talks after his initial promotion with Teacher Luke. They usually spoke about things to come, duties he would be expected to follow through with, and keeping things secret until the final step of Phase 2 was implemented.

Lonnie was nervous that day, as he'd been for every meeting before. He felt a mess of emotions while prepping the face he would wear for the talk. But which one today? When he was with Melinda or other Palace-born, he was to act like one of them for the sake of getting along and fitting in. Everyone wanted to fit in.

For all intents and purposes, he was one of them. But he knew about things that were on the forefront. Things that would likely trouble the already riled-up Palace members. Then, when he was around the teachers or security agents, he was expected to be the strong-willed future military captain for a unit of Palace-born killers. Even thinking it made him feel stupid and gullible. Sometimes he wondered why he was even going along with it, but deep down, he knew.

The constant switching of faces, moods, and emotions was beginning to take a toll on him. Lonnie was afraid that at some point he would have on the wrong face with the wrong person and either alert the Palace-born to what was coming prematurely, or show the teachers he had reservations about what they wanted him to do. Either way, the face swapping was becoming a problem for him. It was too much.

Lonnie was beginning to care for Melinda. He didn't know why, but he knew that he did. Since their talk a few weeks ago, he'd seen her in the hallways and at shooting practice. He'd tried to make eye contact and smile at her multiple times, but she wouldn't even look his way. Every time he saw her, she had her head down and walked at a fast pace, like she didn't want to be seen by anyone, including him.

She was sweet; she cared about others over her own wellbeing. It was what they'd all been taught from a very early age. While he was planning to go out into the world and lead a death squad, Melinda was living up to the original teachings. Of course, the idea was to get back to the lovey "help each other" stuff after the surviving rats were put down. No matter how he tried to shake it though, it felt wrong.

He *had* shared a moment in the auditorium with Melinda the day of the cleansing. He knew it, and she did too. That was clear. He had handled their conversation like an idiot, basically trying to make her believe that he was a heartless bastard who felt nothing while watching Old World members being killed. There was a moment where he had worn the wrong mask.

True, he didn't feel exactly the same way she did. He didn't feel bad for those who'd died. He more so felt bad for himself—for what he was becoming. Or maybe this was what he'd always been, and this caused confusion about his own identity. He felt bad that he didn't feel worse about watching them all die. He wondered if he was detached from humanity. How could he watch so many people be mowed down by gunfire and not even feel sick from at least the visual of it?

Blood had filled the stage that day, so much so that it ran off the sides and onto the feet of the Palace-born in the first row of seats. Some of them hadn't died right away. After the rain of bullets, there were still moans and even a few screams. The security agents pulled their handguns and planted bullets in the heads of those with too much will to live, extinguishing it right then and there.

And still, he didn't feel bad for them. After seventeen years of learning to care about everyone, all of mankind and the planet, he should have been in tears...maybe he should have even run up on stage to save them. Raised his hands high in the air with courageous, loving fight in his eyes. He imagined confronting the security agents, telling them that this was not the way things were done, that this was not the way humans treated each other anymore. If only it could have happened that way.

He hadn't tried to play hero though. No one had. They'd all just watched. Those like Melinda had a heart for the Old World members, they felt bad to see them die. All he could muster was sympathy for himself.

That scared him more than anything else. Maybe the teachers did pick the right man for this job. Who better than a man with no attachment to human life? It puzzled him why he didn't mind seeing them all die. Was it because of Jacob tricking Mary into leaving with him? Or could it have been what he found in Michelle's pod that day? He was not sure if it was either of those things, but deep inside he was hoping that was the case. He was not a monster, but only a monster could be indifferent about such a thing.

Deep in thought, he barely noticed Teacher Simon walking into the small room until the freakishly tall teacher pulled his chair from under the table to sit down. Teacher Simon was not commonly seen by Palace members, as he didn't teach classes. Though he was always present for any Palace-wide presentations or announcements. The classes that Teacher Simon would be teaching in the coming weeks would all be new material. Battle plans and things of that nature.

The lumbering teacher was at least six foot ten, accentuating the fact that he was a very slender man. He wore a black suit and shiny black shoes. Unlike the other teachers, he was bald and had no facial hair. While most of the teachers had an easygoing nature about them, Teacher Simon did not smile, he did not make jokes, and he was not what you would call friendly.

"Hello, Lonnie. How are you feeling today?" Teacher Simon said as he sat down. His voice was deep and always sounded like it was echoing. In that case, maybe it was because of the small room, but regardless of the setting, Teacher Simon's voice always seemed to boom. He had to pull his seat away from the table, as his legs were too long to fit beneath it. Lonnie thought that it looked comical, but he wouldn't dare crack a smile.

"I'm feeling good, ready to learn and ready to serve." Lonnie sat up straight, looking at Teacher Simon and hoping to appear eager for knowledge.

"I'm glad to hear that. My apologies for making you wait. I was taking care of time-sensitive things for Sirus." He placed his massive hands flat on the desk. His fingers looked entirely too long to Lonnie. Everything about Teacher Simon seemed to be an exaggerated version of a man. The teacher slowly rubbed the tips of his fingers over the surface of the desk, almost nuzzling them into the wood in slow, circular motions. Lonnie didn't know why he did it, but he did know it freaked him out and made it hard to focus on the man's face.

"No need to apologize, I know that you have lots to do. What's on the agenda for today, sir?"

Teacher Simon gave one nod in Lonnie's direction. "How has your training been going? Shooting and stamina building in the gym? You will serve as the face of our expectations, so these things are of the utmost importance. Your personal physical development, that is."

"It's all going great. I shoot multiple times a day. All my targets are turned in on a daily basis. I've mastered every type of firearm that we have, including the weapons in the private shooting ranges that only captains have access to. I'm shooting assault rifles, RPGs, and handguns at a ninety-seven-percent accuracy rating, and that's moving up.

"Teacher Paul has the statistics printed out and in a file, I believe. I can get them from him and bring them to our next meeting if you wish." Lonnie realized his hands were gripping his knees. He did that when he was nervous. He thought such body-language made him look weak, so he mirrored what Teacher Simon was doing and placed both hands on the table, minus the finger rubbing.

"That won't be necessary, we've seen the statistics. I was more so wondering how you feel about your development in these activities. Stats can only tell us so much," Teacher Simon said, an emphasis on the last two words.

"I feel great about them. While shooting, I've been keeping my mind clear, seeing targets, not people. Not lives. The way you taught me. I remember the training stuff you mentioned about soldiers from the Old World, how they were trained to view the enemy as something other than equals or people. I've been doing that," Lonnie said.

"I like to hear that, Lonnie. If there is anything we can do to help, please don't hesitate to ask."

That made Lonnie feel good, wanted even. In his short seventeen years of life, he'd never been made to feel special in this way. It felt good. On the inside he brightened up, but on the outside, he kept the same stone-cold face he believed they expected from him. He knew that every interaction he had with those from the Order was being evaluated.

"Today won't be a long meeting, I do need to get back to more pressing matters. Sirus thinks it's important that I'm giving you information on who we are and what we're doing on a planetary level."

"Yes, sir. Such as?" Lonnie was confused. He knew who they were and what they did. He'd been learning about the Order and how they came to be since before he could even remember his own name. *Unless they'd been lying to him, lying to everyone. Like Melinda was saying that day in her pod.*

"As you know, we are the Order, and we're the remaining governmental power throughout the world. Obviously, we're the strongest of mankind and did not succumb to the sickness. We are the ones Mother Earth chose to bring the New World into a new era, which is what we have been doing for the last twenty-some-odd years."

Teacher Simon's voice was void of emotion, almost as if he were reading the words off a page in his mind, and his stare was unwavering. Lonnie wasn't sure if he'd ever seen the man blink. Speaking to him was always unnerving.

"There are a sizable number of Palaces throughout the world. They were created long ago for circumstances such as these. If there was ever a pandemic, or a war such that civilization could not go on, the

Palaces would be of significant use. The world powers were able to come to an agreement to keep this secret. When the sickness came, the plan became clear: power up the Palaces and begin bringing in survivors to begin repopulating the planet." Teacher Simon's hands remained flat on the table in front of him, his chair at least two feet away from the table.

Lonnie knew these things already, but he would not interrupt. He did not want to disrespect the serious teacher or speak out of turn. He knew there would be more to the story.

"Our reach is long, much longer than you know, but you will come to understand who we truly are as a people in time. The vastness of what we can touch is beyond your limited imagination, but it's my job to get you there. We chose you for a reason, because we see something inside of you that resonates with our mission.

"You are not the only person being groomed for this type of promotion. Only the best and brightest can handle what's to come, and we see that potential in you and others." Teacher Simon crossed one leg over the other, keeping his hands on the table in front of him. The visual was so odd to Lonnie. He thought it had to be very uncomfortable to sit in that position.

"Will I get the chance to meet any of the other people who are being promoted? Only to share ideas and such with, of course," Lonnie added.

"No, not yet. When the final steps of Phase 2 are ready, you will meet them, as you will be coordinating plans and assaults together. In the meantime, you can share any ideas with me, and I'll help as much as I can."

Lonnie's stomach tightened at the word "assaults." He knew what that meant. More people would die, and while he did not feel anything for the dead, he wondered if he could truly do it himself. He thought that he could. Knew that he would most definitely try his best to pull the trigger on a human life when the time came...*But how will I feel?*

"You should keep in mind that some things we cannot and will not tell you, for your own protection and for the protection of the cause. If you were to be captured by the rats out in the world, we would not want you to have certain vital information that could put the planet at risk. I hope you understand. If you don't, then that's okay as well, as long as you do understand that the info you receive is on a need-to-know basis. If you ever hear something you were not privy to before, keep this in mind, Lonnie."

"I understand," Lonnie said. Inside he was wondering what type of stuff the teacher was talking about. Why were there things they could not tell him? He knew that everything was on a need-to-know basis, but that didn't mean he didn't want to know. Especially after his conversation with Melinda.

Exactly how long was the outside habitable for people after they were exposed? Were there protective suits out there for people to wear? There were so many questions he wanted the answers to so that he could feel better about doing the job he was being asked to do. He would not voice these concerns though. He would do as he was told and answer the call to be the soldier the planet needed him to be. He would get rid of those that were doing her harm. He wished he could get Melinda to get on board with the importance of trusting the Order; they owed their lives to them. Why couldn't she simply give them the benefit of the doubt?

"We, the Order, can only do so much from where we stand. We cannot go out into the world and fight those that wish to do us and the planet further harm. We need the young and strong to fight on our behalf. We need those like you to help your peers see the enormity of the battle coming on the forefront. Have you been training the hand-chosen group we've put together?" Teacher Simon asked.

"I have. Once a night we speak and train. Just like you said. We never miss a session, sir."

Teacher Simon lifted his wide hands from the table's surface as he rose from his chair. He grabbed the back of the chair, which looked like miniature furniture from the child center in his huge hand, and pushed it into the table. "Great. Keep up the excellent work. I'll need to get going. There are things I must attend to now that I see you are still on the true track.

"We will talk again soon. Just know that we are always watching." The teacher's stare became more focused as he stood over the table like a giant. Then he slowly turned and walked out of the room.

Just like that, Lonnie was left sitting in the room, holding his breath. He was just as confused as he was before the brief conversation even began. He exhaled and allowed himself to come down from the tense encounter. He always got wound up when he had to meet with Teacher Simon. He preferred Teacher Luke, as he was more relaxed, and his stare was not so... creepy. He felt like Teacher Simon could see inside of him. He felt talked at instead of talked to. The energy was different, and something about Teacher Simon scared him.

With every passing day, he wondered more and more if what he was doing was right. Was he just doing it because he was being given attention that he craved? They all craved it. Growing up without parents or anyone to give you special attention outside of the group was missing in their upbringing when compared to how Old World members were raised.

The fear of being hurt or killed by the Order was also a cause of stress for him. He didn't want them to think him weak and decide to remove him. Maybe he was going along for that reason. But no, he'd never been a coward. Death was not a serious source of fear for Lonnie. Over time he came to think of himself as being weak, someone stupid enough to go along with a plan he didn't believe was right.

What he was doing in secret was either a good thing or a very bad thing. He didn't know the answer to that, but he knew it played a part in why he would do what he was told without outright questioning anything. That was the difference between him and Melinda, and likely the reason he knew he was letting her down. That still stung.

He wanted to make that situation right. They needed to talk. Maybe he could apologize to her and clear the air. He didn't know if she was right in her theories, and at that point it wasn't very important who was right. Things would be what they would be, and he did not want to see her get hurt for questioning the Order. He knew what they were capable of. She and the others in the Palace had no idea what was coming.

CHAPTER NINETEEN

Thomas

ONCE, WHEN HE WAS A KID, he found his father's gun. Back before the world turned into something he could barely familiarize himself with. Many of the thoughts and ideas from before were lost or all but erased from his memory, making room for the new stuff. He still remembered that day he found the gun though. That told him the day was a pivotal moment in his upbringing.

Thomas's parents were both at work. They worked at a small diner not far from their little starter home in Cincinnati. He remembered hating that house, not because it was terrible, but because it was much smaller in comparison to the houses his friends lived in. A few of those friends would make comments about it from time to time, which hurt his feelings. But that's how kids were back then, and still are from what he'd seen in the Palace.

It had been a Thursday, which in his house was another name for "the hungriest day of the week." His parents got paid on Fridays, so the day before that was always a struggle. Struggle days meant he would eat spam, raw hotdogs, or peanut butter crackers if he could find them. Spending the whole afternoon opening the refrigerator over and over, as if new food would show up out of thin air.

Looking back on it now, it was interesting how his brain worked as a kid. Maybe it was that every time he went back to the fridge, he would be even more hungry and susceptible to eat something that he'd arrogantly passed up the first few go-rounds.

That day, Thomas remembered looking above and under every surface in the small kitchen. There was not much to it, just a few counters and an old wooden table that had been fading since before his aunt gave it to them some years back along with the refrigerator. It was one of those small refrigerators that didn't hold more than a hundred bucks' worth of groceries, not that they had that much to spend on food.

Between bouts of watching *Saved by the Bell* on TV and becoming an ace detective during the commercials while looking for food, Thomas became desperate. Or brave. Either way, he decided that the kitchen was a lost cause. No way he was going to eat relish on bread. And he would never stoop so low as to crack open a can of spam without his mother there to properly cook it.

The thought had simply popped into his head that particularly hungry day. The type of thought you know is so unreasonable that you'd be better off murdering said thought and burying it in the back of your brain. Desperation allowed such thoughts to thrive and peck away at the brain enough that you would do the deed. Thomas decided to check out his parents' room.

Parents' rooms were off limits among most children in the Old World. There was simply nothing in a parent's room that would interest a child. Under normal non-starving circumstances, that is. But that day was a special occasion, and he knew that no one would be home for quite some time.

He'd seen his mother take a pack of cookies up the stairs last week. Maybe it was a personal stash for her and his father. They were constantly saying he ate just because the food was there, and he always wanted to feed the neighborhood when they came over to play video games. It made sense that they would hide some of the good stuff for themselves. He couldn't remember ever wishing his parents were greedy, food-smuggling demons before, but as he made his way to their bedroom, that's exactly what he wished.

Thomas walked up the steps knowing he was not likely to find anything to eat in their room. If there had been something, his mother would have left it on the counter for him. He knew that in his heart of hearts, and he also knew that she was aware of the fact that the appetite of a twelve-year-old was unmatched. He was always at his hungriest when he came home from school. There had been nothing on the counter when he got home but a note saying they were bringing dinner from work. That was at least three hours away. A boy needed to eat in the meantime. What else would he do with an extra three hours? It was worth a try.

Walking into this parents' room, he investigated underneath the bed and in the dresser drawers. Thomas found nothing but a pink odd-shaped piece of plastic with small bumps all over the tip. The object was hidden underneath his mother's underwear. He would not understand what that was until he was much older. By the time he did figure it out, his mother was long dead and gone right along with his father... and everyone else.

After he'd straightened up everything in the drawers, he checked their walk-in closet. The closet was not very big, just sizeable enough to line some shoes up on the floor and hang shirts and pants. This closet belonged to his father. Most of the clothes were dressy stuff. Button-down shirts, slacks—the type of stuff his dad wore to his old job when he was working as a call center salesman. He hadn't worked there in some years though. He said that people weren't buying things anymore, and because the job was mostly commission, he couldn't afford to do it. That's when Thomas's mother got him a job at the diner.

Looking up at the top of the closet, he noticed a shelf. He was too small to see what was on the shelf, but he could reach a few of the boxes with his fingers if he stood on the tips of his toes. In his young mind, he imagined there could be boxes of snack cakes or cookies up there. He'd already gone far enough to sneak into his parents' room scavenging for food, no point in getting shy at that point. So he attempted to smack the boxes down.

After a few tries of sliding the boxes with the tips of his fingers, he decided to take a leap and knock them all down. He could go downstairs and get a chair when he was done to put them back neatly. As an adult, Thomas looked back on that memory knowing that a chair would have been useful to get the boxes down, but kids didn't use common sense in most cases when they were eager to get to something they wanted. So a leap and smack it was.

Thomas jumped as high as he could, and with his right hand he swung, knocking every box on the small shelf down. Cardboard boxes and shoes came raining down, and he covered up, placing both hands over his head. Something big and hard clunked him on the shoulder, sending nerve pain screaming down the right side of his body. Thomas immediately grabbed his shoulder, running out of the closet and jumping around the bedroom like an idiot, cursing the gods at the pain.

Holding his arm in an awkward position, he sat on the edge of his parents' bed, waiting for the pain to subside and the tingles in his arm to go away. He worried he would have a bruise that he'd have to explain to his parents.

Thomas pulled the sleeve up on his tee shirt to spy the area of impact. It was a little red, but that was it. After a few more moments of rubbing his shoulder, he got back to the matter at hand. Food.

He walked back toward the closet, shaking his arm along the way as if that would make it feel better. It did not. Thomas looked at all the boxes on the ground. He didn't see one Zebra Cake box. Not a hint of a Honey Bun. Not even a box of the cheap cookies they sold at the CVS around the corner.

After a careful glance, he saw what had destroyed his poor shoulder. How had he not seen it from the bed? It was so shiny and big. He knew right away it was a gun. His father owned a gun, he knew that—but he always thought it was in some magical hidden place. Locked away in a strong lockbox and buried beneath the ground or something like that. Not in an old shoebox on the top shelf of the closet.

Reaching down to pick up the gun, he couldn't help but to think about how much of a badass his father was. In his childish mind, Thomas only saw his father flipping the weapon in his fingers like a gunslinger from Gilead, shooting down bad guys left and right. When in reality his father had never shot the gun a day in his life. Hadn't even been his idea to get it. Thomas found out later that his mother said it was a good idea to have protection in the house just in case someone tried to burglarize them.

The gun felt so much heavier than he could have imagined. Nothing like the plastic guns that he played with. He felt like he needed to grab it with two hands to lift it off the wood flooring of the closet. Thomas had a gun like it; he'd gotten it for Christmas one year with a cowboy hat and a cheap golden sheriff badge. The gun was called a revolver, a six-shot revolver.

Thomas walked the gun back to the bed and sat, admiring it. The cold steel in his hand felt so powerful, it felt like it was alive—he could almost feel an energy inside of the gun. For an hour he sat there, studying every angle of his discovery. He took the time to get up and point the gun at his reflection in the tall mirror on the back of the bedroom door. Just like that, he'd forgotten about food, and the hunger pangs in his stomach went away that day.

Today though, Thomas sat at the service desk of a brand-new shooting range, inside of a utopian-like facility in what was once Indiana. Now he loaded up and passed out guns to underage children all day. If there was a god, he had one hell of a sense of humor. The same kid who'd once ogled his father's firearm now had a job passing them out to kids in a world long forgotten.

Funniest thing about it was that he didn't even know why he was doing it, why he even cared to still be in the Palace, working for the Order and doing their bidding. *Do I really care to still be among the living at this point?* he thought while loading a rifle and explaining how the kickback would knock the fourteen-year-old girl a step back if she didn't get snug up on the thing when firing.

When the sickness came to undo all that mankind had achieved in only two days, he was no more than a junior in high school on his way to nowheresville, and with express shipping. Failing out of every class, fighting anyone who looked at him the wrong way, and cursing the memory of his father, who'd gotten fed up with their situation and decided to gather his clothes from the small walk-in closet and run off with another woman from the diner.

Thomas's mother turned to drugs to comfort her after his father left, and this left him utterly alone to deal with the confusion of being a teenager. One day he was smoking on a vape pen in his room, trying to break into an iPhone he'd pilfered out of some kid's locker, and the next he was walking around the block in an endless march, unable to go into his house and deal with his mother's body at the bottom of the steps covered in vomit and blood. She'd coughed up something that was not meant to be coughed up.

He'd walked around the block in his neighborhood for what seemed like fifty times, feeling nothing. In shock and afraid. When the white van pulled up to him as the sun began to fall from the sky and night took its shift, he'd barely noticed the big vehicle. A man called him to the van and asked if he needed a safe and warm place to be, and of course, he took the offer. There was nothing else for him to do. The news channels and websites told him as much. Just about everyone was dead anyway. So he went with them.

While everyone else was being taken to local stadiums for vaccinations and grouped up for Palace consideration, he was taken somewhere different. Thomas and a few others were taken directly to the Palace and told that they were needed for security purposes. They could have a purpose and help keep all of the scared and lonely survivors safe. The alternative was to be released back out into the world with the sickness still active. Thomas had agreed to work as security in exchange for a pod and safety from the sickness.

That was another lifetime ago, at least twenty years ago, or so everyone said. The days all felt the same after the first few years, and it didn't make a difference if it had been ten years or one hundred and fifty years.

"Can I get a box of the hollow-point bullets, please?" a young man of about sixteen asked Thomas from the other side of the service desk.

"Yes, here you are." He dropped the box of bullets on the desk. "You may want to try these out too. I've heard great things about them. They really shred up the targets," he said, grabbing a box of Hydra-Shok ammo and placing it on top of the hollow-points.

"Okay. I'd love to try those as well. Thank you, sir," the young man said.

"Just doing my job while helping you do your own," Thomas said, smiling at the young man as he crossed out the two types of ammo on the daily list. The Order expected him to get rid of so much ammo per day, and he was required to have the Palace members try out all the diverse types of ammo at least once. The young man left with a handful of ammo, walking toward the shooting lanes with a high-powered rifle strapped over his shoulder.

Thomas wasn't sure if he even wanted to live anymore. He didn't see the point in continuing the charade of getting back out into the world. What was once a mission of peace and repopulation had now turned into yet another war. They told him it was to clean up the last of the "bad people," but he was not as young and impressionable as the kids in the Palace.

"Bahahaha!" Thomas sat back in his seat and laughed out loud. Laughed louder than he'd laughed in some time. Thankfully no one was around to see the abrupt outburst. He thought it was humorous that he had the nerve to call the children impressionable, as he'd spent the day passing out deadly ammo to them so they could go train to kill others.

Thomas stopped laughing as fast as he'd began. *What if he took one of these high-powered rifles, loaded it up with the deadliest ammo they had, and started killing as many teachers as he could before being taken down? Wonder if others would see me as a martyr or just some idiot who caused a small hitch in a plan that would be carried out regardless of what anyone did to stop it.*

Tapping his fingers on the service desk and smiling at Palace members walking by, he considered the idea of shooting the teachers down. His imagination went back to that day in his father's closet, and he remembered the shiny revolver in his hands and the power that it seemed to have. He wondered if he could spin the weapons on his fingers like a gunslinger and take down bad guys left and right. The corner of his mouth twisted and curved up into a half-smile, silly thoughts in his mind keeping him entertained as a crew of children no older than twelve or thirteen approached.

"We want to try the automatic pistols," one of the kids said.

"You will enjoy these. I've tried a few myself, and the stopping power is much better than you would think. Just make sure you hold on to the gun tightly. Automatics have a tendency to get away from you. Considering how young and small you are, just keep a steady grip. If you lose control and shoot something other than the target, you can be reprimanded." He passed off ammo and guns to the children as he spoke.

"Don't worry about that, sir. We are grown men and have been handling guns for weeks. We know what we're doing," the boy in front said. The others simply stared at him like he was an idiot for even mentioning such things.

"Just making sure you know. You are free to go shoot. Enjoy your time," he said as he sat back in his seat and went back to the visions in his mind of twirling guns with his index fingers and liberating the world of those he now believed to be the true evil in the world.

Truth of the matter was though, no gun had ever made him feel the way that first one did. He didn't even enjoy shooting them. When the Old World member Jacob had stepped over the line in the central plaza a few days before he was shot down for all to see, Thomas couldn't even manage to pull his gun on him. Those were the orders—shoot and kill anyone who went too close to the exit door in the central plaza. But Thomas froze and did not do his duty. Teacher Simon made sure he knew that the events that transpired with the Palace-born and Jacob escaping were his fault. Had he done his duty and ended Jacob that day, none of it would have happened.

Putting on a security uniform and having a firearm at his side did not make him a killer, and in that moment, his freezing and hesitation told him all he needed to know about himself. He was not what they wanted him to be; he had not lost his humanity. The thought brought a smile to his face as he checked out another rifle to yet another child.

CHAPTER TWENTY

Carla

EVERY NIGHT SHE SAT WITH HER legs crossed beneath her in a meditative position on her bed while she read Bible verses out loud as a reminder of the one true goal, the real mission at hand. Those who had infiltrated mankind and produced a virus to kill off nearly the entire species were not as important as the reasons why God allowed them to do such a thing. *Used them*, she thought. God used them to bring down his punishment.

The pod was darkened, all lights were turned off—the only sound that could be heard was the shower running in the bathroom to her right, and the sink also had a steady flow. She turned on the shower and the sink to block out her own mumblings and possible groans and squeals from the different things she would do to herself when the spirit touched her in just the right ways.

The glow from the moon illuminated the bed with its white sheets and pillows. The white comforter lay bundled up at her feet. She hadn't made the bed that morning, so it looked the same as it did when she'd woke up. The moon's light cast the bed and Carla in a blue hue; the rest of the pod furniture faded out into the shadows of the room.

The Bible lay across her lap while her hands hung at her sides—palms flat on the bed. Her favorite book was bookmarked to her favorite verses. Carla tried not to speak too much about her religion around people, but she felt compelled to do so more often than she would have liked.

Most survivors of the world no longer subscribed to the idea of Christianity or any religion being a viable option. There was nothing like worldwide destruction and death to change your mind about a divine being that loves everyone eternally. She differed from that viewpoint...all she saw was a test of faith in the world before her. Carla looked down to the book on her lap and read aloud, making sure not to speak over the water running in the bathroom.

"For the life of the flesh is in the blood, and I have given it for you on the altar to make atonement for your souls, for it is the blood that makes atonement by the life."

After speaking the verse from Leviticus 17:11, tears began to well up in her eyes as one corner of her mouth quirked up into a grin.

As quickly as the grin appeared on her face, a cold expression replaced the smile just before she brought her right hand up from the bed and slapped her own face so hard that her ponytail whipped to her opposite shoulder. Carla's face did not move an inch; she took the full impact of the slap. It was a small price to pay in comparison to what the Lord Jesus went through for her to have the chance to atone. Her right hand went back to the bed. Carla blinked hard and opened her mouth wide to clear the cobwebs and dull the tingling on the right side of her face.

She moved her bottom jaw around in looping circles to stretch the muscles in her face while going to a different bookmarked page. Since year two of the sickness arriving, she'd performed this routine as well as lots of others. As time went on, some routines of atonement fell by the wayside as she tried new things to punish her flesh for what continued to take place on Earth, but pounding her face was a tried and true way to bring the spirit to the surface.

For the first year of ducking the white vans and sneaking out in the night to find food in grocery stores or gas stations, Carla had the foolish idea that she was alone. Like everyone else, she'd felt self-pity, thinking *woe is me* because she'd been abandoned by her family, God, and everything she thought to be normal. That's the way to think when everything revolves around yourself, as if God created the world and his own rules to your sensibilities. This was not true of course, and over time she figured out that she'd been chosen to bear the cross for her generation. The next time the Lord looked upon her and the planet that he punished, he would see that she was doing his work.

"He is the propitiation for our sins, and not for ours only but also for the sins of the whole world." Carla spoke the words and pondered on the thought. She wondered if Jesus felt the way she did now, taking the responsibility of answering for every sin for every person to live.

Her left hand rose up, making its way beneath her tee shirt. She thought it silly to create too many scars in plain sight of everyone. God knew she had enough, and if they could see the entirety of the atoning she'd put her body through so that they could have a place in heaven one day, they would think her insane.

She thought the opposite of them. How could the Lord consistently show what he accepted and did not accept all throughout history and the general idea still be lost upon the lot? Carla thought there was a reason that people like Jesus and she existed. They were humans with heightened levels of spirit energy or spirit pressure. The link to the Almighty was stronger in her than it was in most everyone else. The things they failed to see were so bright in her view that she could not see around them; that was the difference between her and the flock.

Carla's hand crept up her chest, and her nails rested on her sternum, just between her breasts. She thought about the short-term plans with the Eagle group and what was to come. The little bitch Mary had to go; she did not belong with them. Carla was taking care of that behind the scenes though. She dug her nails into the skin on her chest, feeling them go in deeper as she slowly dragged them downward toward her abdomen. The collection of skin between her nails could be felt, thick and full. Her fingertips were slick with blood.

Her hand made its way from beneath her shirt. Carla could not see her fingers clearly in the darkness, the moon's illumination was not enough to make out the details, but she could see that her fingernails were darkened from the outside. Using her right-hand nails, Carla dug into the nails on her left hand to remove the dead skin and blood, flicking the remains of skin onto the floor next to the bed.

Earlier in the day, after a ten-mile hike through the surrounding woodland area just outside of the city limits with the assault squads, Carla got back to her pod to a very welcome surprise. Tony, a young and impressionable man she'd been showing the ways of Jesus to, had retrieved something from the infirmary for her through his own connection with one of the nurses. A special something that could help with her cause in regard to their new visitor. She had many plans, and this was just one. There was not much to do in the world but plan, plot, and put said plans into action.

Tony was one of her apostles, as she called those who helped her in the spiritual war being waged. It could be seen as blasphemous to some, but she didn't care what others thought. She was created in the Lord's image and doing His work, so to her, it made sense.

In return for Tony's hard work and the risk of being found out, she did small favors for him. Not because she had to, but because she wanted to. He and any of the other helpers needed to understand there were perks to being on the side of the savior. What made one of her helpers happy sometimes didn't make the others happy; that was part of picking out the individuals who could be of use. Men were easy to please, had always been that way since the beginning of time.

Tony required nothing more than a suckle at her bosom. Obviously in the dark; she couldn't risk anyone seeing the gauntlet of pain she'd put her body thought. Carla didn't know if it was sexual for him or repressed mommy issues. Didn't matter either way, anything that could be used to her advantage in the spiritual and physical wars would be taken advantage of. If the young man of nineteen wanted to try his hand at intercourse with her, she would have allowed it. He was an attractive man, but he never took it any further—after sucking and nibbling away at her breasts for an hour and falling asleep on her chest, he would wake up hours later and leave without a word. That was days ago, and today he kept his end of the bargain. Good man.

After freeing her left-hand fingernails of skin, Carla flipped to the next bookmark in her Bible. There were already blood stains on the pages from years of similar self harm. Smearing a bit more on the pages only added character, she thought with a grin.

It was right there in Hebrews 9:12. There was no debate to be had, no confusion. It was right there.

"He entered once for all into the holy places, not by means of the blood of goats and calves but by means of his own blood, thus securing an eternal redemption." She didn't know how much clearer the message needed to be in order for others to simply follow the teachings, to simply learn from the past. Ignorance was a plentiful thing in the world of man, that was apparent, so she didn't bother to convert those who did not possess the mental capacity for such things.

Their souls still needed saving, and she would do that for them because that was her calling. Even a lost soul like that of their visitor, Mary, the one created by those that brought the sickness. The girl bothered Carla in a way that was foreign to her. She didn't know what it was, but she wanted her to go back to where she'd come from—really anywhere but around her and the Eagle squad. Carla thought it a bad idea to help Mary from day one, but Logan insisted that they save her.

Carla closed her blood-stained bible and slid it beneath her bed. Then she swung around and placed both feet on the ground. She wore nothing but a gray tee shirt and panties. Walking over to one of the taller wooden chairs near the sofa, she began repeating the Lord's prayer to herself out loud. Low enough to not be heard by anyone who could be walking the halls, but still loud enough so that she could hear the prayer; that was important.

"Our Father, who art in heaven, hallowed be thy name. Thy Kingdom come, thy will be done, on Earth as it is in heaven." Carla repeated the words at a quick pace as she stood above the chair with her hands gripping the armrests.

Without a pause in the prayer, she brought her ribs crashing down on the back of the chair with as much force as she could muster. The wind escaped from her lungs in a hurry, coming from her lips in a muddled squeal. The pain doubled her over next to the chair. The second she was able to catch her breath, she continued to say the prayer.

"Our Father, who art in heaven, hallowed be thy name. Thy Kingdom come, thy will be done, on Earth as it is in heaven." The words escaped her thin grimacing lips.

Carla slowly rose to her feet, standing above the chair. She gripped the armrests once more. Closing her eyes and taking a deep breath, she quickly got to her tiptoes and again slammed her stomach and lower ribs down on the back of the chair. The pressure and force caused a small scream to leave her throat. She quickly slapped her right hand over her mouth, hoping to quell the sound before it carried far enough to alert anyone.

That was enough for the night. She couldn't take much more and still have enough energy and movement to train the next day. Carla said the Lord's prayer one more time as she went to the bathroom and turned off the sink and the shower. Then she slipped beneath the big warm comforter on her bed. Even though she went though much pain that night, enough pain to send a weaker person to the infirmary or the hospital in the Old World, she lay there with the biggest smile on her face. The same smile she wore every night after finding a multitude of ways to punish herself.

There was also another reason why she was smiling. The plan she had for Mary—that was special to her heart. All things were lining up just as she planned them, and that was a good enough reason for happiness to show on her lips.

If her God was watching, which she believed he was, she knew he would be proud. The meek shall inherit the Earth, she knew those were the words. The weak needed a leader, the herd of sheep needed a wolf. God loved both animals just the same, so being one or the other made no difference to her. She dozed off with that smile on her face, blood drying on her chest, purple bruises forming on her ribs.

CHAPTER TWENTY-ONE

Melinda

M ELINDA KEPT A SMALL JOURNAL OF the things she'd been doing since everything had changed at the Palace. She'd taken part in twenty-nine shooting activities, spent one hundred and seventy-nine bullets, and had watched countless violent and graphic videos on her pod TV. At one time she wondered why they played them twenty-four hours a day when all they'd ever displayed before was "Please Wait." She knew now.

For so long, they'd been fed a bunch of rubbish about being there for one another. (They meant each other, as in Palace-born.) And now that the Order no longer needed to create that link of kindness, they could move on to Phase 2, as they were calling it. The purpose of which, in her estimation, was to make them hyper violent to Old World members.

She sat alone in the central plaza, people-watching and thinking. For the last some-odd weeks, she'd felt so alone. Everyone seemed to be gung ho (no pun intended) about the shooting and killing of other humans, and she just couldn't get on board with that. It simply went against everything she'd been taught up until now. Melinda didn't think you had to be super smart or take a bunch of morning enrichment classes to accept that killing another human or any living being was wrong.

Fear was the motivating factor, she thought. It had to be. She could not deduce any other reasoning as to how those who were peaceful and loving could be so easily converted into killing machines in such a short span of time. It reminded her of stories from the Old World she'd heard, which was ironic seeing as those people were now being made out to be animals without hearts or morality.

Before there was a need for Palaces, watchers, teachers, and quarantine zones, people went to war...quite often. Most who went to war were young, same as what was going on there in the Palace. These young men and women who waged war against each other for little to no reason, or at least no reason that they could understand, were all peaceful and decent people.

She remembered being told that in the daily life of soldiers in the Old World, they would hang out with friends, go to see movies, have relationships with other people, play video games, and all kinds of stuff that was considered peaceful and normal in those times. Then some politician would have an issue with another political figure from somewhere else in the world. Both politicians would call upon these young men and women, who were simply living their lives and minding their own business, to go off to foreign lands and begin killing each other in massive numbers.

Melinda struggled to understand the logic. She thought that in those days, people did it to protect their country. Which was the reasoning behind this new war brewing among the Palace-born and the survivors of the Old World. They were told they were protecting the planet and each other. There was more to it though. From where she stood, nothing was that simple.

As it turned out, things hadn't changed so much with people from the time before to the time she found herself in now. The youth were still being sent to do the deeds of those in power, for whatever reason. No reason would ever be good enough to send Mother Earth's creations out to kill off others.

What if we all decided not to do it? Then what happens? They were not exactly given a choice in the matter. The normal daily activities went away, and then the guns came into play. She could not be the only person thinking that things in the Palace were no longer adding up.

From someone else's point of view, she probably appeared the same way they did to her. Like it wasn't a big deal, like she was okay with what was going on. She wasn't exactly kicking up dust on the topic or stepping up to say that what was happening was wrong. She hadn't even bothered to speak up during the cleansings. Why? She knew the answer to that though, and if she accepted that as the answer, then she'd also have to accept that she was on the bad side of the war. If she had to kill in order to not be killed by those who said they were protecting her, then that made the Order the ultimate evil.

Of course, they did not outright threaten to kill her. And they would not. But it was implied by making the Palace-born witness the cleansings. The way it all went down seemed too put together; it felt wrong and orchestrated. If she was still going through with all the shooting activities and morning enrichments about combat and vanquishing evil still walking the planet, she imagined others who questioned this new system were doing the same. She desperately wanted to find others like her.

Sitting there alone in the central plaza, she noticed how the energy had changed. Where once there were people gathered about discussing philosophy, the planet at large, and how they could not wait to get out there to fix what had been broken, there were now stern faces, secretive whispering, and the sounds of shooting. Palace members now wanted to get out into the world in order to kill...not to fix anything.

They were told that as soon as the last of the sickness was under control, they would begin to move around without protective suits. That time was drawing near. Teacher Paul had said as much in a session just days prior. That was not in her future, she thought as she stood up and walked toward the elevator. The time to get changed in her gym clothes and get to cardio class was coming up. If she was late, she was afraid that could arise suspicion. Last thing she needed was to have eyes on her while she attempted to find others who thought the way she did. It was clear this was what she needed to do before the time came to go out into the world. She did not know how much time was left until then, but she knew it was close.

Thinking to herself, she nearly didn't hear the voice calling from a distance behind her. Melinda slowly turned at the faint sound of her own name to see where it was coming from.

"Melinda! Hey, its me!" She could see Lonnie jogging in her direction from behind a group of girls walking toward her. He was wearing workout attire, and he looked tired from his workout by the way he was jogging. Lonnie passed up the group of girls and made it to her, out of breath. His hands were on both knees as he hunched over, trying build his wind back up.

"You are actually stopping air from getting to your lungs when you bend over like that. Stand up straight and put both hands on the top of your head. You'll catch your breath easier that way," Melinda said. She didn't even know where the advice had come from. She'd seen some of the Old World females do it when they were working out. Maybe she picked it up there.

"Yeah, yeah, I know that's what they say, but it feels better like this." He remained hunched over, looking up at her as the group of females walked by. The girls watched them as they passed, whispering to each other. Lonnie eyed them until they went around the corner of the hall and to the elevator.

"What's up? Why are you running after me like a madman?"

Lonnie finally stood up straight, putting both hands on his hips as he stared down at her. "Am I keeping you from doing something so important in your pod?" he said as a smile formed on his face.

Melinda couldn't help but to smile herself, even though she tried not to. She was still angry with him from weeks ago when they'd had the disagreement in her pod, but he had a way about him that made it hard for her to be mad when she saw that smile.

"There it goes," he said as he touched her arm. "You should smile more, and stop being mad at me. I've been wanting to speak to you about something."

"Well, I've been around, and we've seen each other. If you wanted to talk to me, you could have," Melinda said, finding her cold face once more.

"Well, you aren't very approachable anymore, and I didn't want people to see us arguing if you decided to get loud with me again." He backed up with his hands in the air, palms forward.

Melinda smacked at his hands. "Stop it, you know where my pod is. You could have come to talk to me at any time."

"You kicked me out last time I was there."

"Listen, I'm on my way there now to get changed and into some gym clothes. You can talk to me about whatever you need to while I'm getting dressed. Let's go," she said, grabbing his hand and leading him to the elevator.

SHE STOOD THERE with no clothes on as she searched through the closet next to the bed. Melinda arched her back to get a better view of the different variations of workout gear hanging up, trying to find a nice pair of stretchy pants for running. She knew Lonnie was behind her, sitting on the bed, but she didn't know if he noticed her or even cared. He was two years older, but that meant nothing. They'd never had relations exercise together, so maybe he never looked at her that way.

Again she wondered what it would be like to be with him in that way. She did like Lonnie and was attracted to him. Intercourse was not meant to be for pleasure, but since they seemed to be changing the rules on the fly in the Palace, she didn't see why it couldn't be.

"What were you wanting to talk to me about, Lonnie? If you could, make it fast. I have to go soon." She waited for a response from behind her, but there was nothing. He didn't say anything. Melinda could only hope that meant he was looking at her.

She turned around, holding a pair of blue athletic leggings, to find him sitting on the bed, watching her. He looked away as soon as she caught him staring. *So, he does notice me...in that way.* She turned back to the closet and quickly grabbed a matching shirt.

"Lonnie? What did you want to talk about?" she said, trying to pretend she was all about business while prolonging her nudity.

"Uh, um...I wanted to see if you had changed your thinking on... um, the stuff we talked about that day in your pod...in this pod, I mean." The look in his glazed-over eyes was unfocused. He was speaking to her, but his eyes were not meeting hers. They were studying her body, looking her up and down while talking.

She walked over to him, standing directly in front of him while still fully naked with her pants and shirt in hand. "No, I still feel exactly the same. Have you changed how you feel about what we talked about before?"

"Um...I feel like...ummm..." His eyes moved lower and lower down her body. Melinda was smiling on the inside, but she wore the same stern mask on her face. Her poker face was much better than his own.

"I'm sure you still feel the same, so we have nothing more to speak about on the topic," she said as she turned away from him, pulling the shirt down over her head and purposely leaving the bottoms for last.

"Um...yeah, I still feel the same. Could I change your mind? I think if we talk more about what's to come, you may see my point of view and that of the Order. I um...don't want you to get yourself in any trouble," he said as he stood up from the bed, turning slightly to the side. Melinda thought he was hiding an erection in his pants. She hoped.

"I'll never be okay with hurting other people. I don't care the reasons. There is no reason good enough for me." This got his attention away from her body, and his gaze met hers.

"Not even if it means protecting the planet and every living thing inside of it? That's not worth spilling some blood? To me, it is. I'd hurt someone to protect you and all those I care for," he said, getting visibly angry.

"Oh, so you care about me, huh?" Melinda smiled in a mocking way as she went to step into her leggings.

Before she could get one leg in the pants, he was in front of her, pushing her hand away and causing her to drop the leggings. His lips were pressed against hers before she knew what was happening, right there in the middle of the pod. It happened so fast, she didn't have a chance to mentally prepare for it. But she loved the way his lips felt against hers. Melinda wanted to stay like that forever, their lips touching, their bodies as close as could be.

Lonnie ended the kiss slowly, moving his face away from hers but not backing away. "I do care about you, and I'm about to show you just how much, if you allow me to."

"No one is stopping you," she said as she placed a hand on the back of his neck, pushing his lips to meet hers once again. Lonnie grabbed her in his strong arms in what felt like a bear hug and turned her so that her back was facing the bed.

He kissed her deeply once more before pushing her onto the bed. Melinda's eyes widened as he then dropped his pants and crawled on top of her.

"I won't let anyone hurt you," he said as he stared down at her. "You will never end up on that stage as long as I have breath, do you understand me?" he said in a whisper.

"Yes, I under—" Melinda tried to say, but Lonnie pushed the words back into her mouth with his tongue, his hands running wildly though her hair.

Melinda skipped her workout in the gym. They stayed there on the bed for the remainder of the day, not speaking much, just enjoying each other's energy. She could barely contain her happiness.

CHAPTER TWENTY-TWO

Mary

L OOKING AT HER SIDE PROFILE IN the bathroom mirror, Mary couldn't decide if it was okay to let herself feel happy or not. A part of her loved that the baby growing inside of her still lived, but a part of her felt terrible that Jacob was not around to go through it all with her. She'd never had a baby of her own—not one that she would be responsible for.

Telling the Eagles that she was pregnant was out of the question. She didn't think they were bad people, but if she had learned anything from the Order and those in the Palace, it was not to trust anyone. Especially with the things you held dear to your heart. The child inside of her meant everything; it was all she had left of Jacob.

Looking at her face, she noticed a little pudge in her cheeks and on her arms. Her long black hair now had a shine to it. This meant one of two things: she was either getting out of shape physically, or the pregnancy would be noticeable sooner rather than later. For the last week or so, Mary had been trying to decide if she would stick around the rebels or move out on her own. Being alone didn't sound like a great idea, especially out in an unfamiliar world.

She was now living for revenge and the child in her belly. The two things did not go hand in hand, and she knew it. It was a silly idea to think she would go kick some Palace butt with the rebels while carrying a child at the same time. The child came before any hurt feelings she had about what befell Jacob. She'd need to carry the child to term and raise him or her alone, then exact revenge. The Eagles seemed to know the weak spots in the Palaces, and they had no qualms with killing. Something she was not adept in, but she could learn. Sirus would pay for what he did—dangling freedom in their faces and then blowing out the candle of hope just when it was within reach.

Mary left the bathroom and went back to the bed. She crawled beneath the covers and thought about where she was and how she'd come to be alive with a baby inside of her, occupying a bed in a Palace taken over by rebels. A few months ago, the idea of any would have been absurd.

She wore light-gray sweatpants and a white tee shirt. The room was cold, but she liked it that way. The feel of gooseflesh rising on her arms and legs as she hid beneath the covers and wrestled with her thoughts had always been a way for her to deal with what to do next in life. Things were never so dire before though. There had always been a friendly, trustworthy face around every corner. Or so she had thought.

I have to tell Logan or someone in the infirmary about my pregnancy. There is no other way. I could leave and face the unknown by myself with child, or I can stay where I seem to be wanted. Even though she didn't know what exactly they wanted her around for, and she would wager it was not for a wholesome reason, she did have a place to stay and protection. For the time being, anyway. At any time, the Order could send a security squad to take the Palace back or just kill everyone. She'd heard an Old World man saying as much in the central plaza yesterday.

Mary didn't know if Logan or the others would be okay with her having a child. There hadn't been anything spoken to her to make her think it would be looked down upon, but she didn't know what the food and water situation was in the Palace. Carla said they lacked beds and medical equipment the day she'd first met her. It was possible they were trying to hold on to anything they had in the way of supplies. What if they kicked her out?

Rubbing her belly beneath the covers and creating friction with her inner thighs to calm the goose bumps sprouting all over her body, she wondered about every possible situation. Maybe they wanted to keep her around until they could do something with her, like hand her off to Sirus in order to advance their own agenda. That was a possibility. There was no way around it; she needed a weapon. *Maybe* she'd *ask Logan* if she could *take part in some of the tactical training they did throughout the day. Wonder if he'd even trust me with a firearm. Carla definitely wouldn't.*

Mary thought about the children she'd left behind in the other Palace, the ones she'd given birth to. Wondered what they thought if they knew about the Palace-born woman who ran away. She hoped to see them again one day. That would be nice. She thought about introducing the child in her stomach to the children she would one day liberate from the Palace.

That would happen, or she would die trying to see it through. Those who came from elsewhere, as the Eagles referred to the Order, had created her. In a way. But she would be their undoing. If Sirus was as smart as he thought he was, he would have blown a bowl-sized hole though her body as well. He hadn't though. Either the sniper lacked the stomach for the job, or he was ordered not to harm her. Either way, it was a mistake. There would be a homecoming. She didn't know when, but she knew it was inevitable.

There was no sound in the pod. Just the humming of the air conditioning through the walls and vents. The sound was calming. All that was missing was him. But he'd never be in her life again. He'd left a gift, and that was their child. Regardless of what she needed to do or learn, she would bear and raise that child. She owed it to him and to herself. Mary closed her eyes and allowed the droning of the central air to take her off to the only place where she and Jacob could once again see each other. The only place where she could feel his lips pressed against hers and talk about the excitement of their child to come. In her dreams.

CHAPTER TWENTY-THREE

Sirus

To: Code Origin
Server: Scrambled Server

From: O'Sullivan, Sirus
Date: June 19, 2040 10:29:36 EST

Subject: Smart idea

F IRST, I NEED YOU TO UNDERSTAND this: The only reason that facility is not a smoldering clump of metal and flesh is because I did not know whether my property was there with you. You must know how pointless every life under that roof is to me and my people here with the Order. As easily as one could crush an ant hill while taking a brisk walk, that's how meaningless your scrambled perception of an existence is to me. Ah, that felt good. Now I'll get to my response to your email.

I received your message, and I want to congratulate you on being the beacon of hope within your species. It took intelligence and a certain amount of cunning to contact us with the coordinates of something we have lost. I thank you, and I will grant you what you wish in exchange for her. I'd love to know how you were able to figure out the correct server connections to get an email to me. But that is a conversation for another day. Make sure she does not leave.

Keep your own people in the dark about when and where we will be making our moves. This should not be an issue for you if what you say is true about your place in the hierarchy within the group there. You will not be hurt, and I will have a position waiting for you when the smoke clears. We can always use others like you in the battles to come. I'll let you in on a small secret, maybe it's something you have already realized.

There are many Palaces all over this planet. More than you would believe. I say that to inform you that the battle is ongoing in Asia, Antarctica, South America, Europe, Africa...Anywhere that human life existed, there is a Palace and a battle to be won. And we are winning. Make no mistake about the small victories your people have managed to muster at the expense of your lives. We, my people, cannot lose a battle when all of the fighting pieces are YOUR PEOPLE. For thousands of years, your species has not been able to get it right, and I don't believe you will figure it out now. You made the right decision, now see this through. Return what belongs to me, like you said you would.

We are gearing up to move out and toward you within the next thirty days. I don't want any issues when the time comes. Keep her safe and happy. If she is hurt, I will personally level everything in a one-mile radius of the Palace you have procured. We will talk soon.

Thank you,
A Friend

CHAPTER TWENTY-FOUR

Logan

L OGAN STOOD IN THE MIDDLE OF a huge room with gray cement floors. The walls were metal. He could hear the sound bounce even when he yawned. The structure was a hangar that he had his men build when they took over the facility. He didn't need the hangar for anything other than quiet time, not that he couldn't find that inside of the facility's many rooms, but there was something calming about shooting off weapons in such a big enclosed area that he enjoyed.

For him, it was beginning to feel like the more amenities he was surrounded by, the more he wished for things from the Old World.

It was sad to him when he actually took time to think about who...*what* he'd become. What they all were forced to become. Scavengers, picking and rummaging through the dirt and weeds, desperate to find something to eat or tools to build. That had been his life for the past twenty years. That life had created a new man; it kept him on his toes, kept him sharp. The longer he stayed in the Palace facility with his Eagle squad, the more he felt detached from the world.

Logan knew that was why he constantly had his men building rickety hangars, workbenches, and removing things from his pod that made him feel...posh. The verdict was still out on if they would stay in the liberated Palace they had taken. Many of his men liked it there; it brought smiles to their faces, allowed them to relax and have at least a piece of what they'd lost as children or young men and women.

The hangar was made of all scrap metal, no bigger than a standard barn, but it was his. He spent most of his time there when he was not attending to Eagle business. Testing weapons, testing armor, mostly helmets. And sometimes, he'd sit in the corner of the hangar and cry. Since the day the world ended, a day hadn't passed where he didn't cry. In those moments, he got to be the old Logan again.

A kid stumbling into adulthood, still trying to figure out if he wanted to play baseball for a local D2 school or get a job working for the city with his father and older brother. He was never given the chance to make the choice though; the world made that choice for him. One moment he was planning on hanging out with his best friend Jacob, and the next, Logan was being chased through the woods behind the local Meijer grocery store by men who pretended to be friends. The men who drove the white vans. Those that came from another world.

Sure, they looked like normal people, which was part of the reason their plans worked so well. Who knew how long they'd been living among humans, hiding in plain sight. It was a good plan. It worked, after all.

Logan pulled a small dull-looking metal weapon from his jacket pocket. He stood there in black cargo pants and the heavy black boots he'd taken from the body of a security officer when they killed a handful of the guards on their way inside the facility. His green bomber jacket fit snuggly around his muscular build. The red decoration streaking down the right arm of the jacket signified his place as commander of the squad. All of his tops had the red stitching sewn into them by Diana, who was in charge of attire and armor for the squad. A woman of sixty years old, Diana had lost her husband and every child and grandchild when the sickness came. That was common though.

He brushed the long blond hair from his eyes with one hand and held the weapon out in the other, staring at it, wondering how something so small could be so powerful. How powerful, he did not know, but he would test it out today. In the privacy of the hangar, with no one around to speculate or possibly let their lips speak what was not meant to be spoken.

Logan cracked a sunflower seed with his front teeth and spit the shells on the ground. Wherever he went, there were sunflower shells left in his wake. There was a joke within the Eagle squad: *If you want to find Logan, just follow the trail of shells.*

Logan lowered the weapon to his side as he thought for a moment.

Should I simply allow her to be taken? Or should I keep her on our side? Sometimes tough decisions had to be made for the greater good. Logan knew better than *anyone else* that *the group* came *first; mankind* came *first.* What did it matter *if the colonizers get back something that belonged to them, especially if* the Eagles *benefited from the exchange in the end?* He *could always contact...him...and switch up the plan.*

Logan spit on the floor at the thought, then began pacing around the hangar. The place was empty aside from a table that sat ten yards away with two dead pigs lying on their sides. Pig flesh simulated human flesh almost perfectly. While testing weapons, Logan preferred to use pig flesh if they could get their hands on some. Which wasn't always easy.

When he first learned of the other beings, it was hard to understand or even fathom. For the first year or two, all the survivors thought the sickness issue came about from the government. Everyone saw the YouTube videos of patents on diseases or FEMA camp stuff. When people started dropping dead left and right, he and everyone still among the living thought that the government was killing everyone. The people in the white vans looked to be human as well. The idea of aliens coming to the planet to colonize or kill off everyone was not a part of the general thought process.

As time passed and he met more and more survivors who had their own experiences with the beings, it came to be accepted that the alien theory was what made the most sense. The discovery of the Palaces drove those thoughts home. When everyone thought they were going against their own people or the government, there was not much confidence in survival beyond running every time they came upon a white van. After finding out what was actually in the vans and understanding what they were dealing with, humankind had rallied together like he'd never seen before. They were killing security officers and van drivers whenever they saw them.

Eventually the vans popped up all over the city less and less. They were now the hunters instead of the hunted. The discovery hyped everyone up to fight back for mankind, to take their world back from those from elsewhere.

She's definitely pregnant though...Could he hand her over to them knowing there was a child inside of her? And what if it was Jacob's? That had to be *his* friend Jacob; she'd described him so perfectly. When Logan passed on to the world after this one, could he look his best friend in the eyes knowing that he'd handed his child over to the enemy?

Logan continued to pace around the room, rubbing the odd metal weapon inside his jacket pocket. The material felt warm, not cold like any other weapon he'd ever touched. It almost seemed to merge with his skin. Holding the gun, or whatever it was, sometimes scared him. He felt as if it had become a part of him—or at least had the potential to do so. There was another weapon just like it hidden away in his pod, and he hadn't told anyone else about them.

Not because he wanted to hoard them all for himself, but because he wanted to make sure he knew what he was dealing with before he revealed them. After taking one apart and reassembling it, he knew the weapons were from another planet and somehow interacted with the user. Until he touched it, it seemed to have no energy at all. It appeared to be dull, without a gleam of shine to it. But once he picked one of the weapons up, there was a slight glowing aura around it. He didn't know what caused this, but he knew the weapon was responding to him, his life force even. The found weapons would be instrumental in taking back their small piece of the world if they held the great power Logan thought they possessed.

Moving around the hangar thinking to himself was nothing more than a way of stalling. A part of Logan knew he was afraid to shoot the weapon. He didn't know what firing it would do to him. There was no trigger on the piece, but a voice in his head told him that the thing would fire if he ordered it to do so. The thought was both exciting and dreadful, to think that those from outside of their planet had weapons capable of such a thing. Logan pulled the weapon from his jacket pocket once again, letting it lie in the palm of his hand. The gun with no trigger was no bigger than a Snickers candy bar. He smiled at the thought of a Snickers bar. It had been so long since he'd had one of those. The weapon pulsed with energy.

Regardless of what he decided to do with Mary, having the secret weapons could help humankind at some point. He had no idea how to reverse engineer such things, but having two of them was better than nothing at all. Unless Sirus and the rest of his people had something bigger and more powerful than what he had in his hand. The thought scared him.

Making his way back to the middle of the hangar, Logan breathed in deeply and held it. Gripping the small gun-shaped thing, he pointed it at the dead pigs on the table approximately ten yards away. With his arm extended, the metal of the gun glowed a deep orange, the color pulsing at the same rate as his heart. They were in tune. Making sure to keep his thoughts clear, he only saw the pigs on the table and the big metal wall behind them.

There was a calmness about him, an eerie silence all around. Logan could almost see the atmosphere gathering around the tip of the weapon, seemingly pulling from everything in the area: the dust on the hangar's floor, the gravity, the unseen particles and bacteria that he could not see with his human optical deficiencies. He felt himself slightly weakening, becoming tired. His legs felt somewhat limp. Then he focused, and he shot at the pigs on the table with his eyes—at least, it felt that way. He focused on them with his sight and pushed out at the target with all his being.

Logan didn't see the burst come from the weapon, but he did feel it. Warmth covered his hand and arm. Everything went black when he heard the shot, more like the explosion, of the weapon. It sounded like a bomb going off in his ear. The impact pulled him forward so hard that he tripped and fell to one knee, and then both. The weapon fell from his hand as he put both palms down to catch himself from falling face forward.

Logan opened his eyes, but all he saw were small stars and dust everywhere. He widened his eyelids, hoping that would clear up the fuzziness. He could hear yelling. Sounded like it was coming from his men. For a second, he thought they were being attacked by the enemy. Still looking down with both hands flat on the ground, he began sliding his palms, trying to feel for the weapon. If there was trouble, he wanted to use it on the bastards. If it was just his men checking on him, he did not want them to see the weapon that had knocked him on his ass from one shot. Either way, he needed to find it before someone reached the hangar.

He had locked the door when he came in, so no one should have been able to simply walk in. They would have to kick the door down, which would take a bit of time. Sliding his hands in circles, he finally felt metal. He grabbed it up and slipped it into his jacket pocket while rolling over on his back, staring up at the ceiling of the hangar. Logan felt a warming heat over his face and a bright light on his right cheek.

Closing his eyes once more and trying to calm himself, Logan heard more yelling coming from the right. He knew the entrance should have been on his left from the way he was lying down, but he was sure the sounds were coming from the opposite direction.

"Captain! Captain! Are you okay!" Logan could hear Derek screaming on his right side. How could he be coming from the area of the targets? The entrance was on the other side.

"Go get one of the medics, I think he's hurt. Go now, you fucking idiot!" Derek yelled at someone as he appeared in Logan's vision. The giant of a man looked like a child in that moment. Fear written all over his face, Derek looked near tears. His beard was as long as any Logan had seen, telling him a lot about how long ago the world had changed. The big bald black man leaned over Logan's chest, listening for a heartbeat.

"I'm alright, soldier." He managed to squeeze the words out of his mouth while still struggling to catch his breath. Derek's eyes came to life after hearing the words, the sides of his mouth curving up as big as a clown's makeup.

"Just help me get up, Derek. I'm not hurt, just a bit out of it." Logan offered a hand to the soldier, using his other hand to boost himself from the ground.

"Shit, sir, you scared the hell out of me. What were you doing in here? And what was that explosion?" Derek pulled Logan up, nearly lifting him off his feet entirely. The soldier's strength was otherworldly. Even to someone as physically imposing as Logan, who was a small man compared to Derek. He wrapped one big arm around Logan's shoulder and patted the dust off his back with the other hand. His pats on the back felt like full-blown punches to the vertebrae.

"Whoa, whoa, soldier, I just got blown up. Calm down on the back chops, please," he said with a smile and a playful push to Derek's inside shoulder.

"Blown up by what, Captain? We all heard the loud boom, and then the metal wall went flying. What were you doing in here?" Derek looked at Logan with a smidge of curiosity and skepticism.

"What? Wait, metal flying?..." Logan looked around, his mouth dropping down to his chest when he saw what remained of the dead pigs he'd been using for target practice.

"What created the big explosion, Captain? Are you hearing me?" Derek looked concerned as he put a hand on Logan's shoulder and followed his gaze. They both stared at nothing but the space outside the hangar. There were trees there, and that was it. The puny weapon from the colonizers had decimated the table of pigs. There was no table. No pigs. It was all gone, pulverized, he assumed. Right along with the whole metal wall that once existed behind the target. Completely gone.

Logan looked around in confusion. He nearly fell over, but Derek caught him by the arm. "Slow down, sir. Let's get you to the infirmary. We'll talk about this later. We need to make sure you are okay." Logan allowed the man to help him, and they both informed the soldiers standing outside of the hangar that everything was ok. The men were alert with weapons drawn, looking around the surrounding area for enemies. It had been a big explosion, and no one but him knew where it came from. He wasn't sure if they needed to know, or if they'd even *want* to know what created the destruction. Logan was now truly afraid. If the enemy had weapons like this that they hadn't used yet, he couldn't imagine what they would call their "big guns."

CHAPTER TWENTY-FIVE

Lonnie

SINCE THE DAY THEY'D MADE LOVE, it had been a whirlwind of emotions. There was no doubt that he cared about Melinda immensely, but those same feelings made it terribly hard for him to do his job. Nights were spent making plans with some of the teachers, mostly Teacher Simon and his handpicked group of operatives. His nights were spent sneaking into Melinda's pod, not only to make love (she had taken to calling it that), but also just to be with her. To spend time, to calm her about the goings-on of Palace plans to move out into the world.

A lot of the time they spent lying in bed together with her head on his chest, her hand twisting the tight curls in his hair and talking about how scared she was. How much she did not want to be involved in killing other people. Lonnie tried to get her to understand that this would be a situation where once it was over, they would never have to do anything like that again. If they did not handle the threat still lingering about in the world, then they would all die off sooner rather than later.

No matter how he tried to explain it to her, she would not accept what was to be. He could only say so much to her without going into detail about his role in the whole thing. No one knew he would be serving as a captain when it was time to attack rebel forces in the area, only the men he'd be training with. It was made very clear to him that he would be disciplined if he gave any intel to anyone within the Palace.

In a way, Melinda's inability to accept what was going on with the world was part of why he cared so much for her. Much like himself, maybe even more so than himself, Melinda was unrelenting in her stance on things. She could not be moved. It was doubtful that she needed to constantly swap masks like he did. They'd all learned the value of being someone else while growing up in the child center. Having the ability to play along, to pretend to be happy when you were dying inside, was a survival tool in itself. But at what point did this tool need to go away?

For him, he hadn't come to that point yet. Lonnie believed that what he was doing was absolutely the right thing to do. Survivors out in the world needed to be dealt with, and he was going to do all that he could to make sure that happened because he was a soldier for Mother Earth. When all the smoke cleared, his name would be etched in stone as part of the reason why life could continue. He'd thought about it a lot. So many had perished when the sickness came upon the planet—it would all be for nothing if they allowed the survivors to continue their evil deeds. Tough decisions were for the tough at heart...that was him.

Lonnie grabbed his blue jean jacket off the sofa in his pod and threw it over his shoulder on the way out the door. He had a meeting with a few of his men on the fourteenth floor of the Palace. They had a secret meeting area there, and sometimes met twice a week depending on orders coming up from Teacher Simon. They would go over battle tactics, test each other's knowledge of the area based on maps given to them, and sometimes they would do something entirely different. Today, his favorite thing was on the docket. He'd come to enjoy it.

Walking down the hallway sharing smiles and claps on the back with fellow Palace members, Lonnie thought about a conversation he and Melinda had the week prior while eating together in the central plaza. They'd shared fried potatoes with ketchup—it was her favorite thing to eat.

Melinda had looked at him and said something so nonchalantly that he had to ask her to repeat herself. She just came right out and said, "What if you are wrong? What if we are on the wrong side of the fight?"

The words had hit him in the gut like a knee being driven into his midsection. It was something he never even thought about. At the worst he thought maybe the Order was keeping things from them. Not to be secretive, but for their own good. Some were cut out for certain information, and some weren't; it was just that simple. But the Order being the enemy was not something he could even fathom.

After she repeated the statement, he gave her a halfhearted smile and stopped chewing his food. He wanted to spit it out on the plate in front of him. He recalled stuttering and talking in circles, rambling even...hoping that if he just talked a lot, he could confuse her into accepting it as an answer. He didn't think she bought whatever it was that he'd said. How could she? He didn't even buy it. Melinda likely dropped the topic because it was clear he'd been backed against a wall that he was not ready to face. There was a pinch of pity in her expression as he rambled on and on about Mother Earth, the Order, and any other buzz words he could think of.

The conversation ended abruptly after her question. They both got quiet, looking in opposite directions and finishing their meal. Later that day, they met up in Melinda's pod and made love, and the topic never came up again. He thought about it though, much more than he would like to admit.

Walking off the elevator on floor fourteen, Lonnie rounded the corner, making his way to the hidden area for the meeting with some of his men. After the meeting, he had plans to go running with Melinda, and he was excited about that. Between doing stuff for the military campaign and training, he spent every moment with her. When the rats out in the world were finally exterminated, he wanted to only be with her. No relations exercise with anyone else. That's the way they did things in the Old World, so he wondered if the Order would allow such a thing.

Lonnie stepped into a room at the end of the hallway. That particular door was usually locked, but today it was occupied. The room was dark, and there was nothing inside but another door on the far northern wall. A second door. Lonnie walked across the empty room, taking long measured steps the whole way. His excitement was building with each step; he knew what was waiting for him on the other side of the next door. Feeling his palms getting sweaty, he wiped them off on his jeans before gripping the knob of the second door. He turned and walked in, slowly closing it behind him.

Like the first empty room, the second room was also dark. There was a small lamp, which was lit and sitting on a table in the far right corner. Five of the men he trained with at night were standing in a circle. Their arms were crossed over their chests, and they stood in a wide stance, much like the security guards did outside of the Palace and around the grounds. Lonnie lifted a flattened hand to his forehead and pulled it away quickly. They'd been taught to salute each other that way. All five men repeated the gesture.

In the middle of the circle of soldiers, there was a man sitting in a chair. A blindfold had been wrapped around his eyes, and an object stuffed in his mouth. Lonnie didn't know what had been used to gag the man, and he didn't care. Making his way past the group of men, Lonnie walked in a circle around the room while removing his jacket.

One of the soldiers handed Lonnie a handgun. Soundproof material covered the walls and the door. This ensured no one would hear what was going on inside the room.

"Move," Lonnie said to the men.

They all stepped to the side and put their backs against the western wall of the room, leaving the man exposed in the center. Lonnie could see snot and blood running out of his nose and a deep gash in his dark brown hair. The blood made it look purple in the dim lighting of the dark room.

The man's hands were tied behind his back around the chair, and his feet were tied together as well. He wore a blue button-up shirt that had been torn open, exposing his chest. There was one big slash down the middle of his abdomen, and blood slowly leaked down and came to a resting place on the lap of his jeans. There was also dried blood crusted along the bottom of his stomach; they had been there for some time. Talking to him, trying to convince him to give information about something—the *what* was not important. Lonnie had a job to do.

"You know that there is no leaving the Palace," Lonnie said, walking in circles around the injured man. His five men watched on, looking ahead. He knew that they needed to see him be the leader, to do what was expected of a captain. There were no feelings of empathy or caring, just a job to be done, and he was devoted to the cause.

"I know you can't reply, that's for the best. Honestly, there is nothing to discuss at all. The rules are simple, and we got word that you were planning to run away like Mary did. You should have known better. There are no secrets here." The man whimpered and moaned. Lonnie didn't know if it was from pain or fear. It didn't matter.

He stopped pacing in front of the man and knelt down on one knee. He rested a hand on the man's knee, which was shaking like a dying leaf on a tree in the fall. The man's head was now hanging down, his chin resting on his chest; he knew what was coming next. They all did. Lonnie lifted the handgun to the man's chin, making sure that the unfortunate soul who'd tried to abandon the Palace and the side Mother Earth chose as her champions knew that it was a gun on his face. Lonnie tapped it against his chin multiple times.

"You feel that? That's the consequence of your decision. Maybe in the next life, we will be brothers once again, and maybe you will remember this moment...and you will know, you will remember me. You will choose correctly." Another low, droning moan came from the man in the chair.

Lonnie turned and looked at his soldiers standing against the wall to his left and pulled the trigger. The sound was deafening in the insulated room. A spray of red covered Lonnie's face, the right side of his face. It felt warm and calming to him. After a while, killing became a source of solitude. That day made the third time he had to take life, a life that forfeit itself by the decision made by the victims. He was charged with releasing them to the freedom they wanted so badly, and he would always oblige.

The man did not die right away. He hacked and coughed, gurgling sounds emitting from his neck region. The gunshot to the chin had sent him sprawling backwards in the chair. His foot had nearly kicked Lonnie in the face as he went backwards. Lonnie handed the pistol back to one of his men and stood there with them, watching the life fight to stay inside of the man's body. He kicked and convulsed in the chair, trying to turn over, fighting to get his hands free to grab the wound in his face. That's what people did when they got hurt, placed their hands on the source of the pain. He tried, but to no avail. He lay there on his back and died...died squirming and wailing like an animal. No one heard him though, as the room was soundproof.

CHAPTER TWENTY-SIX

Mary

"I DON'T TRUST YOU AS FAR as I can throw you...and even though I'm much stronger than you, I couldn't throw you far." Carla finished loading the Glock, clicked the safety, and handed the firearm to Mary, pushing it into her hands more than handing it off.

Mary didn't bother responding to the older bitter lieutenant of the Eagle rebel group. Since the back end of their very first conversation, Carla had hated her. It would be pointless to have a back-and-forth with the short-tempered soldier. So, Mary's plan was not to engage her outside of their activity for the day. It would be a challenge; the woman had a gift for pressing every button she had.

Logan had accepted her request to learn to shoot the firearms among the group. Only under direct partnership with one of his soldiers. She told him that she wanted to shoot because she was becoming bored simply sitting around, reading, and answering questions from Dale. She had no idea what they were waiting on. No one entered or left their Palace, but there were rumblings of moving along and liberating more facilities, ridding the area of the others. She had her fingers crossed, hoping that the next on the list was the Palace she came from. Sirus had a debt to pay, and she wanted to collect on it as soon as possible.

She overheard a few soldiers talking about the very same thing happening in Tennessee. The state was fully liberated from the colonizers, she'd heard a young blond man say to a slightly older soldier. The two men slapped high fives with each other and laughed. If what the men said was true...that was something. Some faith that the Order was vulnerable in some way.

Even though she was pregnant and likely doing a poor job of hiding it, she thought learning to protect herself with a gun was of the utmost importance. Being a burden to anyone was not of interest to her; she would never put herself in that position again. Mary had sat in bed weeks ago, telling herself that she would never be a prisoner of anyone again. Not of the Order, and not of the ragtag group of rebels, who did mean well but were not quite educated on what they were up against. A hunger for violence and drive could only get you so far.

Today made her tenth trip to the shooting area of the rebel Palace. They'd converted three classrooms on the second floor into a shooting gallery. Usually she shot with a few of the different gunner soldiers. Carla had been an unwelcome surprise when she came brooding toward her, scowling along the way. The woman's lips were pressed together tightly, her eyebrows in full furrowed mode. Mary thought she tried too hard to be cruel, but on further examination of a woman among many men in a world that saw fit to leave her alone after killing off her family, it seemed that all Carla had left was cruelty.

"I guess it's a good thing that we are not required to like each other. I'm happy to shoot with you today, I hope to learn from your techni—"

"For God's sake. Shut up, kid, and shoot the damn gun," Carla said without looking at her.

They both stood behind a tall wooden box that came to around their hip region. Fifteen feet away, there were ten bottles hanging from thin ropes that were tied to small hooks in the ceiling. Beneath the hanging bottles were all colors of crushed glass, glass from other soldiers working on their training. No one seemed to clean up the mess at any time. She didn't think the glass had been swept up since her first visit. This was a significant difference between the Palaces; the Eagle group had the sanitation level of animals.

"Are you not going to shoot?" Mary asked, looking to her right at Carla. The woman stood next to her, eyes fixed on the target ahead. She rubbed her ribs with her left hand though. In a way, Mary admired that about Carla. The woman worked herself so hard that she often got hurt in the process.

"I've been shooting for the last twenty years. Everyone here knows what I'm capable of. You, on the other hand? We know nothing about you, other than that piece of shit story you told us. I'm here to watch you shoot and report back to Logan on your progress." Carla glared at Mary with contempt before shifting her gaze back to the target.

It took all that Mary had inside of her not to question Carla on her comment. The woman treated her like she'd done something wrong to her or to anyone there for that matter. She never asked them to come out of nowhere and save her, she didn't ask to be hauled off to their home. Mary thought back to a lesson Teacher Paul taught about matriarchal behavior among women of the Old World.

He'd told them that the women of the Old World were very territorial over their place in the group. Especially among men. Carla could be feeling threatened by her being there—jealous of the men caring enough to make her stay comfortable. Something as simple as her getting attention from the men that Carla regarded highly would be enough to cause those hard feelings. It all seemed ill placed to her; there hadn't been an offense to justify the intensity of Carla's attitude.

Logan did embarrass Carla upon his first meeting with Mary, but the woman had clearly been out of line, nearly killing Mary for simply saying a few words. It was not lost on Mary how that heightened tension of their near fight heated her body from the inside out, how it boiled her blood. She didn't think she could take the older machine of a woman in combat or even in a bout of tongues, but in that moment, Mary didn't care if she could or not. The hunger for the fight was all that was on her mind.

Carla stepped a half-foot closer to Mary, squinting at her and smiling. The smile was not warm, it was as cold as the look on Sirus's face the day he made Mary and Jacob believe they would be allowed to go free. Mary wanted to erase the grin right off Carla's mouth. It was haunting.

"I'm NOT like everyone else here, young Mary. I do not take you at your word. I do not believe everything you utter from that young pretty mouth of yours. The serpent is adept at spreading falsehoods."

Carla's hand quickly shot up to Mary's face, but she did not strike. For some reason Mary knew the women did not mean to harm her in that moment. There was no fire in her eyes, just a dull, glazed-over kind of focus. For that reason, she did not flinch or look to defend herself. Carla's fingers lightly grazed Mary's face near her lips.

"No, I do not believe you, miss. I don't want you here, and I cannot wait until the day that you are back with those who released you." Carla withdrew her hand and placed it on her hip near her own gun, lightly tapping the steal with her fingernail. Mary thought the gesture was meant to be a threat.

"You see, even in my youth, lost dogs were better off with their masters, even if you were better suited for them after finding the animal lost, sick, and in need of saving. You are no more than a lost animal; you don't belong here. No matter what others from the group may think of you, I can see far better than they can. We can safely say that I'm touched by God, the God you don't believe to be real."

Mary blinked at her words, but didn't respond. What could someone say in reaction to something like that? Carla went on before Mary could even sort out her crazy talk.

"In another life, another time altogether, I was a young woman like you. And even then, I had a message for those who did not believe. That message is: whether you believe or not, it will not stop what's to come. The Lord's judgement isn't dependent upon what you believe."

Mary smiled, trying her hardest to fight back her anger. The nerve of the strange woman to touch her face, to speak to her in such a way. So condescending.

"You sound as if you want to threaten me. Is that what you mean to do, Carla?" Mary set the gun on the box in front of her, never removing her gaze from Carla.

Carla's eyes got big as she placed a hand over her mouth in fake surprise. Such an animated reaction from Carla could only be taken as sarcasm or making light of Mary's words.

"Oh no, excuse me, Mary. I do not *mean* to do anything. I do exactly what I plan to do. If I wanted to threaten you, I would do just that. If I felt like you were enough of a problem for my squad, I'd get rid of you myself. I'll also let you in on a small secret." Her eyes blazed with excitement.

"I have a mission in this life, much more important than you know. And Logan cannot save you, princess. He is but one man," Carla whispered as she moved even closer to Mary. They were face to face at that point. "My personal quest is so important that I could, say, get rid of *both* of you, and not lose a wink of sleep. There are bigger fish to fry, you know." Carla winked before leering down at Mary's stomach.

She knows. But how? The woman had just *threatened* Mary's unborn *child. How could a person do such a thing?* The thoughts ran through Mary's mind at a rapid pace, but the expression on her face did not change. It was not a bluff for Carla; she would not pretend she wasn't pregnant. If someone who spent little to no time around her could figure it out, then her condition was obvious.

Within a half-second of Carla finishing her evil rant, Mary's right hand sprung from her side with twice the speed at which Carla had reached out to touch her moments ago. Mary didn't aim for the woman's face, however. Instead, her hand found the Glock lying on the wooden box before her.

While still staring Carla in the face, her hand did its business—the business of shooting at the dangling bottles fifteen yards away. Loud blasts from the gun sounded off in quick succession. Neither of the women looked away from each other, neither blinked. The gun continued to go off for what seemed like forever. When the tenth bullet shattered the final bottle, Mary put the gun back down on the desk before laying the same hand over her stomach. It was now her turn to smile, to be condescending, to show her own resolve and strength. She would not lie to herself, it felt good.

It was addictive when she thought about it. The back and forth, the competition between two human beings. She was beginning to see how conflict ran rampant in the Old World. Here she was reactively showing up an older woman instead of simply walking away. She could not help it, Carla brought the worst out of her...or maybe the best, in a way. All ten bottles that once hung suspended in the air now lay on the ground, adding to millions of glass shards. She'd hit a bottle with every bullet she fired. The clip still had five bullets left.

Mary could see that Carla was trying her best not to look at the targets, but they'd both heard the glass breaking over and over. Out of the side of her vision, Carla spied that no bottles hung anymore, and even though she did not look overly impressed, there was a hint of wonder and even some fear. Confusion was probably the best word to describe what was going on in the woman's mind judging from her expression. Mary's lips slowly parted to speak.

"That's the second time you have threatened me. There will not be a third. That is your warning. I'm fair. Child inside my stomach or not. I don't know you well, Carla, and I assure you, I'm a mystery to you as well. Tread lightly." Mary stepped to the side so as not to touch Carla as she walked by. Carla didn't say a word to her as she walked away, and she knew why.

CHAPTER TWENTY-SEVEN

Melinda

ONE OF HER FAVORITE THINGS TO do was to sit among the beautiful flowers and stonework in the courtyard. Small ponds, rose bushes, and walking trails were aplenty. It was a wonderful place to think, and she had a lot of thinking to do on that day.

Sitting on a small stone bench near a pond next to the biggest walking trail in the area, she watched the fish swim around in circles and pondered her life as it stood. Confused was not the word for how she felt inside. Confused would be an upgrade to her psyche. Her thoughts were so disorganized, she could not get them lined up to figure out her place in the world...or the Palace.

Melinda sat there on the bench with her right leg crossed over her left. Her standard-issue white shoes rested on a big brown rock near the pond. The only thing that made sense to her currently was the way she felt about a certain someone. That fact was apparent to her the day of the cleansing; their hands touching had created a spark. That spark could do nothing but evolve into a blazing fire as time went on, and she felt on fire herself when she was around him.

She tossed a small piece of bread into the pond. Small fish swam rapidly to the food, competing for mini bites of her offering. To be a fish was a simple life, she thought as she rested both hands behind her on the bench, staring up into the sky. The only life that they knew and understood was survival; they must eat to live, so they spent the day searching for food. Whether fish had interpersonal relationships or not was beyond her thinking, but she couldn't imagine they did. And even if they did, it still broke down to food and survival. *Was that how it was for humans as well?*

In order to live, humans needed to eat, but in a separate way. For the fish, a piece of bread here and there was the end-all be-all. For complex social lifeforms like humans, "food" was something different altogether. If everything was simplified into a basic concept of survival, humans simply needed to eliminate any opposition. Food was easy to come by, and so was water. The planet was plentiful in those things. Lonnie and the other Palace members saw the survivors out in the world as the opposition, something in the way of their ultimate survival as a people and species.

The only difference between her ideals and theirs was that she could not pretend there weren't tons of gray areas. After all, she had been taught to see the insignificant things. But if everyone else could see the good in what exterminating the survivors could do for the planet, maybe she was the one with the problem. Doubt was beginning to set in.

Spending time in bed with Lonnie over the last few weeks was beginning to allow her to see his side of things. If this was for the better, she did not know, but it worried her. Melinda tossed another piece of bread into the pond. Fish raced to grab their piece, then moved off to another area. If she had enough bread, they would continue to do this...until they died. Survival patterns were weird like that. Even when you didn't need the thing for survival, the pattern would continue. Staring at the fish, watching them do their repetitive movements and routines, it was easy to see how mankind got to the point that they did before the sickness. On a much larger level of course.

Mankind had always fancied itself above the other life on the planet, but they weren't much different. Humans were susceptible to the same routine traps of other lifeforms, like fish eating themselves to death. Melinda tossed another small piece of bread into the pond.

She stood up from the stone bench and walked closer to the water, searching for an outlier to the standard routine going on in the ecosystem before her. Was there a fish that would not come to bite on the bread even though it was there for all to eat? Melinda had an idea. The implications of her standing over the only world the fish had ever known were apparent to her as she held the power to either give life with the food or strip the pond of all life.

Melinda tossed the entire quarter loaf of bread into the pond. It hit the water with a weighted splash. Like magnets, the fish all came with the speed of a bullet to eat...to die. Not one of them fought the urge. She knew the fish would continue to eat the bread until they were belly-up in the water. It's what they did, and in that way, humans were no different. *So why even fight it?*

There was clarity in that moment that put her mind at ease. The alarm going off in her brain for the last two months or so came to an abrupt stop. Maybe it was best to enjoy the life she had. Billions of others had not been awarded that opportunity. Melinda nodded in approval to her newfound ideology on what was to come. Things would be what they were, whether she agreed or not. "Be the fish," she said aloud, and she turned to walk into the Palace. Lonnie would be coming to her pod soon.

CHAPTER TWENTY-EIGHT

Rachel

"THANK YOU FOR BREATHING LIFE INTO every man, woman, child, and lifeform that you deem fit to walk on your skin, drink of your bosom, and eat of your fruit. We are thankful, and we shall never take your gifts for granted, O merciful Mother Earth. Amen." Rachel spoke the Mother's prayer out loud, standing outside of the shower.

She stood there naked, watching the hot water steam up the glass and thinking to herself that enough was enough.

There was a bran muffin sitting on a small plate in the living area of her pod. She didn't bother to eat any of it, she had no appetite for anything. Her weight was down ten pounds in the last thirty days. The stress was killing her from the inside out. Only reason she ordered the bran muffin that morning was to get access to the knife. A knife came with muffins to spread the butter, and those knives were used for other purposes usually once every few weeks. Lately it had been every day, sometimes twice a day. Whoever was in charge of preparing the food for the pods probably thought she really liked bran muffins. Truth was, she hated them.

Tears ran down her face. She'd been crying all morning, all week, all month. In private obviously. The teachers or security would only think her weak and begin a battery of mental evaluations and questioning if they found out she was struggling with the new ways. It would be pointless to open dialogue about how she was feeling. The way they dealt with "different" was apparent, and she would not be made an example of for the purpose of further mind control.

In the best of times in the Palace, Rachel was overcome by stress to fit in, to get into the Greater Understanding Program (which no longer existed). But now, stress wasn't a strong enough word. She was going insane. She would not hurt anyone, and the time to move out into the world and exterminate the survivors was coming sooner rather than later.

Rachel pulled open the shower door and stepped inside. The hot water felt great on her skin and seemed to calm her down a bit as she allowed the nearly scalding stream to rain down from the showerhead all over her long hair and face. For a woman of sixteen years old, she felt as though she'd lived the life of someone thirty years older. She was tired...tired of it all. She wished she'd never been born. Finding a point to life was not possible.

The shower was spacious enough to sit down in. She knew because many times a day, she would do just that. Sitting down in the shower, thinking and cutting herself. Watching the blood create intricate patterns in the water, then go swirling down the drain. If she was being honest, even that was becoming old and ineffective for her stress. Hiding the cuts was a challenge, and with the more frequent "releasing" she had been doing as of late, it was even more difficult to hide.

Sitting beneath the showerhead with her legs crossed under her, the water came down on her legs and feet. Rachel's head and upper body were just beyond the water's reach.

There was something strange that happened when you knew that a certain day would be your last. Everything became that much clearer. Every memory came back with clarity. She could not remember one truly happy day. In a way, every day prior to that one seemed to only prepare her for what she was about to do. The only future she could have experienced was always going to end this way. Since she was ten years old, when she first sliced her arm and felt a release of stress, it was the only thing that helped her deal with the worries of her life.

The day before, she'd sat in morning enrichment class, listening to

Teacher Mathew go on and on about how they were the chosen few to win back the planet's freedom. Freedom from those who sought to destroy her, suck up her resources and kill for the sake of killing. His logic was that death was not to be feared; even killing could be beneficial in dire times. The survival of mankind and the very wellbeing of Mother Earth constituted as dire.

Everyone in the class smiled. A few even cheered at his words. The spectacle made Rachel want to vomit right there in her seat. What had they become in such a brief time?

Teacher Mathew assured everyone that after the threat from the immediate area had been extinguished, all would be calm and harmonious. The regular classes, teachings, and learning would return to normal. But until the threat was taken care of, no one could rest. It was life and death. Rachel thought the class was being sold a product. Sure, the product was important, she didn't doubt that. But the cost of the product was something she could not pay. There were things more important than survival. There were hundreds of people in the Palace ready to go out killing their own kind; she was not needed for such a thing.

Rachel tapped the tip of the blade on the bright white surface of the shower floor. She tapped over and over, creating a rhythm that coincided with that of her own heartbeat. She was biding her time. The reason was not clear in her mind about what she was waiting for. Just building the suspense inside, she supposed.

There was no one to say goodbye to that mattered. She had no friends. Rachel grew up around the same people, and here she was, sixteen years later, without a soul who cared for her. Truly cared, not just in the "we are one" type of way, but actually cared for Rachel. She smiled at the thought of "we are one." They were indeed one—until it was time to go out and kill perfect strangers.

She wondered if words would be exchanged before the shooting began out in the world. Would they simply go out with the rifles and handguns, screaming bloody murder, or would they give the survivors a chance to atone? They didn't give the Old World members a chance to atone for anything, and those poor souls had lived among everyone since the Palace's inception.

Rachel stopped tapping the tip of the knife on the shower floor and quickly dragged it across her calf muscle. Spurts of blood bloomed in a line stretching down her leg. A small river of red ran down to her foot resting beneath the shower's flow. The water mixed with the blood, creating the most gorgeous color of pink she'd ever seen. The smile on her face widened even more. Her eyes closed, and she took in the pleasure of the release.

There were scars all over her legs, thighs, and arms. Only weeks ago, those parts of her body were unharmed. She'd always kept the cutting to the under-arm area because it was easier to hide. But the things that had been transpiring so quickly in the Palace caused her to cut much more, much deeper, and she'd had to spread the wealth to other body parts. Her body resembled a map of squiggly lines, wounds in various states of healing. The day before, she'd nearly fainted while walking in the courtyard with a group of Palace members. She told them it was because she'd been up all night shooting.

Rachel moved the blade up to her stomach, where she quickly slashed her abdomen. The strikes were faster and deeper than any she had ever tried. Before there was the fear of being found out or being so hurt that she could not move around freely. That was no longer an issue or a fear; this would be the last time she had to do any cutting.

The place on her stomach the blade had ripped through showed white, then pink—then finally red. The skin folded back on itself, exposing flesh and a small layer of fat. In that moment, she knew that was the deepest she'd ever gone. It felt good, and it hurt. And there was a lot of blood, more than she'd ever seen before. She tried to lie back and focus on feeling the release of stress. She thought about how this would all play out. She would cut herself like she'd done a hundred times before, but she would not stop. The blood loss would become too much, and then she would faint and fade off, just like that. It would be poetic, in the same way that Michelle had died not long ago.

The pain was unrelenting, but she thought that was normal based on the depth of the cut. She kept her eyes closed, but could feel the blood spurting onto her pelvic area. *Don't think about it. This is what's best. Cut yourself again.* She concentrated on calming herself down.

Her arm was now trembling; a combination of the rapid blood loss and fear had begun to take over her body. She lifted the arm that still gripped the knife and ran the blade over her thigh, not as deep as the stomach slash, but deeper than her usual type of cut. Her body nearly fell in on itself then, her shoulders hunched over, and she dropped the knife at her side. She wished that she could lie down and fade out that way, but her legs were far too long for that.

There was nothing more for her to do than sit back and allow it to happen. It did not feel the way she thought it would. Dying was not poetic or peaceful, at least not the way she had chosen to die. Rachel began to fade out. She leaned against the wall and tried to look out into the bathroom from the shower, but she could not—the steam from the shower trapped her in a cloudy prison of blood and water.

She wondered if they would find her like that, her skin pruney and void of any blood. The thought made her feel like she should panic, but there was no energy for that. The last bit of energy she had inside would be used to think about how relieved she was to not have to go and hurt others. The thought made her smile. Rachel's time in a world where she never felt like she belonged was coming to an end. Before everything went black and her life fell away into the ether with nothing but the sound of water coming from the showerhead above, she thought...

Maybe none of us belong here. Maybe we were never meant to be.

Rachel's head fell to the side and her eyes closed. There was one last bloody eruption from her abdomen before her body relaxed for the final time. Every muscle inside calmed and allowed her limbs to settle. In the end, all she ever wanted was to relax and for the sirens in her head to subside. She granted her own wish that day.

CHAPTER TWENTY-NINE

Sirus

To: NCP GROUP [Official]
Server: Unknown OC

From: O'Sullivan, Sirus
Date: Aug 18, 2040 07:48:11 EST

Subject: Early movement

Due to circumstances within the capital Palace, I've decided to push Phase 2 through to completion. There have been multiple deaths on sight, and if lives are going to fall, I'd rather them do so out there, taking down as many survivors as possible.

While we did not expect survivors to become as formidable as they seem to be today, we did know that at some point we would need to grind them down. They still live by the old ways, and the attacks on Palaces have proven that. Allowing them to die off is no longer an option.

I have my captains in place, and everyone is trained up enough to clear out this region. I've gotten word back that Old Maine has terminated all survivor life and is now in a clear status. Indiana will be the next to achieve that feat. By next week, we will have Mary back, and the rebel forces causing the majority of the issues in this region will help to take down the others. From my intel, there are twelve different rebel sects operating in the area. Most of them are tiny in comparison to the group that took the Palace not far from my own. I have that situation under control, and I'll retrieve her without loss of life on our side.

I know that in order for the experiment of this planet to work, we will need her. That is not lost on me, and obviously I have my own personal interest in having her around.

There is something else that you should know about Mary. The Old World member impregnated her before they moved to escape. My contact within the Palace she has been staying in has told me as much. She has not come out and told anyone there, but for a woman who has been through the reproductive process multiple times, there is no way she does not know. That leads me to believe she doesn't trust the rebel team who's been caring for her. I believe I can use that to my advantage. I'll have my contact force the termination of that pregnancy; the child cannot be allowed to survive. Mary has a long and storied life ahead of her, and that time cannot be spent raising children.

The next time I contact you, it will be to say that all is back to normal and the key has been put back into place. There is no need to send reinforcements, and we will not be using the Lohar weapons. If the engineered humans were to see us do such things, it could sway their opinions on our nature. That would derail the experiment, and I'd rather not reset everything again. I'll be in touch soon.

Thank you,
O'Sullivan, Sirus

CHAPTER THIRTY

Mary

"WELL, FIRST OF ALL, LET ME say that it's a good thing you've brought this to our attention. I'll add that I'm very happy and excited for you," the woman said to Mary with genuine excitement on her face. Her short blonde bob bounced as she quickly rose from her seat to come around the desk and gave Mary a hug.

The hug felt weird to Mary, but it was reassuring that someone was happy about the news. She thought they would be angry about it. There was still a chance Logan would be unhappy when he was informed. She didn't know, nor did she care. The secret was out of the bag anyway. Carla was in the know, and for all Mary knew, Logan was as well.

"Thank you for that, Ashley. I really should have come to you sooner, but..." Mary paused, not knowing how to finish the sentence without offending the woman and her squad.

Ashley smiled while making her way back to her own seat. "I understand where you are coming from. You don't need to say it. You're new here, and the place that you came from is a point of bad feelings within the squad. You weren't sure if the news would affect your time here or make some even more abrasive to you. I get it." Ashley sat down in her seat, clasped her fingers together in a ball on the desk, and smiled. "Now, let's talk about the baby. That's the fun part."

Mary's face lit up. She was so happy to be able to talk freely with someone about the baby. It had been a secret for so long that sometimes she would forget she was pregnant. In the Palace she'd grown up in, mothers were basically waited on hand and foot as far as nurses, check-ups, evaluations, and things of that nature. Mary thought that she was around four months pregnant, and it was a relief that she would finally get some of the care she would be needing. For her and the child.

"Okay, I'd like that."

"Let's start with when you conceived? If you can remember," Ashley said.

"'It was four or five months ago, if it was the night that I believe conception took place." Mary could not forget that night...it was still so close to her heart. She could remember it like it was yesterday, lying in bed with Jacob after the most passion-filled lovemaking of her life. She remembered listening to his heartbeat, rubbing her fingers through his beard, being the happiest she'd ever been before. The thought in that moment ached to the core of her heart.

"Okay. That puts you around four months or so. Can you do a favor for me, Mary?" Ashley said while opening one of the drawers of the desk and retrieving a small plastic cup with a big top on it. She set the cup on the edge of the desk.

"Can you please stand up and lift your shirt? I'd like to see how you are showing." Ashley smiled as she spoke.

"Yes, of course." Mary rose to her feet and lifted her gray long-sleeve top. The word *Roseanne* was written across the front. She had no idea what it referred to, but it had been given to her by a nice woman in the rebel Palace along with a bag of other pants, shorts, and shirts from the Old World.

She felt silly standing there with her shirt lifted above her belly, so she looked away from the nurse, staring at the assorted medicine bottles on a nearby sink.

"A little higher please. Lift the shirt above your breasts—or you can take it off entirely. No one is coming into the room with us. I've locked the door," Ashley said. Mary thought the woman could sense her unease.

"I'm sorry." Mary took the shirt off and set it on the back of the chair behind her. She studied the nurse to see if she could make out any expressions on her face about how her body looked.

Ashley got up and walked to Mary's side of the desk once more.

"Do you mind?" she said, bringing both hands up, palms exposed.

"No, I don't mind."

Ashley began to touch, squeeze, and poke at Mary's breasts. She walked a circle around her, making humming and mumbling sounds as she took inventory of Mary's body.

"Is everything okay?" Mary asked, beginning to feel nervous. The nurses in her old Palace never did such things while evaluating the body during pregnancy.

"You can put your shirt back on and have a seat, Mom. You look great. Very healthy, and everything looks good. Just making sure you and the baby are fine. I remember the shape you were in when you came here. I thought it necessary to check out everything." Ashley touched her gently on the shoulder and went back to her seat while Mary pulled the shirt back over her head before sitting down.

Ashley scribbled something on a stationary notepad while nodding. Mary didn't know what she was nodding for, but she was happy that everything looked good to the nurse. The near-death experience after coming out of the forest did leave her worried.

"Now that we have examined your body, I'd like to talk to you about how you plan to care for the child once he or she comes into the world, which will be a great day, right?" Ashley raised both eyebrows to her forehead, giving Mary a thin smile with no teeth.

Mary hadn't thought very deeply about such a thing. She knew that things would be different from what she was accustomed to as far as having a child. No one would come swipe the baby away and rush it to the child center directly after birth, but she hadn't truly given thought to how life would play out for herself to be a mother.

She'd watched some of the mothers in the rebel Palace with their children, and it was beautiful. They were around their children all the time. Teaching them, disciplining them, hugging and kissing them when they needed to be calmed or shown affection. She was excited to have those moments with her own baby...with Jacob's child.

But what of the rest of her life? How would caring for the child coincide with her personal mission of avenging her love's loss of life? How could she liberate the Palace of her youth with a child strapped to her back? She could not.

"Mary?" Ashley said, snapping Mary out of her own thoughts.

"I'm sorry, I was thinking about something."

"About what? Talk to me. That's what I'm here for. Anything we talk about is between you and me. I promise you that," Ashley said. She set her notepad on the desk next to the small plastic cup and offered Mary a look of concern.

"This is all so new to me. I come from a place where mothers have no contact with their children. I'm happy about raising my child, I just don't know how the logistics of everything will work in the real world. I see mothers here with their children, and it's beautiful...but...is that all they do? I'm sorry if what I'm asking is hard to understand. I don't know if I'm making any sense." Mary smiled uneasily and felt embarrassed. There she was again, looking like the unintelligent Palace-born idiot. She wanted to kick herself.

"Well," Ashley explained, "the mothers here do a lot. They help with the day-to-day things among the company. They help cook the meals, wash clothes, prep shooting galleries, and they train. They help create maps of the surrounding areas too, things like that. If push came to shove and we were invaded by the white vans or even another rebel company, they would be ready and able to defend themselves and each other with lethal force."

"Okay, that's good. I would like to do things like that as well. I was only concerned that I would not be able to help with some of the important work if my child was latched onto my hip at all times. In the Palace...well, the way I grew up, all people were pushed to become independent entities of their own. That went for the adults and the children. Getting out of that thought process and more into a mother's role will be a new experience for me. I'm very happy for the experience though." Mary smiled across the desk at the young nurse.

Speaking on the situation with Ashley made something apparent to her right then. If the child in her belly did not belong to Jacob, she would almost certainly find a way to get rid of it. There were ways to do that; she knew because some of the Old World women in her Palace talked about it from time to time. There was one woman in particular who was said to have terminated multiple pregnancies right there in her pod, but that was only talk.

Nothing came before wanting to end what the Order were doing to the planet except giving birth to and raising the child she'd made with Jacob. If that child was created by anyone but him, she would not be going through this mental bout of how to care for a child while taking up the fight against those who sought to darken and destroy the lives of innocent men and women.

"I see where you are coming from, and I want to assure you that women in the 'real world' have a purpose outside of raising their children." A touch of attitude finally showed in Ashley's tone.

"Out here, we don't have a child center to raise our children, and honestly, even if we did, none of the mothers would take advantage of it. Giving birth and nurturing your own child is one of the greatest experiences a woman can have. It's to be taken seriously, not worked around for your own personal needs...or wants." Ashley smiled at Mary, but it wasn't genuine this time. The smile was brief, and the woman's eyes said something else altogether.

Mary could see Ashley was offended, and she didn't want to make an enemy of one of the few women to be kind to her.

"I'm sorry if I offended you with my words. That was not my intent whatsoever. Things are just different here than they were in my Palace. I was only looking for clarity. I'm sorry." Mary slid both hands into the pockets of her jeans, feeling embarrassed and guilty for making the once excited woman angry with her.

"Oh no, I'm not offended at all. I need you to understand that real women in the world do not put their children off on others. If you lie down and create them, it's your job to take care of them. There are sacrifices involved in that, but what you get back in unconditional love from that child makes it worth it." Ashley picked up the pad and pen, jotting something down while turning the pad to the side so that Mary couldn't see.

171

"I'm sorry, but did you write something down that could paint me in a bad light simply because I have questions about how motherhood works out here? Can I see what you wrote, please? Mary began to raise her voice. She didn't want Logan to think she would be an issue living among them. It was very important for her to be there, to have her child there where there was medical care and warm living space. Her time in the forest showed her that the world could be cold and unforgiving. She had no desire to have a child alone in the world with no way to feed or care for it. Trying to feed herself for a few days had nearly killed her.

Ashley looked as though she couldn't believe what Mary had asked. She closed the notepad and laid it face down on the desk with the pen on top. The young nurse crossed her legs and squinted at Mary.

"I will not show you my notes. It's none of your business what I write in my own personal notes, nor should it matter. I've been charged to keep a log of everyone we see in the infirmary. This comes from Logan at the very top of the ladder. If you have an issue with how we do things here, you can take it up with him. Or better yet, you can go back to where you came from," Ashley said in a low voice.

"Go back to where I come from? Are you serious? You talk to me this way because I asked a question?" Mary removed her hands from her pockets and gripped the arms of the wooden chair she sat in across from the angered nurse. She could feel her own temper rising as her knuckles became white and her eyes focused in on the woman looking down on her.

"I'm just saying tha—" Ashley began, but was cut short by Mary, who leaned over the desk.

"No, I'm talking!" Mary screamed. Ashley flinched back into her seat. Her arrogant disposition shifted to one of concern, and a little fear showed in her eyes.

"You see yourself and your people in a light that makes you believe you can talk down to me if my views and questions rub you the wrong way. No, you will not do that. And you will not preach to me about what a mother does and doesn't do. I know all about how mothers did things in the Old World. No, there weren't child centers in the same way the Order has them, but there were millions of daycares, schools, and after-school programs. Don't talk to me about the gift of a child and conveniently leave these things out." Mary was so angry that spittle was flying across the desk while she screamed the words at the nurse. She was seeing red, and it was taking everything she had inside not to physically harm the woman.

"I'm not the child you believe me to be, so never speak to me that way. Climb down from your high horse and look into mankind's past before you start throwing darts. You think I don't know about the millions upon millions of abortions, adoptions, self-administered miscarriages, and many other things mothers did when they did not want to care for their children?

"Do not confuse me with the history of your own ilk. I do not want to give my child away, and I don't want to abort my child or neglect him or her. I asked a simple question to someone I thought was qualified to answer such a question. I don't need your attitude and self-righteousness."

Mary got up from her seat, still leaning over the wooden desk. The nurse put both hands up in the air while trying to get a word in, but Mary would have none of it. She was not done saying what she had to say.

"You people have a pattern of taking kindness for weakness, and in that way, you are no different from those that you detest. The Order did the same things to us in the Palace. I was a victim to this before, and I will never be that person again. You will speak to me with the respect that I give you. I don't care if you tell Logan, Carla, or anyone else here. I do not fear the Order, and I definitely do not fear a ragtag group of rebels finally climbing out of the grime of their own demise. Do you understand me?!" Mary flung the last of her sentence across the desk like a fast pitch. She was breathing hard, veins bulging from her forehead, arms shaking from gripping the edge of the desk so hard.

There was an awkward silence in the room. Mary noticed that Ashley's seat was at least three feet back from the desk, and her body was pressed up against the chair. The nurse's face was red, and she looked to be on the verge of tears. Mary did not feel bad for her; she was fed up with the rebel people. If all they understood was unabashed strength in the form of anger, then she would give it to them in spades.

It had become much harder to control her anger-fueled outbursts since losing Jacob. It didn't take much, but implying she was doing a disservice to her child or threatening that child were low blows, and she was not going to stand for it. From anyone.

Finally, Ashley was allowed to speak. "I'm sorry, Mary. I didn't mean to come off in that way to you."

"I know what you meant, and so do you. Again, don't speak to me as though you are speaking to a child. I likely know more about your own history than you do. I've spent my life learning about you and your ways. We did not work, we did not waste time doing things that had no purpose. We learned, we gained knowledge, we pushed ourselves to be more than what humans of the past were willing to push themselves to be," Mary said in a calmer voice, but still glaring at the woman with fire in her eyes.

"We did not have a choice in what happened with our children. They were taken, we did not choose to give them up. I did *not* choose to give my children up." Mary could feel a tear escape from her eye. She quickly wiped the tear away and straightened her posture. "In the future, maybe you should try empathy and understanding before making judgements hidden behind your idea of educating someone you assume doesn't know any better." Mary sniffled loudly as her nose began to run. She pushed her long dark hair from her face and turned to leave the infirmary.

"Mary, I need you to urinate in this cup for further testing before you go," Ashley said in a quiet and hurried voice.

"Pee in the cup yourself," Mary said. She then slammed the door behind her so hard that the glass shattered.

CHAPTER THIRTY-ONE

Melinda

THERE ON THE TV, AN IMAGE appeared of an airplane flying lower than a plane should in what was called New York in the Old World. The plane crashed into the top of a building, a big building that had a twin next to it. Two identical buildings called the Twin Towers. After another plane crashed into the buildings, they came tumbling down.

Well, not tumbling, but small explosions could be seen from the windows on descending floors, spreading down the massive buildings. To her, the buildings came down in what looked like a demolition. The type of demolition explosions used to bring down old structures that needed to come down so that new buildings could be erected. The Twin Towers crumbling reminded her of that. Melinda watched intently.

She would not remove her eyes like she had done every day before. She needed to see it, to see what mankind was capable of—to see what they were up against. Melinda knew she was a part of the solution now, the solution to getting rid of what had caused the planet so much harm. A part of her was still apprehensive about doing what needed to be done when the time came. The televisions were showing the images for that very reason: to educate them on what they were up against.

These were not the blameless, innocent people they wanted to believe they were. She knew that now, and for that reason, she would not look away from the TV.

The acts of only a few were able to send 2,996 lives to the afterlife, or wherever souls went off to when it was over. This was the heart of the people who were still out in the Old World, the survivors out killing Palace security. Killing was all they knew. For their own good, they had to be stopped. Lonnie had said as much to her, and she now saw that to be the truth.

When she thought about it, that was the reason why she would never watch the images on the televisions before. She didn't want to see what was happening, didn't want to regard them as what they truly were. That was a weakness in her own heart that needed to be dealt with in order to do what was needed in the near future.

She wanted to be there for Lonnie, to support him in his beliefs. It was slow going for her in the beginning, but she was coming to stand on the same side as him and everyone else. After all, there wasn't a single fish that would not eat the bread. They were one, and nature would decide the outcome. She would not be the fish.

The next image on the screen was that of a man inside of a tall building in what was Las Vegas, shooting out the windows at hundreds, maybe thousands of people dancing to music at some kind of event. Red letters at the bottom of the screen read *59 killed*. One man was able to hurt that many people by himself in such a brief time. Melinda thought about that and how terrible it would have been to live in such a time.

What they were doing was the same, but it was also different. There was a noble reason behind the deaths to come. It was for the preservation of the species and the Earth as a whole. History had shown the nature of those from the Old World. They were not willing to learn, they were not willing to submit—and for that, they would be erased.

From what she knew through learning of their history and the videos shown on television, the people of the Old World killed for the sake of it. There was much to be said for mental illness, but that was no excuse for the amount of carnage and fallout left lying in the wake of mankind. She knew Lonnie felt the same way. When all of the ideologies and lectures were spoken and fading off in the wind, it came down to removing them, or waiting for them to remove you along with everything else.

The next thing to pop up on the screen was an airplane flying across the sky. The plane dropped something, and then there was a humongous BOOM! A huge mushroom formed high in the sky. It looked as if it were made of smoke. The caption at the bottom of the screen read: *Atomic bomb of 1945. Over 220,000 died instantly*. There were images of dying men, women, and children. Skin falling off, arms or legs missing. There were people covered in rubble and ash. So many dead in the street, and for what?

Those of the Old World seemed to *do* simply because they *could*. A justification would be created after the fact. So badly Melinda wanted to turn away from the screen, to not see the children born years after the atomic bomb—it was sad what some were willing to do to their own brothers and sisters because one man or a few said to do so.

Melinda continued to watch scenes of gang violence in the cities of the Old World. *Are we willing to kill simply because one man or the few orders us to?* She didn't quite believe that was the case, but she could see how someone would surmise that idea. The teachers and Sirus were giving the orders because they were in charge, but all the Palace members had seen the work of the Old World. They knew them to be violent for the sake of violence; the status of the planet was proof of that. Those in the Palaces were different, she told herself. *I'm different.*

Lonnie had told her he was playing a bigger role in the battle to come than most others. He was not ready to tell her what role exactly, but she could sense that it was weighing heavily on him. She'd learned in the short but meaningful time they'd spent together not to push him to talk about things he was not ready to get into.

He would tell her more when he was ready for that. With Lonnie being deeper in the battle than everyone else, she wanted to be there for him, to support him. She found herself there on the sofa in her pod, powering through the most terrible videos she'd ever seen before. And she would watch those videos and more a million times over if it meant she was making herself better for him.

There would be no doubt on the battlefield, no time for challenging ideologies and what could be wrong. She knew the second she stepped outside the Palace with weapons and plans to kill, she was for better or worse the predator, the killer, the taker of life, and finally, she could accept that. If she was being charged with getting rid of people who were capable of what she was watching on the television, she could live with that.

In the end, when everything was over, when all were gone who were best beneath the Earth, then what? Would she and Lonnie be together? Would that even be allowed? This was something she thought about on a regular basis as of late. Nothing or no one meant anything to her but Lonnie; he was the end-all be-all for her. She was willing to kill, die, and jump whenever he said so. Whether he knew this or not, she couldn't be sure, but she thought he had a clue of where she placed her loyalties.

All that she'd learned in her life was now null and void. The game had been changed, and they were all headed in a different direction. Would they make it back to the loving teachings that were once the peak of learning in the Palace? She didn't know, but she hoped for it. Hoping would not win the battles though, nor would it keep Lonnie safe in what was to come. She could try to help keep him safe if she went with them.

Watching a man with a shirt tied over his face decapitating a woman, Melinda began to feel no emotion. The man had to dig the large knife into her throat and cut deeply, sawing at the muscle and bone while pulling her hair from the top. The woman's legs kicked like a donkey, and her arms shot out in every direction. Melinda didn't think someone was able to scream with their head halfway connected; she was wrong though. The woman screamed bloody murder, seemingly even after her head was swinging from the masked man's hand. At least that's how it seemed. Melinda did not look away; she wanted to watch it.

She grabbed the cup of coffee off the table in front of her and took a sip, feeling the hot liquid traveling down her throat, moving around her chest, and then down to her stomach. She liked her hot liquids as hot as possible without burning her taste buds off her tongue.

For the remainder of that morning, Melinda watched the videos on the television, repeatedly. The same videos were aired in a thirty-minute loop, and by the time a few hours had passed, she felt nothing. She watched, she saw what the survivors were, and without feeling any hate or malice in her heart, she knew that they were right in what they were planning. Someone had to protect the planet and the species of the planet, not just the humans. Who better to stop the threat of the human species, than the human species? A more updated and logical version of the human species, to be exact.

CHAPTER THIRTY-TWO

Carla

I<small>T'S BEST TO ELIMINATE HER NOW</small>. *The longer she stays, the more ground I'll lose*, Carla told herself. She was waiting in the darkened hallway of the crypt that was once a child center. Carla picked at the peeling paint on the wall and wondered what the Palace looked like before the monsters went scurrying down to the area where they kept the kids, burned every soul, and killed themselves. The thought sent her temperature through the roof.

She was conflicted with her thoughts on the Palace-born children. Mary was one of those children, but she hated the woman. She knew that the dislike associated with Mary was based on keeping her foothold within the group. That was selfish and would be judged as a weakness and shortcoming in the eyes of the Lord. Surely, he would understand her end game, and it was not to simply be a lieutenant in a rebel group.

Since the moment she got together with the Eagle company, there had been one goal, and that goal never changed. Carla walked up and down the hallway waiting, kicking broken pieces of plaster, moving rocks around with the bottom of her boot. Tony should have been there by now. The thought crossed her mind that he could have been found out. That would be bad...the boy did not have the heart for much of anything, definitely not interrogation. He would spill the beans if questioned.

She decided that while she waited for Tony, she would go into the child center and walk around to pass the time. If she sat around counting the seconds until he came, she would worry herself to death.

Since they'd taken over the Palace, Carla had not come into the child center. She allowed Logan and some of the other men to secure that area alone. Anything involving kids was a weak spot with her. The reminder of her own daughters would come flooding back to her brain. *Not with Mary though...I don't care what happens to her or her child.*

Carla stepped into the child center. As her eyes took in the terrible imagery, her knees went limp and she nearly fell to the floor. In order to keep her balance, she reached out to a charred wall to her right to keep steady. With all the atrocities she'd seen, and even taken part of in her life, what she was looking at now was by far the worse. Because it was done on purpose. Those...*things*...purposely burned those children.

She put her back against the wall and slowly slid down. The scars and open wounds from her atonement activities burned as she made her way to the floor. Carla sat there, unable to walk further into the child center. She needed time to breathe and think. A single tear went rolling down her cheek. She didn't bother to wipe it away. There was no one around to see.

Resting her chin on her chest, she allowed her hair to fall over her head and into her face as she stared between her legs at the blackened carpet. She couldn't recognize what the color had been at one time; everything was black. Everything was a crumbled remnant of what it once was. No different than the outside world, she thought while flicking small pebbles with her fingers. Carla thought about how Mary grew up in a place like that.

On one hand, the mother in her felt bad for a child that had grown up among the monstrous colonizers through no fault of her own. But the petty, selfish, purely human part of her was jealous that while everyone on the outside was dying of the sickness, being robbed for goods, raped, and anything else you could think of, Mary was growing up in a wonderland of sorts. No, the Palaces were not the utopias the colonizers fancied them to be, but even the fucked-up nature of a Palace facility was an upgrade to the outside world.

There was more to her dislike for the young Mary. It wasn't simply that she was there and being shown favor by Logan. It was deeper. Carla picked up a handful of rocks and shook them in her closed hand like dice. It reminded her of playing Monopoly on Saturday nights with her family. She quickly shook away the memory. Too painful. Carla threw the rocks to the far side of the child center and heard them skitter across the floor in the distance.

In a weird way, Mary reminded Carla of herself at that age. Young, hardheaded, full of herself, and eerily dangerous in a mysterious type of way. Carla lost track of her body count around year four of the sickness fallout. There had been countless battles with other rebel groups, fights against men looking to take her as their own. That happened more in the beginning. Male survivors had a tendency to revert back to cavemen, with sex and food being their only interest. She'd neutered or fully killed a handful of would-be Fred Flintstones.

Carla got to her feet, closed her eyes, and said the Lord's prayer. It felt right, given the situation. To do what needed to be done in the near future, she had to let go of certain things that lingered from the time when she was a mother and Sunday school teacher. Even though it was hard to step farther into the child center, she was glad that Tony chose this area to meet up. It was fitting, divine intervention maybe. Her Lord and savior Jesus Christ were always doing things like that to show her that she was on the right route.

Two birds with one stone, she said to herself, taking a few more steps through the charred room, kicking aside a plastic toy that was burned and melted so badly she couldn't make out what it was before. All at once, she could conquer her own insecurities and fears while waiting on Tony to complete a small part of her ultimate plan. Without this moment, she might not have been able to go through with it. *The brain has a funny way of stopping you from doing what your heart knows is right. Separation of church and state,* she thought, the corner of her mouth turning up in a grin.

Carla was dressed in her standard green army fatigue pants, green tank top, brown bomber jacket, and black combat boots. The weight of the boots made crunching and cracking sounds as she stepped on burned pieces of wood, pieces of the ceiling that had fallen down over time, and other random pieces of nothing she could make out.

She could see her children there. Not literally there, but she could see them running and playing with other kids in that space. Her brain created a setting of colorful walls and rainbow carpet. Areas of focus for the kids like block building, puzzles, and TVs to watch *Teletubbies* and *Barney*. She wasn't sure if it was actually like that in the child center; she would bet it wasn't. But in her mind, the child center looked like the many daycares she'd worked in as a young woman in the Old World.

For the next fifteen minutes, Carla walked a few laps around the remains of the child center. It was hard at first, but it did become easier. The challenge was not in seeing what had become of the area, but in disassociating her children with every child that suffered. The day she'd had to bury her kids at the church, the morning that she'd lost everything and everyone—it left an imprint on her brain. She thought of it like a brand. She'd been stamped: USDA BROKEN. That's how she felt. But her God would help put her back together. The road had been long, but she thought she was at a crossroads that day, walking among the burial ground of so many children and not fainting from the horror.

There were times during the walk that her knees threatened to give out, but she stood strong and continued. If Jesus could walk with a cross on his back while being beaten, she could do this. She had to. It was important work; it was the Lord's work.

Carla noticed a red clump of twisted metal on the far-right side of the center, in the same area where she'd thrown the rocks earlier. She walked over to the thing, bending down to pick it up with both hands. Immediately she recognized it; the clump had once been a red tricycle. The thought made her release a small laugh as she turned the piece of metal this way and that, surveying the sides and figuring out which part was which. Her husband had bought their oldest daughter one of these tricycles for Christmas when she'd turned four.

"Carla!" She heard the voice, but thought it was in her mind.

"*Mark?*" she said to herself. Was he speaking to her? She looked up at the ceiling. Was her husband speaking to her from the heavens?

"Carla, what are you doing?" The voice was louder and getting closer to her.

"Yes dear, it's me...Is it really you?" She dropped the burned piece of metal to the ground. It banged against the floor with a loud clank. Carla raised both hands into the air as her body became filled with joy. She couldn't believe he was finally speaking to her.

"Come to me, please!" she begged. "I'm here, I'm right here." She patted her chest with both hands, as if that would allow a figment of her imagination to see her. "Mark! Can you see me!" she bellowed out with all the force in her lungs.

"Carla, stop screaming! You're gonna get us caught." The voice was a harsh whisper now. Carla felt a hand grab onto her arm and whirl her around. The years of fighting, defending herself, and killing at a moment's notice were not lost on her cat-like reactions. Even while having delusions of hearing her deceased husband's voice, she would not allow herself to be caught off guard. Carla pivoted to the left.

"No, It's m—"

The man tried to speak, but she cut him off. Her feet and hands were already doing what came naturally. The same movements that had gotten Carla out of many potentially fatal situations had already begun. Muscle memory took over, and there was no stopping it once she got started.

Carla pushed the arm away so hard that the man stumbled backwards, causing him to drop something. Before she even saw his face, she was closing the distance between them and driving a hunting knife between his ribs on the right side of his body.

Her face was so close to her victim's that when she twisted the knife, she could hear the wind escape his lips. Carla snarled as she pushed the knife deeper and then pulled it out, releasing a warm squirt of blood. The man fell as Carla backed away from him. She felt like a cornered animal, close to the point of jumping on his body and stabbing more holes into him if need be. While in a murderous frenzy and taking note of the man's size, height, and clothing, she finally got a chance to notice his face...

"Tony...?" Carla said. The familiarity of his face brought her out of her blind rage. The young man lay on the grungy floor of the child center that was once again serving as the backdrop for even more violence. His eyes bugged out, looking up at her with what resembled fear and disbelief at what had just occurred.

Tony tried to say something that sounded like her name. But what came out of his mouth was an inaudible blob of sounds and blood. Carla put the knife back into the side pocket of her fatigue pants and quickly dropped down to him.

"Oh my God, Tony...I'm so sorry. I didn't know," she said.

Her young apostle continued to try to speak, but his mouth was filling with blood. She had buried the knife deep, and he couldn't get a word around all the crimson liquid coming from his lungs. His hand was reaching out to her. He wanted help—he thought that she could help him. Carla held onto his hand and repeated her words over and over.

"I'm so sorry, I'm sorry..." That was all she could say, because there was no hope in saving him. The maneuver she'd used was meant to kill. Not wound or disarm, but kill. And in quick order. Tony did not have much time. He was beginning to panic. His legs were kicking forcefully, creating clouds of ash and dust every time one of his boots went into the air and came crashing down to the ground.

Carla grabbed both of his hands and held them in hers as she did all that she could. She said a prayer over him.

"Our Father, who art in heaven, hallowed be thy name. Thy kingdom come, thy will be done, on Earth as it is in heaven. Give—"

Tony cut her off mid-prayer by spitting blood into her face as she leaned over him, holding both of his hands. She noticed then that she was more so holding him down than holding his hands to comfort. Carla thought that if she wasn't anchoring him to the ground with her own weight, he would be popping up into the air with how his body was bucking.

To make sure the blood didn't get in her eyes, Carla closed them but held on. She was sure she could make out Tony cursing her between all the thrashing and choking. Her blade had pierced and ripped open a lung. She got him good, she knew that. Carla did not fault him for cursing her or spitting on her, it was what she deserved. She'd taken a life out of fear and ignorance from someone who was on her side, someone who did not deserve death. That life was not hers to take in pursuit of the goals she'd created for both herself and for the Lord. Her own tears mixed with the blood all over her face as she finished the prayer.

"Give us this day our daily bread. And forgive us our trespasses, as we forgive those who trespass against us. And lead us not—"

One of Tony's hands slipped loose from Carla's grip. He reached out and slapped at her face, trying to push up from the ground. His slaps were weak; he didn't have the energy or strength to do much of anything. Carla easily wrangled in the unbound hand, closing them both back within her own. "Shhhh," she whispered. "Shhhh, just let go, Tony."

She wanted so badly to ease him off into the afterlife, but he would have none of it. Even while he was down to his last bit of energy, his legs flopped around as he shook his head back and forth. He was flinging blood all over her, himself, and the ground. The choking sound eventually stopped, and his body relaxed. There were still mild jerks for what felt like an eternity, but was actually only a few seconds. Carla kept his hands within hers as she cried and laid her head on his chest. Tony was no longer moving.

"And lead us not into temptation, but deliver us from the evil. For thine is the kingdom, and the power, and the glory, forever and ever." She thought that closing his eyes after the prayer was a good idea. She'd seen it done that way in movies a million times. When she lifted her bloodstained face to do so, she noticed that his eyes were already closed.

How foolish was she to have thought that her dead husband was speaking to her? The only soul that could have been saying her name was Tony. He was the only one who knew she was there in the child center, waiting for their planned meeting. She knew that, but had still allowed feelings from her old life to create such destruction in what she thought was her rebirth, her new life. Carla picked herself up and dusted off her pants.

It was clear to her at that moment that no matter how much she wanted to distance herself from the past—her husband, the kids—she couldn't. It was all-encompassing. She had to be both a tool of the Lord and the Sunday school teacher, because she did care...just not for everyone. And there were tolls that had to be paid.

She bent down and used Tony's pant leg to get the blood off her face and hands before noticing a syringe on the ground a few feet away. He'd brought what he said he would.

"Thank you, Tony. I'm in your debt, and I'll pay it back in spades. In this life or the next," she said out loud.

Carla placed the syringe into the wide pocket on the side of her jacket. Looking around the child center, it was clear there was no shortage of places to hide the body. Patting the pocket containing the syringe, Carla wiped the last of the tears from her face and forced a smile. She had what she needed to complete the plan. At least something good had come out of the travesty. *It won't be in vain, Tony. I promise your sacrifice won't be in vain.*

After dragging and hiding the body beneath three hefty rock slabs and the remains of a burned table, she made her way back to the hallway that led to the staircase. That staircase led to a back room near the kitchen area, where some of the moms prepared meals that were ordered on the nutrition dispensary gadgets in each pod.

There was a woman in that kitchen by the name of Sheila who owed Carla a favor. She'd caught the woman smuggling extra food from the kitchen to her pod, and Carla had been nice enough to not alert Logan to the thievery. Out of the goodness of her heart, of course. That relationship with Sheila would see that the contents of the syringe would find their way into a certain someone's food, and the rest would be history. Unrecorded history. The world had been lost; no one was recording what happened during this time, the time of reorder. Carla would make sure that she was at the forefront of the new world though. The way the good Lord intended.

CHAPTER THIRTY-THREE

Mary

"WE'RE GLAD YOU TOLD US ABOUT the baby. I feel bad that we didn't create an environment where you felt comfortable enough to tell us about something so important to you. Important to the world, really." Dale sat on the edge of her bed with his legs crossed, his left ankle resting on his right knee. The young makeshift psychiatrist of the Eagle squad had showed up that morning, knocking on her pod door with no pad or pen. Strictly a social call, she thought.

"I'm very sorry about that. Hopefully you can understand why I chose to wait before releasing that kind of sensitive information," Mary said. She sat at the small white table near the sofa, picking at a bowl of apples with a spoon. Morning sickness was still kicking her ass, but she knew she had to eat something. Diced apples with cinnamon in a light syrup was usually her favorite thing to eat in the morning. But that morning, she wasn't feeling it.

"Of course, of course. Say no more. I get it."

"It wasn't personal. I know you're a respectable individual, but you aren't the standard for those among you. Not that the people here are bad, I don't believe that—although I'm sure you know I've had some issues with a few Eagle members." Mary dropped the spoon into the bowl of apples. The metal clanged against the glass dish.

She turned in her chair to fully face Dale, wondering if he'd come to give her the "having kids is a big responsibility" talk.

"Really, I am relieved to come out with it. I know it won't be easy for someone like me to raise a baby on my own. I know this, so I hope that's not why you came to chitchat. It is true that I've never cared for any of the children I brought into the world before. I know that." She began talking faster, trying to get it all out before she was cut off. "But I did what was expected of me in the Palace; I did what was customary. If there was an option to be with your children, to care for them, feed them, nurture—"

Her voice broke. Mary stopped talking and turned to the bowl. She grabbed the spoon and scooped an apple up, then dropped it back into the bowl and turned to face him again, trying to gather her emotions. Dale hadn't interrupted. He was allowing her to speak and work through how she was feeling. That was another relief to her.

"I'm sorry, I'm just trying to say that, just because I'm a Palace-born person does not mean I'm any less human than you or anyone here. As a mother, I wanted so badly to be with my children. I can't count the amount of times I went down to the observation area to watch them play, smile, cry...In a weird way, I was with them. I could not go inside and touch or speak to them, but I was there every step of the way. As much as a parent could be in the Palace."

Mary spoke proudly. She wanted Dale to know who she was, what she was made of. To see that she was no different than him. She knew they all looked at her like some kind of weird science experiment, and to some extent they were right. If all the implications were correct, she was engineered by beings from outside of the planet, but her makeup was all human. How she was raised was vastly different, but that could not remove base human intuition. Especially that of a mother.

"I understand, Mary. I really do. I did not come here to give you a lecture or anything like that. I came to congratulate you and—"

"Please, let me finish, Dale. I need to get this out. Not sure if it's one hundred percent for you, or if some of it is for me as well. Let me finish, please." Dale's lips formed a hesitant smile, and he nodded, encouraging her to continue.

"The child I'm giving birth to means everything to me, literally everything. No one will take this one from my arms, and I will get the other two back as soon as I'm physically able to. Whether your group goes after the Palace I came from or not, I will. No one will stop that. What I've suffered at the hands of the Order, what those I grew up with suffered—it's unthinkable. It must be made right."

She took a deep, determined breath and continued. "Logan will not stop me, your lieutenant Carla cannot stop me. I will do what needs to be done to liberate everyone in that Palace, and I will hunt Sirus to the ends of this planet or wherever he comes from. I've thought of nothing else since watching someone I loved very much die on the grass like an animal. He did not deserve that...none of them do. And if they burned this child center just because you all took control, that tells me they have no qualms with doing something like that again. That mixed with what I've seen with my own eyes and heard with my own ears—I know that this must be done. With or without the Eagle squad's help."

Mary turned back to her breakfast, allowing the awkward silence to blanket them both. She'd said what she needed to say, and it was up to Dale to respond or not. She didn't care either way. Mary picked up the spoon and scooped up a bunch of apples with syrup and popped them into her mouth. Saying her truth to someone had somehow lifted some weight off her mind and relaxed her.

"Are you done?" Dale asked.

"I am," Mary answered while chewing up the apples. She did not turn back to face him. Instead, she went for more apples. Her appetite was coming back.

"Good. And I agree with all that you said. We are in fact going after every Palace in the area, and we look to liberate all of Old Indiana. Which is why having you on our side is very important." Dale raised his voice and assured her, "*Not* because you are some kind of freak or whatever you believe we think about you. But because you have vital inside information on the layout of that Palace and how things work there. Schedules, teacher count, Old World members, Palace-born members, things like that."

Mary pushed the bowl of remaining apples to the opposite edge of the small table and gulped some of the orange juice down. She grabbed the napkin that had been sitting beneath the juice glass and wiped away the orange juice mustache from her top lip before turning back to Dale to finish their talk.

"We will make sure that you have all the care and support you need throughout your pregnancy. The nurse says you are around four to five months along. It's always exciting to have another child in the camp." Dale stopped talking for a moment, tilting his head. "Well, we're not so much a camp anymore now that we have this Palace. Old habits die hard, I guess. All those years living as a traveling group of mercenaries made a lot of us get used to that way of life. Even in our speech, it seems."

Again he paused, clearing his throat before he continued. "You mentioned some people here that you have had issues with. Are you talking about Ca—"

Mary began coughing. Her hand shot out in a gesture, asking him to wait. She jumped up from her seat and walked toward the bathroom.

"Mary, are you okay? Maybe get a drink of your orange juice. It's right there on the table." Dale uncrossed his leg, a touch of concern on his face.

Mary put a hand over her mouth to cover the violent coughing while shaking her head no. Her stomach didn't feel right. Dale's eyes followed her across the room. Just as Mary got to the bathroom doorway, she fell to one knee, clutching her stomach.

"Mary! Are you okay?" Dale sprung from the bed and put an arm around her shoulder. He patted her on the back firmly. "Oh my God, are you okay? C'mon, you gotta get up."

Mary's stomach felt like it was eating itself. She'd never experienced a feeling like that. Even when she'd eaten the bad berries out in the forest, it hadn't felt anything like what was going on inside of her at that moment. She felt like she had to vomit, but nothing was coming up. She lay on her side with her legs pulled up to her abdomen in a fetal position. She couldn't tell Dale to get help because she couldn't stop coughing.

Suddenly, a panicked thought came to her mind, and she knew what was going on. Someone had put something in her food to kill her. Lying there on the carpet of her pod, all she could think of was her child, and Jacob. She thought herself reckless and dumb to have ever trusted the Eagle group. Her insides twisted, seeming to wrap themselves around her lungs. She could feel wetness between her legs. Dale got up from the floor and went running out of the pod, screaming for help. Then the room began to go dark.

Mary lay there on the white carpet of the pod in a ball, both arms clutching her belly as tears streamed down her face. As she faded out, she could hear footsteps running toward her along with Dale's shouts. "She's in here, hurry! She's pregnant. You have to help her now!"

Then there was no sound, no pain, and no more worries.

CHAPTER THIRTY-FOUR

Trust No One - Lonnie

"COULD YOU PLEASE PUT A SHEET or towel over the TV? Just drape it over the top. I'm not in the mood to see this stuff anymore," Lonnie said. He was annoyed, and had been for days. He knew Melinda noticed his attitude. She was going out of her way to be extra nice to him. It made him feel good to know that she cared, and made him feel bad at the same time. It would be easier if she wasn't...her.

"Of course I will," Melinda said as she quickly scurried out of the bed. There was a towel near the door, the one she threw there after they'd showered together earlier. Melinda draped the towel over the front of the damn screen.

"Is that better? I was tired of looking at it as well. Let's talk. I had a few things I wanted to ask you about next week," she said while nestling her face beneath his chin. Lonnie knew that she enjoyed lying on him. She'd told him the feeling of being that close to someone was amazing, and he agreed. It was amazing for someone to want to be that close to him. Her hair tickled his chin, and her right leg looped across his body and found a home on his pelvic area, covering his manhood.

Lonnie stroked Melinda's hair and rubbed her shoulder. "I don't really want to talk about any of that stuff. That's all I talk about when

I'm not with you. It's so close to the time of moving out of the Palace, and I just want to enjoy the time we have."

"I'll be going with you though, right? Teacher Luke said it was okay if I was in your unit. You said so last week." Melinda was talking fast. She angled her head so she could look up at him. Lonnie thought she looked absolutely afraid. He looked away from her, stroking her hair with his right hand.

"Of course, Mel. You're in my unit. We'll be together." It certainly sounded like a lie coming off his lips as soon as he let the words go. He wondered if she heard the lie.

She didn't notice. Her eyes twinkled upon hearing that she would be with him when they went to battle. From the corner of his eye, he saw the look on her face and returned a warm smile. That much was sincere, but he knew that she could not go with him.

His orders were firm. Lonnie had tried and tried to change their minds, but they would not relent on what was next. Last night he lay in his own bed, in the darkness and solitude of it all, and he cried. He cried until he could not cry anymore. He thought that his tear ducts were simply out of tears.

In the meeting with the other captains, he was the only one who'd objected. Everyone else seemed to be okay with what they were being asked to do. A few of the men even smiled.

His objection was light of course; he didn't want to look like he was going against the teachers, or the Order. He knew the rules of getting out into the world and doing what needed to be done were coming from the top of the pyramid.

When he asked Teacher Simon if there was another way, the man sat there massaging his fingertips into the surface of the big round table. "No, there is no other way. There is no better way to get yourself ready for what's to come." That was the end of it. The conversation moved on, and they never returned to the topic.

While the other seven chosen captains and Teacher Simon went on with their tactical questions and answers, he sat in his seat, staring at them all but hearing nothing. He was a million miles away. Mostly he focused on keeping his heart from bursting out of his chest and not screaming at the top of his lungs in the middle of the meeting.

By the end, he'd accepted what was. If he'd learned anything in the past few months, it was that the plan would be seen through whether he was involved in it or not, and he very much wanted to be involved. He was involved, and he was possibly the most important cog in said plan. His unit was the lead unit to engage the Palace that had been taken over by the survivor scum.

The captains were slapping high fives, patting each other on the backs, and giving each other words of confidence as the meeting ended. He took part in this, but inside, he wanted no part of it. He was once again wearing the mask. The one true thing that he'd always done well. Deception was his talent; being conniving and making those around him believe he was whatever they wanted him to be. At times he had trouble discerning his true self from all the different masks in his possession.

Here he was again, lying, wearing a mask, even when he was with the person who meant the most to him. Deceiving her into thinking something would happen that actually had a zero percent chance of occurring. He couldn't bear to tell her the truth. He could barely face the truth himself.

"I've been shooting multiple times a day, you know. When you are off doing your thing, I go to shoot. I want to make sure I'm ready when the time comes," Melinda said as she laid her head back down on his chest. Her hair tickled his chest as she moved around, trying to find that sweet comfortable spot that she loved.

He thought of the letter she'd written him some days ago. Reading it had made him happy. She talked about how much she cared for him, how scared she was to say the word love. That was a word the people of the Old World used, and it had caused them so many problems. She said she was close to saying it to him, but she didn't want him to feel disrespected if she did utter the words. Lonnie could not stop smiling while reading the letter.

Melinda went on and on in her writing about her feelings for him, how she enjoyed being in his presence and lying with him. Lonnie read that letter over ten times that night before burning it in the sink. As he'd rinsed the small blackened pieces down the drain, he thought about how he felt the same way. He planned to tell her that he loved her after the meeting. He didn't care what the word meant to those from the Old World; the way he felt about her could only be explained as love.

He'd also planned to ask her if she wanted to try being together as a solo couple. Like the few from the Old World who'd once lived together in the same pods...before the security team killed them all. The idea of being together in that way went against everything they'd learned, but so did killing. And yet, there they were, a week away from days of murder and carnage. If that was something that could be accepted, he didn't think it was out of the question to ask for prolonged companionship.

But the meeting had ended so badly that he couldn't say he loved her, knowing what he would have to do. In fact, he didn't even make it to her pod that night. He hadn't been able to face her.

Lonnie now lay there with her, stroking her hair, listening to her go on and on about how much she'd been learning to kill in a more efficient way. It was a good thing she couldn't see his face because one or two tears went running down his cheeks, finding a home in her hair. What had her love for him turned her into? That saddened him. She cared so much for him that she went and became someone else to appease him. He felt bad for that. In his own way, he had played a part in that change.

Melinda had always insisted that what they were doing was wrong. She was all about love and sticking to the teachings of empathy and understanding. While it bothered him at times, it was part of what captivated him about her. She was a person that stuck to her guns (for lack of a better term), unlike him. He was all too happy to flip-flop on the teachings and become a killing machine simply because they'd asked him to.

In his heart, he knew he was a coward. Not in the way of doing his job of killing, of exterminating, of defending what he believed in. But he was a coward in the way that he had no strong thoughts outside of what the Order told him to think. They could change his mind back and forth like a light switch. Lonnie didn't know if it was his upbringing in the Palace or if it was just the way he was, but it bothered him.

He bent his head down and kissed the top of her head. She was still going on and on about all of the new things she'd learned while shooting. How the rifles were very high powered and would cause maximum damage if used at close range. He answered with canned responses, but he wasn't truly listening to her. The words coming out of her mouth didn't matter. Lonnie just wanted to enjoy the time they were having together. While they still had time.

CHAPTER THIRTY-FIVE
Melinda

S OMETHING IS WRONG, SHE THOUGHT TO herself after closing the door. Lonnie had just left her pod, and something was off with him. Something was different, she could easily see it. Since the night he didn't come over like he said he would, he'd been distant.

It could be that he was getting in the zone for the battle coming up. That was a real thing. Melinda had been reading anything she could get her hands on about war, the psychology of it and things of that nature, and sometimes people had to get into a zone. It felt like more than that to her. She hadn't been close to him for long, but she thought that she knew him better than anyone else in the Palace. Melinda went back to the bed and lay on her stomach with her face in a pillow. She so wanted to understand him and what was going though his mind.

Lonnie was the same outgoing happy guy when others were around, that wasn't the issue. It was when they were alone. He didn't speak much, he seemed sad—and she couldn't do anything to bring his spirits up. The last thing she wanted to do was call him out on it or create friction when they were both so close to leaving the Palace.

The shock of leaving was enough to deal with. They'd never been outside of the hundred-yard radius. To see all the buildings, streets, and structures would be a system shock in itself. Then add on that they would be killing other human beings, something they had no experience with; it was a very scary thing.

For the last week, Lonnie hadn't been going to any of his morning enrichment classes or doing anything in the way of stress relief. If he was not with her, he was having battle meetings, shooting with his squad, or making plans for the battle efforts. She was happy that the Order saw him as someone special enough to lead a big portion of their men and women, but the toll it was taking on him was visible. Maybe no one else noticed, but she could see it.

Melinda turned around to lay on her back and stare at the ceiling. She did her best thinking staring up at the white ceiling. It cleared her mind so that she could think about the matter at hand, and that was Lonnie. Melinda pulled the white comforter over her legs and upper body. Only her head peeked out of the top, like a turtle. She smiled at the thought. Lonnie said she looked like a turtle when she pulled the covers over herself like that. They laughed about it a lot. She wanted that Lonnie back, but she feared he was gone forever. If planning a battle, if practicing shooting changed him in the way she could subtly see, what would actual war do to him?

It didn't matter to her. Whatever he became, whatever he did, she would be there. It made no difference to her. She loved all that he was, all that he would ever become, and she would be there in the worst of times. There was nothing that would stop her from protecting him out in the world.

Melinda was known as the best shot at the range when it came to many of the handguns and some of the different rifles. Lonnie could use that kind of help, so she would be that person for him. She would become whatever he required, because she did love him.

Why didn't I just tell him tonight that I was in love with him? He would probably think her *a young fool if* she *said such a thing.* Melinda rolled on her side and thought more deeply about the idea of saying the words to him. Before, she didn't think it would be a problem to say it to him, but with how somber he'd become over the last week or so, she thought saying something like that could make him worse. Or cause him to get angry with her. Soon they would be involved in a life-or-death situation. His mind needed to be clear.

Melinda fell asleep thinking about Lonnie and how she could be there for him. Wondering how to make him happy, how to protect him from the survivors out in the world, and protect him from himself. It was all she thought about as of late. Melinda had literally lost herself while falling in love with Lonnie, and she would have it no other way.

CHAPTER THIRTY-SIX

Logan

THE REBEL LEADER SAT IN A meeting room with the most important members of his squad. The table was created by his men with the old war-room tables in mind. Big and rounded on the edges, dark wood with a map in the middle. The map was of the surrounding areas, and three pins signified the locations of the three Palaces that were not yet liberated.

They were not there to speak about Palaces though. This topic was just as important as far as Logan was concerned. He was worried that what befell Mary could get in the way of his future plans. He didn't know what had happened to Mary, but Dale said that it looked like poison. She was eating at the time just before falling and choking. They thought she would die, and yet she had not. That said a lot about her.

That made two times that death came knocking at her door, and two times she did not answer. She was special, he knew that. But he wondered just how special.

"So, what are you trying to say, man?" Derek said to Dale, almost barking across the table at him. "Are you saying that someone here tried to hurt the Palace-born woman?"

"I'm not *trying* to say anything, Derek. I'm saying that from my analysis of her body after the fact and being there during the ordeal, it was most definitely poison, or something very similar to it," Dale said in a calm voice. He did not look up to regard Derek, but stared down into his notepad, scribbling and circling things as he spoke.

"Well, I think that's bullshit!" That would mean one of the cooks in the kitchen poisoned her.

Dale looked up over his glasses without moving his head up and responded with the same nonchalant tone. "Not necessarily. I've been down to the kitchen to speak to the cooks. From my questioning, I don't think that's the case."

A balding man at the table by the name of Tanner spoke up. "If not the cooks, then who?"

"I have no idea. I'm guessing that's why we're all here," Dale said. He looked back down to his notepad.

Logan scanned the room, observing the faces of everyone. Watching, listening...chewing and spitting shells on the ground. There was power in being a better listener than talker.

At times like these, it was beneficial to simply look upon the faces of those who could be guilty of the thing. Words meant little to nothing, but the eyes were a dead giveaway. So, he watched them. To see who avoided eye contact, to see who excessively blinked when they spoke. There were a few there he thought knew more than they were saying.

It was Dale who'd asked him to set up the meeting. The young intel specialist had a sweet spot for Mary. Logan decided to grant him that courtesy. Having someone in his unit who moved on their own accord was more important to him.

"Hold on, if you are saying that your analysis shows Mary was poisoned, but no one in the kitchen did the poisoning, then how did someone else manage it?" Carla asked, placing both hands on the shiny dark oak of the round table.

"There are ways," Dale said without looking up.

"Before we go down the road of deception among the ranks, is it at all possible that she became sick from a different cause?" the top medic of the unit, Marcella, suggested. "Those born in Palaces are made to have children at a very early age. We're talking sometimes as young as ten years old. That type of trauma to the reproductive organs at such a young age is severe. I wonder if the possible trauma has caused issues that brought on a reaction. Is it possible that her eating at the time of the choking and such was pure coincidence?"

"No telling what those...things do to Palace-born humans. Who are we to say what could be going on inside of that woman's body?" Carla said, sitting back in her seat.

Logan watched them all, listened to them all challenge each other and try to come up with ways that Mary could have had such a reaction. These were his most trusted men and women, but someone knew something, or maybe someone had done something.

"It's no secret that there are certain people in our ranks that do not like Mary being here. I know this to be true. Can we cut the shit and be honest for a second?" Logan finally spoke up.

"That is true sir, but do you think that dislike is so thick that someone would poison the girl?" Derek answered, throwing both hands in the air. Logan slanted his head to the side raised both eyebrows with a "you never know" gesture.

Dale placed his notepad on the table with the pen clipped to the top. He removed his glasses and laid them on top of the notepad. "Listen...I have investigated everything for the last day or so. I even had the bowl of apples Mary ate tested by a friend down in research." His voice was stern and cold. "They were poisoned, and the substance used can only be found in the infirmary." He looked at Marcella. The woman jumped back at the implication of his words. Her eyes morphed into globes as they widened, and everyone at the table turned to look at her.

Logan didn't think it was Marcella; she'd always been too sweet to hurt anything. Poisoning a human was far from her sensibilities. He had a promising idea of who did the deed. Letting the blame game play on was beneficial though; it allowed him a look into how they all thought of each other, so he allowed it to play out right there at the table.

"That's impossible," Marcella protested. "My people would never do such a thing, nor would I. What are you trying to say?"

"Are you sure, Dale?" a lieutenant by the name of Matt said. He sat next to Logan and was as reliable as any in the group.

"I'm more than sure," Dale said.

"Who in research told you that? Give me their name right now. I'd love to have a word with them," Marcella said as she stood up.

"I will not, the point is moot. The test was run twice. Speaking to the research team won't change what is." Dale put his glasses back on and pulled the pen from the notepad before flipping it open and jotting something down.

"Why do you want to speak to the person in research? They are just doing their jobs, and if they say the poison or whatever it is came from the infirmary, then it did." Derek looked at Marcella, then Logan.

Logan noticed the group instinctively leaned toward Marcella or someone in the infirmary as the culprit. They would be wrong, but it was the easy out. When given the chance, people always went with what was easiest. The eyes never lie though, and her eyes told no lies. In situations such as the one she found herself in, it was easy to look guilty. If you got offended or angry, it came off as guilt; if you tried to play it cool and simply deny, it came off as arrogant guilt.

It was clear that Dale thought she was guilty of the crime, but he could not be relied upon for objectivity. He simply wanted someone to pay for what happened to Mary, and Marcella was the easiest mark based on her running the infirmary. Never mind the fact that she had no motive, no stomach for such a thing, and she had no way of getting to food in the kitchen. There were a few at the table, however, who did have friends in that area of the Palace.

Logan had figured out the trick to the special guns they'd discovered, and it was all he'd been thinking about as of late. So much so that he'd forgotten his place in the group as the leader. That lapse in leadership allowed Mary to be hurt. He was glad she was still alive, because he had plans for her, and they would only work if she was still breathing. Someone else there at the table had plans for the young woman as well.

He saw now what his old friend Jacob had seen in Mary. The woman was unique in a multitude of ways, some he was just beginning to understand. He'd thought about telling her that Jacob was his best friend before the sickness came, that they'd grown up together, but he thought telling her would create a bond that wouldn't benefit either of them. He was not that person anymore, and he could imagine that Jacob was someone totally different before he'd died. *It wasn't for nothing, Jacob, I promise you that*, he told himself as his lieutenants and other trusted peers fought amongst each other, trying desperately to push the blame away from themselves.

That was a typical response. Logan sat back in his seat and watched them go back and forth but get nowhere. Placing the blame this way and that, turning on each other with passive-aggressive finger-pointing. The meeting ended the same way it started—with no one knowing exactly what had happened. Just a lot of hurt feelings and angry people with guns going in opposite directions.

The meeting had served its purpose for Logan, though. He was now sure who the culprit was. Sometimes it was the person who spoke most; at other times it was the person who said the least. When those from elsewhere came for them, he wanted to know where all the chess pieces were on the board. Dale would recover from his anger and heartbreak from seeing such a thing happen to Mary.

Mary lived, and that was a good thing, at least for Logan's plans. She could have lost her life. Logan didn't know Mary that well, but he did know that she would trade her life for the life of her child. Dale told him as much when they found out she'd lost the baby, which had died as a result of the poison in her stomach. The medics had tried their best, but nothing could be done. He thought that he should be the one to tell her, and he knew it would not be an easy thing to do.

CHAPTER THIRTY-SEVEN
Lonnie

"WE MOVE OUT IN THE NEXT three days. You do understand that, right?" Teacher Simon said.

"I do, and I'm going to get it done. I was waiting for...I don't know what I've been waiting for. I know what's expected of me as the leader of this battle campaign. I guess I've been waiting for the right moment." Lonnie moved around in his seat uncomfortably, finding it hard to wear the mask in that moment. But he did.

He'd come too far to turn back now. Too many lives had been lost, too many training hours spent, and the survivors out in the world had committed too many crimes against humanity and the planet. He knew that he'd been chosen for a reason, and allowing his desires to take precedence over that would not be accepted. Not by the Order, and not by himself.

"Are you sure this is something you can do? If not, we don't have a problem promoting one of the other captains. You could be reassigned." The word *reassigned* sounded more like *killed* to Lonnie's ears. It wasn't always what was said, but more how it was said, and he'd found out enough about the Order to know that it was far too late to turn back now or acquire a conscience.

"Oh no, sir, it's no problem at all. I knew that I had more time to get it done. I've been keeping myself busy reading up on the battle plans and preparing my men. I'll take care of it tonight." He said the words like it was no big deal at all. He was ashamed of himself, at what he'd become. Sitting there paying lip service to a man who'd played with and sculpted his mind to become a killer. They hadn't left the Palace yet, and he was already responsible for taking four lives. He knew it was meant to be practice for the business of taking lives. And he was good at it, better than he'd thought he would be.

"I'm happy to hear you say that. Report to me after you do what is necessary, and I'll be sure to let Sirus know that you are ready. We're just waiting on you to finish up," Teacher Simon said.

"Tonight... It's done tonight."

CHAPTER THIRTY-EIGHT

Carla

CARLA SAT ALONE IN HER SECRET cave just a few miles from the facility. The facility she loathed, with people she worked with and protected but secretly thought of as vile creatures. They fought and killed with no direction. There was no goal in mind in how they went about their business. Kill, take over, kill, take over...rinse repeat. To her it felt like the same thing humans had been doing before the sickness. Had they learned nothing?

She found herself sitting on the blue milk crate again, holding on to the flat brown wallet with pictures of the family she once belonged to. Ghosts from the past that felt more real than anything she'd experienced since the day she'd buried her children and walked away from her husband's body. She needed to see them again, to talk to them and ask for advice.

Carla wiped tears from her face with dirty hands, smearing dirt on her face like so much mascara. She cried not because she was sad, or because she was lost in the world. She cried because the plan was in place. Sure, her plan had failed to an extent, but what she was able to accomplish was meaningful. There were other plans anyway.

There were many plans that could bet set in motion, and a multitude of possible outcomes. In another day or two, she expected the proverbial shit to hit the fan. She could feel it in the air.

Even though the tears were falling, there was a big smile on her face. All of the time spent waiting, planning, and dealing with people who were not on the righteous path had taken a toll on her. But soon she would not have to praise the Lord in the way that she did—in private. She would not have to worry about how others felt, those who didn't understand the war they were fighting. Blind, the lot of them.

They were fighting a holy war if she'd ever seen one. She was the one to be at the helm of such a war. Her children had told her so, her husband even agreed. They spoke to her in dreams, through the pictures, and in her mind. Her family was the only truth in her life besides the words of the Good Book. Everything else was an obstacle, and obstacles were for crushing.

For days she had punished herself for what happened to Tony. It wasn't right, and he didn't deserve the fate that befell him. It was an accident; she hadn't meant to hurt him, but that fact would not bring him home. That night she pulled out two teeth from the back of her mouth with pliers. It was the most physical pain she'd ever felt in her life, but it was the price to be paid for such a mistake. A mistake that had cost a man, a good man, his life.

It was unfortunate he couldn't receive a burial. He deserved that much, all men did. She would right that wrong as soon as she could, and the time of her reign was a lot closer than anyone thought. The world needed a new leader, someone who understood the sins of man, someone just and righteous enough to dole out punishment. If a leader was not willing to punish themselves for less than perfect actions or thoughts, then they were not fit to hold anyone else accountable.

Carla had created a small fire in the cave when she'd arrived. The fire served two purposes, to warm her because it was cold in the cave, and to help her move on from the physical things in her old life that she still clung to.

Carla kissed the pictures, holding her dried lips to the flimsy, crackled paper.

"I've heard you, my family." She spoke out loud. There was no one to hear her or call her crazy. "I know that it's time to let you go in this form."

She kissed both pictures repeatedly, holding on to them so tightly with both hands that her intense grip threatened to rip them.

"You will never leave me...I've transferred you from these pictures into my mind. You will be with me every step of the way. I've only managed to survive this long because of you. I know that...we can never be separated, so please don't think I'm abandoning you. I could never do that."

Carla placed the pictures to her heart, crying uncontrollably.

"I must focus on the physical world. I have a mission, and you are just as much a part of that as I am. There is a rebirth that's to take place very soon, and I have to kill off the weakness inside of me. You are my weakness, and I must let go. I'm sorry."

She rose from the milk crate and kissed the pictures once more before angrily kicking the crate into a dark corner of the cave. Doing what needed to be done was harder than she thought it would be. With everything inside of her, she wanted to compromise and keep the pictures, maybe even just one.

That wouldn't be right though, and it would be starting off on the wrong foot. There were so many thoughts running through her mind that she began to doubt what she should do. Carla closed her eyes and screamed; she needed to stop the voices in her head. Not the voices of her family or that of God, but her own voices. Voices of doubt.

Carla quickly stepped toward the fire and threw both pictures into the flames. She looked away because she could not watch the fire destroy what meant so much to her. She could smell the burning of the plastic, could hear the twisting and crackling of the pictures. It was a lot for her to deal with, so Carla moved to the entrance of the cave.

Resting her hand on the rigid wall, she stared out at the surrounding wooded area. Breathing deeply, taking in the fresh air in hopes of avoiding the burning plastic stench—the smell of her family burning in the back of the cave.

She walked fully out of the entrance, dragging her hand along the jagged wall on the way out. *Just one last punishment*, she thought. She couldn't help but to do it. The hardest thing she'd had to do since burying her daughters was now over. It hurt her to the core—it was a shock to her that she hadn't fainted. *That's a testament to your growing strength and resolve,* she assured herself while walking along the path leading back to the facility.

We are with you, Mommy, always and forever. She heard her children speak in her mind. *Do what you were chosen to do, dear. Only you can live this life. I'm proud of you,* her husband said. Carla talked with her family during the walk back to the facility. They spoke, and she responded.

HE HAD FOLLOWED Carla from the facility to her secret cave again. Same as he'd been doing for the past six months. He'd just spent an hour listing to the woman talking, laughing, and crying like a lunatic. And she continued talking to herself the whole way back to the Eagle squad. As he followed quietly through the woods, he could see and hear her going through every conceivable emotion known to man. She'd always been on the edge of snapping, he knew that. But that day, it was clear to him that Carla had finally lost touch with reality.

CHAPTER THIRTY-NINE

Sirus

To: Code Origin
Server: Scrambled Server

From: O'Sullivan, Sirus
Date: Aug 29, 2040 17:57:09 EST

Subject: Tomorrow

HELLO, MY NEW FRIEND. I'M CONTACTING you to let you know the day has come. I'll be there tomorrow afternoon to take my property. The fate of your people has already been decided. I want you to know that you have made a smart decision in contacting and working directly with me. Some things can't be changed or altered, but you can look out for yourself in the storm to come—and you have. Bravo to you.

I will come to the landing field of your Palace with a small security squad. Please have Mary ready and cuffed for me when I arrive. She will not be interested in coming with me, and I'd prefer to not deal with a childish outburst. Keep your squad inside of the facility...I say this for your safety, not mine. I take the smallest of movements as aggressive actions. Let's not turn a simple transaction into a blood-bath. That will take place the day after, when I have my property, and you have your assurance of the position you desire within my group.

I don't know what your opportunities will be as far as getting Mary outside, cuffed, and probably behaving like the child she is without the whole of your squad seeing the goings-on. It's not my problem; the only reason why I haven't ordered that Palace to be blown from the face of the planet is because she is inside of it. I will come tomorrow, and I will get my property one way or the other. I'm making sure you understand my position.

I received your message about the loss of the child. That does not bother me in the least. The lofty plans ahead of her will not coincide with raising children, so that is good news.

My units will move the day after tomorrow to take back the Palace from your people. They are finally trained up, and I look forward to seeing them in action. If you are lucky, I'll allow you to watch from a distance with myself. The genetic engineering in Palace-born humans is something to behold. Not sure if you have noticed anything...special about Mary from the time you haves spent in her presence. Probably not; your kind are on the more unintelligent side of the spectrum in respect to life in the galaxy.

That's enough chatter for one email. There are other things on my agenda for the day. I'll be seeing you tomorrow. Do your job, and you will have all that was promised.

PS. There will be another message coming to you later in the day. I've received intel on something you may want to know about someone living among you who has plans. Big plans. All of the details will be listed. Can't have someone ruining what we have planned. Take care of it as soon as you can.

Thank you,
O'Sullivan, Sirus

CHAPTER FORTY

Lonnie

WALKING INTO MELINDA'S POD, HE DIDN'T know if his facial expression gave him up. She was good at reading him, better at it than anyone he'd ever known. They'd spent a brief time in each other's lives, but the time they did spend was during a vital and trying situation. He thought that made an enormous difference. The trauma made them closer, which was why doing what he had to do was beyond hard.

Lonnie forced a smile. Walking to her bed, he removed his black hooded sweatshirt and draped it over the white sofa near the TV, which still played the violent videos—as if they hadn't seen enough to be thoroughly brainwashed yet.

"Happy to see you, Lonnie." She walked over to him and laid a kiss on his cheek, getting on the tips of her toes to do so while placing a hand on his shoulder. "I thought we were going down to the gym for a run though...put your sweater back on," she said as she slipped her jacket on over her white tank top.

"We are. I'd like to talk first, if that's okay," Lonnie said softly.

Melinda looked at him like she knew something was wrong. He could tell she sensed something. He knew her body language as well as she knew his.

"Of course we can talk. I've been hoping you would say that. I can tell something has been bothering you for the last week or two. Let's talk." Melinda pulled her arms from the sleeves of her jacket and hung it back up in the closet.

She walked over to the foot of the bed and sat, tapping the bed next to her, beckoning him to have a seat. Lonnie smiled and made his way over, the whole time wondering how he would ever be able to go through with it. The look on her face was pure concern for him and his needs.

He sat next to her and tried to speak, but nothing came out when he opened his mouth. He sat there like an idiot with his mouth agape, trying to begin—he didn't know how though. Melinda placed a hand on his knee. "C'mon, you know you can say anything to me. I know that you have been going through a lot, what with the battle coming and the important role you will play in that." She looked into his eyes.

"Well yeah, it's partly that...I guess." Lonnie didn't know how to start the conversation with her. He wanted to say so much, but he didn't know how to say something he'd never said before. Lonnie looked down at his knees.

"I know it's tough. Everyone in the Palace has been talking about you being the leader of the campaign. I don't know how you even get around this place without being mobbed on a daily basis. I know it's a lot, but people are just happy for you and the chance to serve under you when we all go outside. Now that the sickness has been fully lifted from this area of the planet, we won't need those huge protective suits. At the very least, that's worth a smile." Melinda put on the biggest smile she could conjure and clipped his chin with her index finger, prompting him to look up at her.

And there she was again, being the cutest, funniest, and most deserving person he'd ever met. He returned the smile and gesture, touching her chin with his fingers while placing a peck on her lips.

"I don't want to talk about any of that battle or war stuff. I just want to talk about us and how I feel about you." Lonnie's smile faded. "Is that okay?"

"Yes, I won't mention it again. I just know that its clo—"

"Stop, Melinda. I know what's coming, and I know what my place is at the core of it. I want to tell you how I feel about you." He grabbed both her hands and pulled her down to the bed with him. They both lay there on their sides, staring into each other's eyes.

"I'm just gonna come out and say it. Let me finish, then you can talk. How's that sound? Can you do that, Melinda?" Still holding on to her hands, Lonnie kissed them as he became emotional. He knew that she could see the tears forming in his dark brown eyes, because she began to cry in response.

"I know what love was. It wasn't a good thing, I know that...but what I feel for you cannot be named anything but that. I love you...I do. The way I feel about you is magical, something I didn't think existed. We grew up exactly the same way. Fending for ourselves down in the child center, then being thrust into the pods at ten years old. No one ever loved us, and I think that was a good thing. It taught us both how to find ourselves, our true selves. Honestly, I don't know if I ever accomplished that, but I'm working on it." Lonnie kissed both her hands again and smiled.

"I think they had it wrong though. Love early on can be a bad thing, but later in life, it's a different thing altogether. There is nothing wrong about what we have found in each other." He looked away for a second. He knew he was assuming her feelings, but he had a good idea that they were mutual. Melinda confirmed that when she squeezed his hands, causing him to meet her gaze once again.

"I love you, Lonnie, you know that. I'm not sure when it happened, but I've felt that way for some time. It feels good to be around you, and I feel safe when you are near. I suppose we could come up with a different word for it, but I see no reason to do such a thing. I'm in love with you, and nothing can change my mind about that." Melinda pulled her hands free from his grasp and placed them on the sides of his face, cupping his lower jaw and chin in her palms.

"I'm never leaving you, no matter what. Where you go, I go. If you die, then I die. Do you understand that?" When she said those words, Lonnie could no longer contain himself. He cried, and he cried loudly, pulling her close and hiding his face in her chest. The only thing he could think to himself was *why?* Why like this?

Melinda rubbed his head for a while, allowing him to get it all out and calm down. She said nothing, only consoled him. Lonnie didn't know why he chose to handle the situation in the way that he was, but it felt right. He wanted her to know how he felt about her; it was important. And hearing how she felt about him meant something to him—weird as that was.

"When it's all said and done, when the battle is over...maybe we can leave," she said.

"That's not possible, Melinda," Lonnie mumbled, his head buried in her chest. He picked his head up and looked her in the eyes while rolling on top of her and removing his shirt. He threw the black tee shirt on the side of the bed. With tears still in his eyes, straddling Melinda, he said he loved her again.

Melinda looked up at him, smiling, her cheeks wet from tears. She was beautiful to him, and he knew that in time, he would become even more wrapped up in her than he was at that moment. That was the reason he'd been ordered to do it. The order made sense, but it did not make doing the deed easy.

Hearing her say that she loved him was all he needed to hear, and he needed her to hear how he felt about her. That was important, more important than anything else in his life. No one else would ever hear those words from him again. He knew that.

"But we can try though, right?" Melinda said, staring up at him.

"In another life, in another time, we could have. They would never allow it, and sometimes things have to come before your own desires." Lonnie looked down at her, wanting to only remember her that way. In love, smiling, hopeful of the future. He leaned over her body to kiss her forehead, sliding his hand over the pillow next to her.

Again she grabbed his face, moving it down lower to kiss him. It would be the last kiss that they shared. Lonnie sat up and looked to his right, because he could not watch. He didn't have the heart to see it. His hands knew how to do the job without the use of his eyes.

Lonnie lifted the pillow and brought it down on Melinda's face as hard as he could. He thought about smothering her on the way up to her pod while on the elevator. One plan was to punch her in the face so hard that it knocked her out, then use the pillow to smother her. That plan was impossible; he could never strike Melinda in the face. The second idea was to bring the pillow down with such force and ferocity that the impact would daze or knock her out.

This would make the smothering easier. Lonnie did not want to feel her moving around, kicking and flailing for her life. He thought that a part of him would feel sorry for her and remove the pillow. He'd thought about that all night. What if he couldn't finish the job? It was a real source of anxiety for him. He was wrong though, on both accounts.

The way he'd forced the pillow on Melinda's face did not knock her out. That was stupid to think that it ever would, but only a stupid person would be in this situation to begin with. That was him: Lonnie, stupid with loyalty for those who'd created him and wanted to keep his people alive. To keep the planet alive. The pillow did nothing but make her panic, same as it would any living, breathing being.

Melinda screamed, or tried too, but the pillow did do a good enough job of muffling that sound. She did kick and flail about for a lot longer than Lonnie thought a human should without breath. He tried not to watch, but after a while of holding the pillow over her face, she got more scared and began to buck up from the bed, pushing him into the air.

Then the tears stopped on his end. It was no longer about Melinda and losing her. In his mind she was already gone. Then there was only the job of finishing the job. He didn't mind as much as he thought he would once he viewed it in that light. Lonnie forced his weight down on her body to stop her from moving, using his upper body strength to press the pillow harder against her face. That allowed him to finish the job.

Was that all she'd become to him? A job...? That didn't sound right to him, but he thought that maybe it was the correct term to use.

Teacher Simon said that there would be many sacrifices for the greater good. His own life may be forfeit at some point in the coming days or weeks, possibly months, depending on how many rebels were out there. Melinda was the first meaningful sacrifice he would lay at the feet of the Order, but he hoped she would not be the last.

CHAPTER FORTY-ONE

Mary

GAIN, SHE WOKE UP TO A bright light shining in her face in the infirmary of the rebel Palace. There wasn't a room full of people or any confusion on her part this time. Logan sat next to her, holding her hand. Mary quickly pulled her hand back from him.

"Where is my baby?" she said to him, staring a hole into the side of his head. Logan did not look her in the eye; he didn't look in her direction at all. Didn't speak. That was cause for concern. Mary began to sit up in the bed, but Logan placed a hand on her arm.

"Be careful, Mary, you aren't ready—"

She smacked his hand away from her arm. "I asked you a question. Bring me my child. I know how many months I was, so I know that it's possible the child still lives. I want to see him, bring him to me." She looked straight ahead at the white wall, trying not to lose her cool, trying to focus on the words and not the thoughts.

"Mary, you have to understand." Logan looked right at her as he rose from his seat.

"I don't need to understand anything. I need to see my child. Either bring him to me, or get someone who can. Bring me a nurse," Mary said.

Logan stood over her in his typical clothes. He wore a white thermal long-sleeve shirt and black cargo pants. His long blond hair was tied in a ponytail that went down the length of his back. He clasped his hands together vertically as if he were praying, placing them in front of his face. He did not speak right away. Mary began to shake. She grasped the sides of the gurney, trying not to blink, knowing that if she did blink one good hard time, the flood would follow.

"There is no baby...I'm sorry."

Mary exhaled. She was finally able to release the breath accumulating in her chest. She was certain she'd been holding her breath since the moment she woke up. The feeling of being empty weighed heavily on her the second she awoke. She knew the baby was no longer inside of her, but there had still been hope in her mind that she'd delivered early and the child was on a breathing machine. It was a farfetched thought, but it was all she had.

She had failed Jacob. He had died. And she couldn't even keep herself safe long enough to allow his child (a son, she thought for some reason) the chance to live. Mary lay back down on the gurney, pulled the white sheet over her face, and balled her eyes out. It was all she could do. While she cried, the Eagle leader stood there next to her. He did not move to touch or console her, and he did not speak. He simply stood there. What happened was no fault of Logan's; she would not take her grief out on him.

"I know it wasn't you. Who did it?" she seethed from beneath the sheet.

Still, Logan did not speak straight away. She could see his silhouette through the sheet, moving uncomfortably as he shifted his weight from one leg to the other.

"I'd like to tell you, but the truth is, I don't know. I have a few ideas, as I'm sure you do, but I don't know enough yet to say for sure." He paused. "I wish I had more information for you at this time, but that's something I'll have to get back to you on."

Mary watched as his form moved toward the exit door. From beneath the sheet, his shadow was just as imposing as his real-life body. The door opened and closed, leaving her in the infirmary all alone. Truly alone. First it was Jacob, and in short order, their child had also left her...No, was *taken away* from her. The difference meant everything. She had a good idea of who'd poisoned her food. She didn't need to ask how, she just knew. The second she'd started choking and feeling her stomach folding in on itself, she knew it was poison.

She turned on her side, facing the wall. Mary removed the sheet from over her head, feeling like a child for doing such a childlike thing in the presence of Logan. In her attempt to not look weak, she'd likely done the weakest thing she could have in the moment. She hoped that he could understand.

In all honesty, she wanted to feel worse about things than she did. She wished the child was there, wished that she could give birth to what she and Jacob created. But someone had made sure that wouldn't happen. Her mind was already moving on to something different, and that was adding a name to the growing list of people she wanted dead before she met back up with Jacob in another world.

CHAPTER FORTY-TWO

Carla

"YES BABY, THE PLAN IS IN place as we speak. And no, I did not forget the explosive charges. How could I?" Carla cackled loudly, no longer afraid of being heard. It would all be over soon anyway. Who cares if someone thought her a bit untangled? She'd been talking and laughing with her family all evening. Their company was the best company. They knew her so well and believed in what she was doing.

An AK-47 lay on her bed, along with a pistol equipped with an extended clip. Those were the weapons she planned to start the coup with. There were other stashes in the facility for her apostles to get to when they heard the shooting start. Her most trusted man was on standby, and he knew that the day of the changeover was tomorrow. She'd met with all five of her men the night before, and they'd all recited the devotion prayer. For her, that was enough.

Now that she was free from the shackles of her past, she could better focus on the plan, and it was a great plan. They only needed to take out the leaders in order to have full control of the squad. The majority of those within their group were scared men and women who would do anything for someone's approval, anyone's approval. It just so happened to be Logan's, because he was the leader...for the time being.

Truth was, every survivor was so decimated both mentally and emotionally that they were looking for something to believe in. Why not her? She was righteous and had a great message, one of salvation and togetherness.

She thought the time she was living in was the modern-day dark ages. The flock had become scattered, and they were afraid, lost even. It was her fate to bring them out of the darkness and renew the light of God. With him, they could achieve anything. There had to be a reason for the sickness, for all the death. She saw no other conceivable reason for such a thing other than the reckoning and rebuilding of the Lord's people.

"Hey Mark, you remember the priest who married us?" Carla laughed so hard she had to sit down on the bed. "He looked just like your uncle from Montana—it was so funny! I wish I still had the pictures."

After laughing so hard that her belly began to ache—some from the laughter, and some from the self-punishments she'd administered the night before—Carla got back to her feet and began laying out her attire for tomorrow's assault.

She had a bulletproof vest and tactical pants with plenty of hidden places for knives and small firearms. There was also her brown bomber jacket to cover the bulletproof vest. She'd have to wear it the entire day, as the assault was not planned until late afternoon. If Logan or any of those close to him saw her wearing a vest, they would become immediately suspicious. Talk had already begun circulating about Tony. No one knew where he was. The common consensus was that he took off on his own. Little did they know, Tony was buried beneath a few slabs of cement in the old child center. That would be made right within the next few days though. He deserved much better.

Carla made her way to the small white table near the sofa. Her Bible sat there opened to a passage, one of her all-time favorites.

"Luke 21:36. But stay awake at all times, praying that you may have strength to escape all these things that are going to take place, and to stand before the Son of Man." Carla spoke the words, placing a hand over the Bible and bowing her head in recognition to the glory. There were many smiles on her face that night, smiles that seemed to belong to multiple people. She hadn't been so happy in a very long time.

223

With her weapons and attire laid out for the next day, she was like a child the night before the first day of school. She could barely contain herself. For the remainder of the night, Carla stayed up talking about the old days with her family. Arguing, laughing, crying, and reflecting on the past along with what was to come in the future. A beautiful and enlightening future, if she had anything to say about it. And she did.

CHAPTER FORTY-THREE

Logan

H E KNEW WHAT NEEDED TO BE done, and he was sure that the right decision had been made with both the weapons and another decision he'd been going back and forth with for some time. Good things only lasted but for so long. His father used to say that all the time, and it was true. If given enough time, people would find a way to muddy the cleanest of surfaces. The world as it was that day was more than enough evidence to prove the theory.

Logan lay in his bed going over his thoughts. Tomorrow would decide the future of so many that he'd come to love and care about. He knew that sleep would not find him in the near future; he likely wouldn't sleep at all. If his decision was wrong, everything they'd achieved up to that point would have been for nothing.

He was not proud of the things he'd done in the last few days. If his father was looking down on him, he would not approve. But...if things went the way he planned, he just might be able to change the tide of the current situation of the world. Then his father would be forced to reassess his feelings on the decisions his son had to make.

Being a leader was never something that came easy to him. Growing up, it was always Jacob controlling the reins of anything they did together. Jacob was the captain of every baseball team they'd played on. He was the one who made the decisions about every activity they did. Logan had never really thought about it until he became the leader of the biggest rebel unit in the Midwest region of what was once Indiana.

Logan wished they'd taken over the Palace that Jacob and Mary had been in instead. Yeah, the colonizers had killed everyone before they could get inside, but there was always a chance that Jacob could have fought his way free. The thought made Logan chuckle under his breath. *To see Jacob over the age of forty...that would have been something to see.*

To think that his old buddy had been alive the whole time and living not far from him. While Logan was out fighting, killing, and trying to survive in the wasteland of the Old World, his old friend had been living it up in a plush Palace. Spending a lot of time with Mary, no less. Jacob had a way of getting the lucky draw on things like that. Logan smiled at the thought.

Everyone thought that leadership came naturally to him, but it didn't. It was something he had to work at—building trust, getting others to believe in his ideas and mission when they'd lost hope in everything they'd ever believed in. If he was being honest with himself, he had no idea how he'd managed it.

During that time though, he'd become very good at reading people. Seeing through the smiles, well-wishes, and pretty words. The real character of every man or woman hid somewhere behind their eyes. That person could not hide even if they tried; the eyes told the tale. He'd never been wrong about this.

Most would never act on their thoughts of deception and jealousy; the average man would always be willing to go with the flow. There were others though, others who could not rest until they got what they felt they deserved. In the last twenty years he'd, come across more than a few of them living among him and his people. Without fail he'd been successful in rooting out those characters. Tomorrow would be different though. It was time to do something bigger, on a grander stage than any before.

Logan smirked once more while sweeping the long blond strands from his face. He'd become so accustomed to sleeping outside in the cold, it made him feel uncomfortable to use the covers, so he lay on top of the blanket and sheets. His barrel chest and shoulders moved up and down slowly as he breathed calmly, and he laid his hands on his abdomen as he thought.

Hope that I made the right decision.

He wondered and hoped, but all there was to do was wait and see how things would play out. There were many events on the horizon. Not all of the moving pieces knew about each other, but he knew. And he was prepared. The one thing Jacob could never best him in was a certain game, a board game. That game was chess. Jacob never thought before he acted, and Logan overthought and planned out every single possible step before taking the first.

CHAPTER FORTY-FOUR

Mary

BACK IN HER OWN POD, MARY took a long hot shower. She needed it as badly as she had the day she arrived at the rebel Palace. The medics did a good job of keeping her alive, but keeping her clean was not high on the list of priorities it seemed. There was dried blood all over her lower body.

After the shower, she paced around her room, thinking of what she would say to the Eagle squad during the morning meeting. Logan had left a note under her door, alerting her of the meeting. The letter said there would only be a few key members present. He wanted to get to the bottom of what had happened to her.

At that meeting she planned to speak to Carla. She didn't know how she would get the terrible woman to admit what she'd done, but if Mary had to beat it out of her, then she would.

Dale had come to her pod earlier in the day. After she was released from the infirmary, he was waiting by the door when she got off the elevator. He was the kindest person she'd encountered in the rebel Palace. The intel specialist shared with her that he had a small list of those he thought responsible for her poisoning.

Mary had told him she had no interest in discussing such things at the time. She wanted to get showered and get some rest before taking on the world. Dale smiled and asked if he could get her anything before leaving. Mary assured him she was fine and gave him a big hug for caring. The man had blushed like a child as he made his way to the elevator.

She didn't care about his list. There was no reason for her to have a list; she knew who it was. Every member of the rebel group had come to visit her when she was in the infirmary after losing the baby. Everyone but Carla.

After her shower, she went to her closet to get comfortable clothing to sleep in. There were two articles of clothing she'd never seen before: a deep red leather jacket, and green fatigue pants with pockets, like most of the Eagle squad wore. The jacket had a folded piece of white notebook paper attached to it. Mary grabbed the hangers and draped the jacket and pants across the white sofa.

She snagged the folded note off the front of the jacket and read it.

Wear these tomorrow. It's time you start to look like a rebel if that's what you are going to be. No longer a Palace-born, you're part of the Eagle squad now, kid. We are on your side.

Mary didn't know how much she wanted to be a part of the rebel squad, but she didn't have much choice. From her perspective, there were two factions to choose from in the area, and the Eagle squad was the lesser of the two evils. After she righted the wrong done to her and Jacob's child, she would be more up to talking about being a rebel. There could be no unity until that debt was paid.

The loss of the child's life was not as tough on her as the loss of Jacob; it was almost as if she expected something like that to happen. She never saw herself as a mother. Maybe that just wasn't in the cards for her. There was a place for her in this life, and it would not be as anyone's woman, mother, or anything like that. She decided that while recovering from the poisoning. There were more important things that needed to be taken care of before any happiness could be achieved... by anyone. Mary decided to craft herself into a tool, a tool of redemption and payback.

Not just for herself or for Jacob, but for everyone. The sickness was brought on by Sirus and the others. She didn't know where they came from or what they were, but she knew they were not human. They were the enemy. Trying to be anything in life would be halted by them. The goal could only be to vanquish the planet of their presence. Her shot at love ended the day that Jacob died, and her thoughts of being a mother were squandered just days ago at the hands of someone there in the rebel Palace. There would be no more delusions of grandeur for her.

Mary stopped pacing, halting at the edge of the bed. She sat down and lay back with her feet still on the ground. Looking up at the ceiling, she thought about her new goals. Carla...Sirus...then every teacher in every Palace she could find. Every security officer in every van still roaming the world, looking to kill or kidnap any survivor they could find. That was the new mission.

She was tired of being looked at like a child. The day she lost the baby would be the last day she would ever be anyone's victim. Now was the time for her to become all that she could be, to force her will on all others. Lying there on the gurney crying, screaming to Jacob in her mind to forgive her, she'd made up her mind that she was tired of crying.

There was a lot lost on her end, but she'd gained things as well. One was her freedom, and that could be whatever she willed it to become. She could change lives with the things she knew and the different talents she had. It had not been lost on her or most of the Eagle members that she was a deadeye shot with remarkable reflexes, and a knack for hand-to-hand combat. Those things had value.

Mary scooted back on the bed and wrapped herself in the comforter. For the first time in her life, she did not have trouble falling asleep thinking about silly things like the Greater Understanding Program, love, escaping, her baby, or survival. She had everything anyone could ask for in this new world. Her mind, her health (most of it), and access to weaponry. Everything else could be achieved as long as the other three were present. That night, Mary slept like a log. She didn't toss or turn, she had no dreams...just silence.

CHAPTER FORTY-FIVE

Lonnie

THE TWO MEN SAT AT THE same white table, in the same small room with no windows in a secret area of the Palace. Teacher Simon sat at one side of the table, and Lonnie at the opposite. Lonnie kept both hands by his sides, his finger tapping the handgun on his hip. He enjoyed the sound of the steel against his fingernail. The tapping was rhythmic and distracted his mind from thinking about other things.

Teacher Simon sat a foot away from the table because of his long legs. His fingers, doing that odd thing that they did—massaged the tabletop in small circles. The habit no longer made Lonnie sick, it simply annoyed him. He wanted to shoot a hole in the man's forehead. Maybe one day he would do just that.

"Tomorrow we move out. Are you ready?" Teacher Simon said.

"Was the body not delivered to your office?" Lonnie said in a cold voice, staring the very tall and slender man in the eye.

"Why yes, it was, but that was not my question."

"I heard your question. The fact that you received the body should answer your question. I would not have killed someone I cared for if I was not ready. Can we not waste planning time on such nonsense?" He did not flinch while speaking. Studying the face of the teacher, Lonnie finally saw him for who he was.

All of the teachers were no more than instruments of the Order. He didn't know if they were ever decent people; sometimes he didn't know if they were people at all. That day and every day after, he didn't care who or what they were. Lonnie decided to devote himself to the cause. All strings had been severed.

He was no longer Lonnie, man of African descent, living inside of a Palace facility in Old Indiana. He was no longer chasing the Greater Understanding Program to go out into the world and fix what was wrong. That could be someone else's calling. He was now Captain Number One, leader of the Order's ground forces. Nothing else mattered but accomplishing the goal of destroying every survivor living out in the world. After the immediate area was safely cleaned up, he would ask to be moved to other parts of the planet to do the same thing. Until his last breath, he would be a hunter of those who sought to destroy the planet. That purpose was worthwhile, at the very least it would keep him terribly busy.

"I see. My apologies, Lon—"

"Captain! Captain Number One. Do not call me Lonnie. From hence forth, never use that name again. That person is no more. Understand?"

"I do, sir," Teacher Simon said, removing his hands from the table and placing them in his lap.

CHAPTER FORTY-SIX

Mary

THE NEXT MORNING THERE WAS A knock on her door. It was Dale. He asked her to get dressed and to wear the clothes that were put in the closet for her. She knew there was a meeting scheduled for the morning, but no one had ever come to get her from her pod. Mary quickly brushed her teeth and got dressed. Her long dark hair hung behind her in a thick ponytail. The jacket and pants were a perfect fit. She'd never worn anything like either of them, and they felt good. They felt right.

When she walked out of her pod, Dale was standing there to the left of the door.

"You look great, Mary." Again, he blushed and struggled to keep eye contact. A far cry from the know-it-all intel specialist she'd met only a short time ago.

"Thank you, Dale, I appreciate those words. Is there a reason why you came to collect me from my pod? Is everything okay?" Mary asked, looking concerned. She didn't want anything to get in the way of her finding and questioning Carla. It took all that she had not to go find the woman the night before.

"I'll fill you in on the way outside. Here, put this on your side there." Dale strapped a handgun to a clip hanging from the top right of her fatigue pants. The weight of the gun felt right on the pants. It made her feel safe, even powerful.

"Will I need that this morning?" she asked, looking left and right up the hallway. No one was walking the halls this morning as they usually did.

"Always best to be safe, Mary. You are a rebel now, and we must always be ready for anything. Let's go." Dale began walking toward the elevator. Mary followed closely behind, listening to the jingle of the pistol hitting against the metal latch of the clip and the sound of her boots clicking against the floor as she kept pace with him.

It was hard for her to believe what she'd become. The things that she had to go through in order to find herself. She was now the closest thing to her true self that she'd ever been. Even with Jacob, she felt like a child trying to appease an authority figure. Not that he'd made her feel that way, because he hadn't. It was her own self-doubt and insecurities. Conclusions from her upbringing in the Palace helped to cloud her mind as well. All that was gone, and what she was left with was someone she could be proud of.

The elevator door opened up as soon as he touched the button. They both walked inside.

"All of the Eagle squad except a few chosen members were told to stay in their pods until one of the lieutenants or the captain said different. Everyone is down on the field with Logan, waiting for you. The meeting will take place there." Dale looked worried.

"Why outside?"

"He didn't say why. All I know is what I just told you. Everyone is in the dark. He's never done anything like this before." Dale pushed the first-floor button. The elevator came to life and began moving down the quiet floors of the Palace.

Mary and Dale got off the elevator and headed to the central plaza, which had no security. That was also strange. There were always armed guards there in case a white van came by or the colonizers made a move to take the Palace back.

They walked out the front doors and headed out to the field, where no red flags stood. The flags that once symbolized the quarantine area were gone; they never meant anything to begin with. Everyone that was ever meant to die from the sickness was dead. The Order had packed survivors inside of those facilities for their own experiments to create what they felt were perfect humans.

Walking down to where the others were standing, she thought to herself, *There is no such thing as a perfect human. By nature, they are flawed... we are flawed.* Anything more or less was no longer human at all. Maybe the human race was not meant to live forever.

"Are you okay?" Dale asked.

"Yes, I'm fine. I'd like to know what this is all about." She noticed a small object in the knee area of her pants jabbing against her. Mary stopped and went to unbutton the pocket there.

Dale grabbed her hand. "We don't have time for that now, Mary, we're already late. You can mess with your clothing when this is all said and done. I know you don't commonly wear things like that, but Logan thought you would feel more like a part of the group if you dressed like us."

"Okay, okay, it's just something hitting against my knee," she said as she began walking, jogging a bit to catch up to his quickening pace.

As they got closer to the group, she could make out who was there on the field. She saw Logan in his green jacket with the red stripe going down the side, his blond hair tied in a tight ponytail that blew in the wind behind him. There was Carla, wearing a jacket as well. Hers looked like Logan's, minus the red stripe. She was no captain. Soon she wouldn't be much of anything. Mary clenched her fist as she bit her lip and did all she could not to take off running at the group and attacking the woman.

Derek was attending as well. She remembered the big bald gunner who'd carried her away from the other Palace she'd collapsed outside of. He stood next to Carla, and Mary wondered if he would protect the woman if she attacked. The two seemed close enough; he definitely listened to whatever the snake said. Mary thought that when she attacked Carla, it would be best to hurt him first...killing them both was not out of the question. If he was a friend to Carla, then he was no better than her. Mary spit in the grass as she walked toward the group.

The top medic, Marcella, was there, wearing a long black jacket over a flimsy white hospital coat. Mary thought the woman looked utterly ridiculous. There were two other men, one bald, and the other a redhead with freckles. Both as big as Logan. They stood close to him.

When Mary and Dale merged with the group, no one spoke. Mary walked up to Carla immediately. She didn't care what the meeting was about or what Logan had to say. She could only focus on one thing.

"Why did you do it?" Mary asked pointedly. Derek moved closer to Carla.

"I'm sorry? What are you talking about, little girl?" Carla said with a look of surprise on her face.

"Don't play games with me. I know it was you. I don't need anyone to tell me any different. I'm asking you to your face, giving you the opportunity to be straight with me. You must have some kind of morality." Mary began to step between Carla and Derek.

Logan moved quickly to her side and grabbed her arm, easily moving her back. She tried to pull away from his grasp, but to no avail.

"Wait, I'm not done talking," Mary said loudly.

"Control her, or she will get hurt," Derek barked in her direction. "Don't go throwing around accusations. That's not the way we move in this squad."

"Mary, relax. That's what we're here for," Logan said calmly. He spit a sunflower seed out of his mouth. "Don't ruin it," he said in a lower voice.

She calmed down and stopped fighting a losing battle with his strong grip. Dale moved close to her and placed a firm hand on her arm. The others looked confused, staring from person to person.

"What's the meaning of this, Logan? We've never had a meeting quite like this. And why were the other members ordered to their rooms? What's going on, sir?" The curly redheaded man was saying what they all were thinking.

Logan lifted a hand to the man, gesturing for him to wait. "All answers will be revealed here shortly. Just wait."

"Wait for what?" Carla sneered, looking in Mary's direction.

Logan smiled, giving her the same hand. Mary looked to her left at Dale and mouthed, *What's he doing?* Dale shrugged his shoulders and lifted his eyebrows. He was lost as well.

Just then, a humming sound could be heard, coming over a group of trees to the north of their standing position. The sound became louder as a flying object appeared in the sky.

Logan pointed at the thing buzzing and humming in their direction. "Our final guest has arrived." He spit out another sunflower shell. Everyone looked in the direction of the object coming toward them.

"Is that a chopper?" Marcella said.

"Yes, that's a chopper," Derek said. "Who is it though? And why are we standing out in the open like dodo birds?" The man was looking to Carla for what seemed to be direction. Mary noticed that Carla subtly shook her head. That put Mary on guard, and she slid her hand down the side of her body near the gun.

"Before anyone does anything stupid, listen up." Logan looked around to the group.

"I have ten snipers in the windows of the Palace. Please don't attempt to run or pull a weapon. If you do, you will be shot dead right here on the field. We are going to get to the bottom of this now. By the end of the day, everything should be...better for everyone."

"What type of treachery is this, Logan? Who's in that chopper?" Carla stepped toward Logan, but Derek grabbed her arm, pulling her back to his side.

"As I said, we are going to get to the bottom of this. And I have an idea. Shut up and wait."

They stood silently for what felt like five minutes but was probably only one. The tension was thick, and everyone was on edge. The only person who knew what was going on was Logan, and Mary didn't know if she could trust him or not. Who could be coming in a chopper? Maybe someone from a different rebel team? They all stood with their backs to the Palace, facing the chopper as it moved closer to them, emitting a sound louder than any she'd ever heard. The engine of the flying object was deafening.

The blades on the helicopter swung so hard and wide that the wind nearly blew her off balance. She reached out to grab Dale's arm to steady herself. He looked as nervous and curious as she did.

"What's going on, Dale! Tell me!" she screamed over the sound of the helicopter, which was landing by that point.

"I don't know, I swear!" Dale screamed at her while blocking his face with both forearms. The wind was severe. They all had their arms up, trying to block the gusts of air from whipping against their faces. Everyone but Logan. He stood tall, cracking sunflowers seeds with his front teeth and spitting them to the side like he always did.

That's when the chopper door opened and the blades came to a slow spin. When she saw them, her vision went red and her adrenaline spiked. She immediately went for her gun, but Logan raised both hands. "Do not pull your guns. I told you what will happen if you do so." There were others on the field who'd had the same idea when they saw the people coming from the chopper.

"What are we doing, Logan? Tell us something," Dale said, loud enough to be heard by the group. No one looked back at Logan as they settled into their attack stances, hands hovering over their weapons.

"I won't repeat myself. If you touch your guns, you will be shot down. Just wait...No one is in danger," Logan said as he began walking toward the group of men. There were four Palace security agents, and in the middle, there he was. Sinister smile and all. The same smile he'd showed her when he gave his word that she and Jacob could go free. The same smile he probably wore as he'd ordered her lover to be shot like an animal on a field much like the one she stood on now.

It was Sirus. Sirus and his security. Mary felt as though she would faint at the sight of him. She wanted so badly to pull her gun and squeeze the trigger until no more bullets came bursting form the barrel. He was there in her presence. She didn't have to get into the other Palace—he could be killed right now, if she only had the courage to do so.

Mary started moving toward Sirus and the team of security that accompanied him. Dale pulled her back. "Don't move, Mary. Logan isn't messing around. Our snipers will shoot you if he gave them orders to do so. Who is that with the security? And why doesn't he wear a vest or have a weapon?"

Mary swung around to face him, her eyes on fire. "That's Sirus, the creator of the Palace program. The architect of the sickness that killed everyone you loved. He's the reason all of this happened. That's him."

Dale, Carla, Derek, and the other two men whose names she didn't know quickly snapped their necks to look at her. Some in disbelief, some in shock. Everyone but Logan; he walked toward Sirus and shook the program director's hand. Marcella gasped at what she saw.

"He's a traitor...I knew it," Carla spoke up.

Logan waved for them to come closer. "Get over here. Let's talk... That's why he's here. Maybe we can all help each other." Logan smiled while looking directly at Mary. The rebel leader turned back to Sirus and said something she couldn't hear. Sirus nodded in agreement and patted Logan on the back as he walked past him and came toward the Eagle group. Her stomach went weak. *Does he mean to give me back to Sirus and the Order?*

CHAPTER FORTY-SEVEN

Mary

S HE COULDN'T BELIEVE WHAT LOGAN WAS doing. Why would he shake Sirus's hand? Mary starting to fear she was being double-crossed. There was nothing to talk about; they should be putting a bullet in his head.

They all stood in a big circle. Sirus planted himself near the middle of the circle, facing Mary, staring at her and smiling. The four security guards waited behind him with their weapons drawn but not pointed at anyone. Logan stood about a foot in front of her, but to the side. Dale stayed right by her. Mary was surprised that the loudmouthed Derek had said nothing, and neither did Carla.

"Mary..." Sirus said, allowing the word to slide out of his mouth. "I've missed you, dear. How are you?"

She was close enough to take one step and spit in his face, and she desperately wanted to do so. Anger wasn't the word. Mary was boiling inside. There was no longer fear or wonder for Sirus, it was all hate and fury. That wouldn't move him though, she knew that. He wouldn't respond to such immature emotions, nor did she want him to see how much he was affecting her by just being in her presence.

"I've been doing okay, Sirus. And how are you? What brings you here today?" she asked in a voice as calm as she could manage.

"Well, let's see," Sirus said in a high-pitched playful voice as he kicked the grass with his shiny black shoes. "I've come to retrieve something that belongs to me, of course."

Carla stepped forward. "You're here for her? Take her and leave now."

Sirus did not look in her direction. He moved closer to Mary. Dale followed suit and did the same, moving closer to her side.

"Captain Logan...that is your name, correct? Muzzle your animal." He tilted his head slightly in Carla's direction without taking his eyes off Mary. "She should know to speak when spoken to." He moved around Mary in circles, looking her up and down.

"No man speaks for me," Carla growled.

"If you continue to address me without my permission, no one will speak for you." His neck snapped around so that he could face her. The movement looked unnatural. He winked and gave Carla that winning smile. "Final warning."

Derek whispered something to Carla. She nodded and did not respond.

Sirus turned his attention back to Mary. His eyes roaming all over her body made her feel disgusting. Logan said nothing.

"Anyways...How is Jacob?" The smile on his face vanished and left nothing but coldness it its wake. His head slanted to the side, studying her to see how she would react to such a vile question.

Still managing to keep her calm, Mary slid her hands inside of her jacket pockets, hiding her shaking fists inside. "He is no longer among the living. I'll see him again someday, I'm sure of that. Work to be done here first though."

"Touché, my dear. Touché. Hey, maybe a version of you is still with him in a parallel universe. Anything is possible, am I right?" Sirus spun on his heel, meeting the gaze of everyone there on the field.

"Logan, why are we all here?" The redheaded lieutenant looked at Logan. "What are you doing here, man? This is the enemy."

"I'm doing this for all of us," Logan said while looking at Dale. The two were close. Mary knew that.

"I'm no one's enemy, here. Father would be a better moniker for me as far as you all are concerned, but I forgive your ignorance. Let's get

241

down to business." Sirus made his way to Logan and grabbed both of his gigantic hands.

"Thank you, my son. And the rest of you should thank your captain as well. He saved all of you from dying. You owe him many thanks." He dropped Logan's hands, and within a few steps made his way to Marcella's side with unnatural speed.

"What the..." Derek said, taking a step back from the circle. The large man was clearly confused by the speed of someone who looked Sirus's age. Mary knew Sirus was much older than any of them could guess. Not even she could understand the scope of his existence and how far or deep it transcended time and a billion universes.

"Marcella, I know you, and I know you have no place here. You, my dear, are innocent. A mindless worker bee who has always done what was asked of her. Sturdy and reliable." He touched her face softly. "Do as you have been doing since I arrived. Keep quiet and watch the show." In another step or two, Sirus appeared next to the redheaded lieutenant. The man nearly jumped out of his skin at the sight of the Palace creator standing at his side when he'd just been clear across the circle.

"Michael, besides taking advantage of some of the women in your camp on dark and lonely nights, you are not disloyal to the cause, as pointless and hopeless as it is. You are a team player. Do like Marcella and keep quiet."

Sirus brought his index finger and thumb across his lips, telling Michael to zip it. "I know that you all view me as the enemy, as one of you so eloquently put it, but I'm here to help with some dissension among your ranks. And I'll get what I came for." He looked over at Mary. "And you, Captain Logan, will find out who poisoned the young lady, causing her to lose her child. The same person planning to take leadership for themselves."

Mary's mouth opened slightly, and she immediately closed it, trying to hide any reaction.

"Yes," Sirus continued. "I know about that. Then I'll leave, and you all can get back on track as far as creating failing plans to stop what cannot be stopped."

Logan spit out a mouthful of shells and stepped up calmly.

"I'm sure you have things to do, I know that I do," the Eagle captain said. "Who tried to kill Mary, and who is threatening my group with mutiny? I'd like all of my men to hear the truth, then you can take her and go back to wherever you come from." Logan did not look in her direction. He'd been avoiding eye contact with her since Sirus began speaking.

"You are not taking Mary anywhere. I don't care what anyone told you. Over my dead body," Dale said as he jumped in front of Mary.

"That is likely, young man," Sirus said.

Dale flinched at the notion. Upon noticing his failing posture, he put the stick back in his spine and stood up straight.

"Mary has a way of making the men fall in love, as you would say. Another man in love, another man dead by the end of the day." Sirus burst out in laughter.

"Well, do what you must but I will not al—" Dale began to say.

"That's enough of this!" Carla suddenly pushed Derek to the side as she spoke in a loud voice.

Logan raised his left hand. He held no weapon, so the gesture confused Mary. Then it occurred to her that he could be sending a signal to his snipers, if there really were any.

Carla pulled a small handgun from her hip that had a clip longer than the actual gun attached to it. Before Sirus's guards could react to her movements, it was too late. Derek tried to grab her, but she was too fast.

There was no sound but that of multiple gasps from the crowd and clicking. Repetitive clicking. Carla stood there in the middle of the circle, gun aimed at Sirus's head, squeezing the trigger over and over. But the gun only clicked. She quickly tossed the weapon to the side and pulled a bigger handgun with a regular-sized clip from her jacket. Again, the gun did nothing but click. No shots were fired.

"I thought I asked you to make sure this did not happen?" Sirus stared at Logan, shaking his head back and forth.

Logan just lifted both hands in the air and shrugged his shoulders.

"Well, I guess we know who planned to kill Mary and take over the group. If any of you haven't been keeping up, it's the gun-welding mountain lion there with the broken firearms." Sirus turned to one of his security guards and nodded as he moved out of the way.

"Proceed," Sirus said once he'd stepped to the side.

The security officer lifted the semi-automatic rifle and aimed it at Carla, who stood there holding the gun that would not fire, looking dumbfounded. The rifle erupted, sounding like thunder rolling over the horizon. Multiple bullets tore into Carla in a vertical line. The bullets landed in her stomach, moving all the way up to the top of her skull. The impact lifted the skin off her head, hair attached and all. When it was done, the top of her head rested against her face, like a baseball cap turned to the side.

It all happened so fast, no one said anything or even moved. Including Carla. She stood there like the rest of them, unaware that she'd died. Her eyes went from Derek, then to Mary. Her hand moved up to touch her face, which had a hole through the cheek. Pulling her hand away from her face, she looked at the blood there and crumpled into a clump of limp muscle and bone.

Marcella screamed and took off running toward the Palace. Mary caught a glimpse of her face as she ran by, and there was pure terror in her eyes. The bald lieutenant whispered something to Logan, then ran after Marcella.

"No reason to run my dear! If you don't attempt to hurt me, then I won't have them hurt you. We are supposed to be playing nice!" Sirus screamed after the woman as she sprinted toward the Palace doors. Then the program director turned to Derek.

"I know that you loved the woman there." He pointed to the twitching body on the field that was once a fierce lieutenant for the Eagle squad. "But she was never going to be with you in that way. No matter how much you went along with her constant droning on and on about her God." Sirus made a pouty face at Derek, purposely goading the big ill-tempered man.

"You people really should get rid of the TVs in your pods. Even though they are not operational on your end, I can still view and hear you through them. Believe it or not, Carla was mainly interested in talking to her dead family members in her mind and beating the hell out of herself. She thought one of your gods wanted her to punish herself.

"If you live through this encounter with me and get the chance to take her body back to your facility, you will find evidence of self-abuse. There's also a body buried in the child center. The young man she killed and buried went by the name of Tony. So, in a way, I've done a service for you all." Sirus bowed.

Derek didn't seem to hear anything that Sirus said to him. He stared at Carla's body and began shaking. Mary had heard enough about the man's temper to know what was coming. His eyes turned from Carla's body to Mary, and she could see the hopelessness in his gaze. At that point, she knew he had no interest in living anymore.

"Derek, don't do it," Logan said. "It won't work."

The words didn't get through to Derek, who pulled a shotgun from beneath his own bomber jacket. Mary had no idea how he hid such a big weapon in the jacket, but he was a monster of man. He was big, but he was no fool. Instead of aiming at Sirus, Derek turned and began letting off shells at the security team that accompanied him.

BOOM! There went a leg, flopping through the air. Another BOOM! A shotgun shell smashed the skull of another man. Bone and brain fragments went flying. Derek was screaming while shooting. He killed two men before rapid rifle ammo peppered his body like Carla's.

Mary had no words. She was so fixed on what was happening she never noticed that Dale had grabbed her and pulled her down to the grass. He was covering her body with his own. From the ground, she watched as Sirus stood there in the middle of the firefight between Derek and his men, and not one bullet struck him. They all seemed to go around or through him. He only smiled, looking back and forth at the carnage and smiling.

Every shot riddled Derek's upper body. There had to have been ten to twelve shots in his chest before he dropped down to one knee and let the shotgun fall from his hand. His eyes went dead, the brown irises looking milky, almost translucent. He swayed back and forth on one knee, heaving and trying desperately to catch his breath.

"Go on, kill each other. I do not care for these security officers. They are your own people. They have no genetic enhancements. Dime a dozen, all of them! Do what you do best; kill, and then kill some more." Sirus slowly walked over to Derek and pushed his body over. "Meat bags that never learn. I'm disappointed in myself for not designing you all better," Sirus said.

Logan stood to her right. He'd pulled something from his jacket pocket. It was small and seemed to glow. It didn't appear to be a gun. Maybe a bomb or something like that. His face was focused as he kept his sights on Sirus.

"Kaden, shoot the others, now!" Logan screamed at the last standing lieutenant on their side. "Shoot them! I'm going to take this fucker out while we have the chance!"

It all happened in slow motion. Mary wanted to get up and help. She wanted to get at Sirus, but she wouldn't have known what to do to hurt him. He was some king of god, impervious to bullets or any kind of harm. All she could do was watch.

The redheaded Kaden pulled two handguns from his pants and began shooting at the two remaining guards. He was able to down one of them with a well-placed headshot. The bullet went through the glass face shield the guard wore, leaving it cracked and filling with blood as the man collapsed to the grass. The second guard was not so easy to kill. After taking two bullets to the chest, the guard continued to shoot at the lieutenant, spraying wide with the rifle. He got lucky, and one of the bullets clipped Kaden in the throat. Blood squirted out as the man dropped his dual pistols and grabbed at his neck. He looked like he was trying to keep the blood inside as he rolled around on the grass, trying to scream. His mouth was wide open, but no sound came.

And still, Sirus stood in the middle of the firefight, looking pleased by what was happening, not bothering to move or get out of the way. Logan ran across her field of vision and dove over her and Dale. In one hand was the glowing mystery object. The other held a revolver. When he dove, she heard a loud sound that could have been a cannon being fired. *BOOM!* The side of the remaining guard's head exploded. The man fell to the side, leaving no one but Sirus, who was turning in circles and laughing. She'd never seen him so happy.

Mary moved from beneath Dale, screaming and pushing him.

"Let me up, Dale! Let me go, please! I have to help," Mary said.

"I can't, Mary. There is nothing we can do to stop him. Just stay down!" He lowered his voice and spoke in her ear. "Let Logan handle this. He has a plan. He lured Sirus here by lying and saying he would hand you over. He just needed to get close enough to use the weapon on him."

"What weapon?" she said.

"The glowing thing in his hand. It's enormously powerful. We have to stay out of the way. And Lieutenant Kristopher followed Marcella back to the Palace not to console her, but to put the soldiers on standby. I'm sorry, but I had to lie to you. We knew about Carla, after the poisoning, not before. Logan used her and her hot temper to test out his theory about Sirus—that no manmade bullets could hurt him."

While he quickly explained what was happening in an attempt to keep her from interfering or getting herself killed, Logan and Sirus were speaking to each other. They both stood about ten feet apart. Logan's body was turned in such a way that the small glowing weapon could not be seen in his hand.

"I thought we could avoid all of this," Sirus said.

"Me too, but here we are, and what else is there to do? You don't have a weapon, and I do," Logan said as he grinned at Sirus.

"You can't be that dumb, can you? How about this...you give me what belongs to me, and I allow you to live, at least a little longer than you will if you keep up this attitude."

Logan tossed the revolver to the ground. "You aren't leaving here with Mary; she's one of us now. I'm sorry to have lied to you, but I had to get you out of that Palace somehow."

"But what's going to keep me from simply taking her? You three can't stop me." Sirus laughed as he took a step toward Logan.

"How about this?" Logan lifted his hand and brought the hidden object into Sirus's view, pointing the glowing weapon directly at his head.

Mary's body filled with joy at the sight of the smile melting away on the program director's face. The hideous, murderous smile crumbled when he laid eyes on the strange weapon. Veins bulged in his forehead as he took a slight step backward.

"Where did you get that?!" Sirus screamed. The panic in his voice was music to Mary's ears. "Tell me *now!*" He took another step backwards. "YOU CANNOT WEILD A WEAPON OF THE LOHAR!"

"Found it in the basement of the facility we took over," Logan said with the calmness of a Sunday morning. To hear him speak was an oddity based on the situation. The man never spoke with urgency regardless of what was going on.

"There were two of them. I have one, and the most trusted member of my squad has the other. I wonder...Does each Palace have weapons like these? I've shot it before, and it's very powerful. So powerful that it knocked an entire wall off my shooting hangar with one shot." Logan took a step toward Sirus.

"You don't know what you are doing, human. Trying to use such a weapon that is not calibrated to your body could kill you. You don't know what you hold there in your hand." He took another step back.

"Oh, I know. As I said, I shot it once. It knocked me out for a little bit. The way I see it though, if I focus all of my own energy into another shot, it may kill me or hurt me badly but...what would the shot do to you? I know that manmade bullets can't hurt you, but based on your behavior now, I think that this may hurt you." Logan took another step in his direction. "If not kill you."

"Don't be silly...kill me? That's not possible." Sirus bluffed a smile as he lifted both hands into the air. "Don't shoot," he said as he looked at Mary.

No sooner had he raised both hands in the air than they all heard the sound of a horn. A loud horn. It sounded off over and over. Sirus kept both hands in the air.

"What is that?" Logan asked Sirus.

"I have no idea, my son. Why don't you put the weapon down before things get out of hand. Don't kill yourself for no reason. I can't be killed—that's not a lie. And if you cared to check the current situation, you would see that the odds are not in your favor."

"Logan, look!" Dale screamed. He reached up with his right hand and pointed over the horizon. In the far distance, there were hundreds of what looked like soldiers coming toward them.

Who are those people? Mary wondered.

"Looks like some of my friends have shown up. And guess what?

Much like Mary being outside of the Palace, their—special talents—are no longer suppressed by the force field we built around the structure." Sirus looked over at Mary and offered a slanted grin.

"Surely you have been feeling your strengths come to life since you have left the Palace you were born in? From insignificant things like easily assessing others' height and weight, to bigger things, like increased speed, strength, and...how should I say"—Sirus paused—"a hunger for violence."

Mary was shocked by the accuracy of his description. She realized that the things he said were quite true.

"You see, my children, the irony has always been, while it was true that the hundred-yard radius was never in place to protect my Palace-born from a sickness, we did build the safeguard to protect the outside from them. I like to call this new experiment Homo sapiens 4.0." Again, Sirus laughed maniacally. While laughing, Sirus raised one of his hands to the sky. "Look up."

During the arguing, killing, and being dragged or slammed to the ground, neither Mary nor Logan nor Dale noticed that the once-bright morning sky had become dark as night. The field was covered in darkness. But it wasn't only the field—as far as the eye could see was darkened. She'd been so focused on Sirus, she'd totally missed the change.

Mary and Dale rolled over just enough to look up into the sky. She thought she was dreaming. What had parted the skies was so big, it was hard to even fathom.

It was a ship of some sort. A *spaceship*, she thought. It was the shape of a triangle, but it was massive. The size of a mountain, if she had to compare it to something.

"Oh my god...what the hell is that?" Dale said. The fear could be heard in his voice.

There was more than just the one black triangular flying object cutting through the clouds. There were even smaller ships of the same shape. The sky was littered with them. Before she knew what was happening, Dale was upright, grabbing her hand and pulling her to her feet.

Mary could see that he was scared, she was too—but she did not want to leave Logan by himself with Sirus.

"Mary, let's go. I have to keep you safe!" Dale screamed to her.

Mary shook loose from his grip. "No, I'm not leaving. This is my moment to do something, and I will not run. You go back to the Palace and tell everyone to stay inside."

"I'm not leaving you," he said.

Mary saw Sirus making a move while Logan was preoccupied looking up into the sky at the humongous structure descending upon them.

"Logan! Watch out!" But it was too late. Sirus was too fast.

By the time Logan could set his sights back on Sirus with the glowing weapon, the much quicker being was already upon him.

The glowing object dropped from Logan's hand, instantly losing its aura. It went back to looking like a dull piece of metal before it hit the ground. Sirus's back was to her as he and Logan were chest to chest, almost like they were in an embrace. Logan tried to speak, but there was something shiny in his mouth causing him to choke on his words. Mary began to walk toward him, but she was afraid.

"You should have given me what was mine, and you could have lived, Captain. There are no heroes here. She is flesh of my flesh, blood of my blood, the first of her kind. Created with my own DNA. She belongs to me in every possible way!" Sirus screamed into Logan's face as he pulled the sharp knife from the bottom of his chin.

Blood splashed onto the front of Logan's jacket. The rebel leader fell to his knees and then forward. Face down, he lay in the grass, much like Jacob had. The sight caused Mary to relive the event over again.

Sirus's back was still to her as Dale tried to pull her away. But Mary would not run way again. She turned to Dale and pushed his arm away from hers. "Go now! Go back to the Palace and get everyone as far away from this place as possible. If there is an underground exit, take them to it. Go Dale. No point in us both dying."

The biggest ship in the sky emitted a disturbing sound. It was similar to that of a horn, but it was inhuman. The sound seemed to hurt Dale's brain. He grabbed his head and went down to one knee. Mary helped him up.

"Please, Dale, just go!" The man did not answer. He just took off running toward the Palace. Mary turned back toward Logan and Sirus.

Logan was crawling toward her, coughing up so much blood and gore. Sirus went to where Logan had dropped the weapon and kicked it away. He looked up into the sky and raised his hands into the air once more. The ship let off the squealing horn once again.

"I-In-In...yrr *pokrrt*..." Logan tried to talk through the blood, but she couldn't make out the words. Mary ran toward Logan, sliding on her knees in the grass. With her face close to his, she tried to comfort him, but he pushed her away.

"No...no...p-pock...pocket. In your pocket!" The words seemed to bubble from his mouth, but she could make out his message. "You...it's you, Mary. I...trust...trusted you. I...don't think the...w-weapon...will h-hurt you." She could see that trying to speak was taking a lot out of him. Logan rolled over onto his back, breathing heavily.

Still on the ground, she felt for the object that was hitting against her knee earlier as she and Dale had walked onto the field. There was something there. Mary unbuttoned the pocket and pulled out the small piece of metal. At once she felt one with the object. The feeling of power emanated through her body as the thing glowed in her hand. She looked down at Logan. He was smiling.

There was one last cough, which brought a gush of blood from his lips and onto his chest. Logan's body went still. She'd seen that happen once before; she knew that no amount of crying or pleading would bring him back. It didn't bring Jacob back, and he would be no different.

Sirus still hadn't turned to look at her. He was staring up into the sky, interacting with the huge ship in some way. The thing was screaming into the atmosphere. The sound didn't bother her though, not like it had Dale before he went running back to the Palace. She knew that Sirus was somehow creating the sound.

Mary rose to her feet, looking at what she heard Sirus and Logan call a weapon. It was beautiful. The thing glowed every color she'd ever seen and a million more that she never even knew existed.

In the distance, a small army marched in her direction, on the same path of her new home, full of new people who had cared for her. People who deserved to live. There had been too much murder already.

"No more..." Mary said, lifting the weapon into the sky at the ship.

"This stops now...NO MORE!" She could feel the thing in her hand calling out to her, begging to borrow her power, to access her life force.

"NO MORE!" she screamed even louder.

Sirus turned around to see her aiming the weapon.

"No, Mary! Stop! Don't!" he screamed as he tried to make up the distance between them. This time, he was not fast enough.

Mary's scream was as loud as the evil horn coming from the ship. It felt like she was screaming with her whole heart. Letting out every bit of pain and grief that consumed her.

The weapon turned into flame in the palm of her hand. It formed a beam of light the darkest black she'd seen. The color of a black hole if there ever was one. The color of death and nothingness all wrapped into one beam, traveling at the speed of sound.

The beam from her hand tore through the entire ship that loomed down upon the area like a hanging mountain in the sky. The dark light split the triangle in half instantly. There were explosions and pieces of the ship breaking off and falling from the sky.

Sirus fell down to one knee, holding his head with both hands. She could barely see his face, but it looked to be changing from one image to the next. One moment it was his normal face, then it was the face of someone different, then someone else the next moment. Each expression was more pained than the last.

This was her shot. This was her chance to kill him, while he was weak and in too much pain to use his speed. Mary lowered her hand, the black arura clinging to her fingers. She was no longer holding the weapon, it was a part of her. She walked up to Sirus, his face still changing through a million different emotions. He rocked his head back and forth in an inhuman way. He was pure evil, and she knew it. Now she could end it all.

As the ship crumbled in the sky, pieces the size of houses fell miles away from where they were standing. She somehow knew Sirus was feeling the pain of the ship's destruction. Destruction at her own hand, from the weapon Logan had entrusted to her. Logan had known it was meant for her.

Mary pointed the palm of her hand at the director's head.

Surrounded by the dead bodies of Eagle rebels and security guards, she found solace in that moment. Mary had come full circle, back on the killing field where she'd lost Jacob. Now it was Sirus's turn to fall.

Mary called out to her life force once again, beckoning the energy to destroy her enemies. She screamed, screamed as loud as she could, holding her palm over Sirus's head. Mary screamed time and time again...but nothing happened. The black beam of light did not return. Sirus dropped to the ground and convulsed as small explosions lit up the ship. The smaller ships circled it, shooting blue beams of light at it. They seemed to be trying to repair it, but the damage was too great. Sirus was proof that the blue lights were not helping matters.

The army that marched for Sirus were getting closer. She could make out some of them even at that far distance. She could see farther than she ever could before. Mary didn't know if it was the power of the weapon, but she could see the faces of people she'd grown up with. Only Palace-born members were marching. There were none of the Old World members with them. Immediately she knew what that meant. Sirus planned to use Palace-born members to kill off any survivors.

She would not hurt them. She didn't know if she could even if she wanted to. The power she'd felt moments before was not working, and she could see that they all had weapons. The man in the lead looked like the guy who'd found Michelle dead in her pod. Lonnie was his name.

Mary turned and went running back toward the Palace. Death and destruction were all around. Flaming pieces of wreckage fell from the sky in the far distance, along with dead bodies and pieces of men and women who were among the living just minutes ago. Sirus lay there in the grass, shaking uncontrollably as she sprinted past his body. Hopefully he was dead or dying. If his power was linked to the ship's, then her well-placed shot should kill him as well.

Mary came bursting through the glass double doors of the Palace, out of breath. In the central plaza stood approximately three hundred Eagle members, all suited up in gear with guns at their sides. Dale stood at the front, waiting with them. They all looked at Mary, in awe of what she'd done. They must have watched it all happen from inside.

"What are your orders, Mary? We stand with you," Dale said. Every soldier in the plaza saluted her.

Mary stood up straight, her hand still glowing assorted colors. The black mist of the beam swirled around her fingertips. The world outside of the Palace seemed to be on fire. The sky burned red as flames rained down on the land. The Palace-born army could be seen heading in their direction. Mary turned to look out through the glass doors.

"Your orders?" Dale repeated. "We are yours to command."

ABOUT THE AUTHOR

A SELF-PROFESSED OUTGOING PESSIMIST, J.M. CLARK is a word enthu-siast, and an up-and-coming science fiction author in southern Ohio. J.M. studied English literature and writing at Northern Kentucky University. Now, a member of Cincinnati Fantasy-writers and Sci-fi and Fantasy-writers of America, J. M. indulges in his passion for writing and critiquing work in the realm of fantasy fiction. An avid reader, and transitional professional from lyricist to author, J.M. loves interacting with friends and other writers. He continues to deliver hesitantly opti-mistic advice, and produce work that keeps fans constantly wanting more.

Join the mailing list and receive free giveaways and exclusive content.

Website: http://www.writtenbyjmclark.com
Email: writtenbyjmclark@gmail.com

facebook.com/writtenbyjmclark

twitter.com/jmclark35

instagram.com/writtenbyjmclark

ALSO BY J.M. CLARK

THE ORDER OF CHAOS SERIES

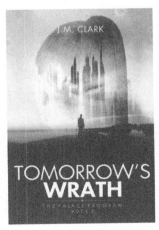

Join the mailing list and receive free giveaways and exclusive content:

Website: http://www.writtenbyjmclark.com

Email: writtenbyjmclark@gmail.com

Made in the USA
Monee, IL
14 April 2022

94021350R00152